LUKE IRONTREE & THE LAST VAMPIRE WAR

Book 0 - The Centurion Immortal
Book 1 - Dark Fangs Rising - March 22, 2022
Book 2 - Dark Fangs Raging - April 19, 2022
Book 3 - Dark Fangs Descending - May 17, 2022
Book 4 - Blood Empire Reborn* - August 23, 2022
Book 5 - Blood Empire Avenged* - September 20, 2022
Book 6 - Blood Empire Burning* - October 18, 2022
Book 7 - Blood Empire Collapsing* - November 15, 2022
Book 8 - Ancient Sword Falling* - February 7, 2023
Book 9 - Ancient Sword Unyielding* - March 7, 202
Book 10 - Ancient Sword Shattering* - May 9, 2023

The Luke Irontree Historical Adventures
Rise of the Centurio Immortalis - April 5, 2022
Fall of the Centurio Immortalis* - May 31, 2022
The Moonlight Centurion* - December 27, 2022
The Highway Centurion* - April 11, 2023

*Forthcoming
  Titles and release dates may be subject to change.

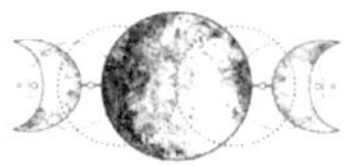

RISE OF THE CENTURIO IMMORTALIS

A LUKE IRONTREE HISTORICAL ADVENTURE

C. THOMAS LAFOLLETTE

RISE OF THE CENTURIO IMMORTALIS
C. Thomas Lafollette

A Broken World Publication
13820 NE Airport Way
Suite #K395495
Portland, OR 97251-1158
Rise of the Centurio Immortalis
Copyright © 2022 by C. Thomas Lafollette
ISBN 978-1-949410-50-1 (ebook);
ISBN 978-1-949410-51-8 (paperback)

Cover Design: Ravven
Edited by: Suzanne Lahna
Copy Editing & Proofreading: Amy Cissell

CONTENTS

CONTENT WARNING

This book contains some gore and body horror. There are also battle scenes with brief, minimally-described scenes of animal injury and death.

For Liana
You're an amazing stepdaughter

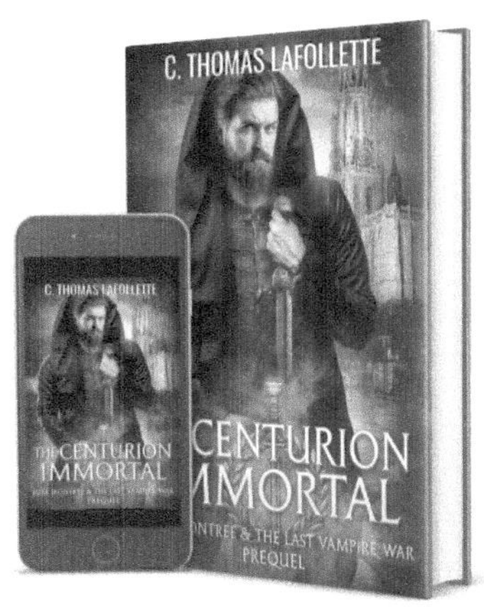

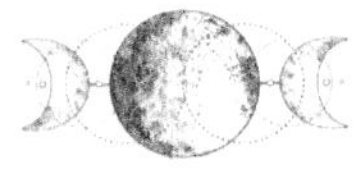

Your Free Book Is Waiting

THE CENTURION IMMORTAL returns to the land of his birth, but he never suspected he'd be drawn into a supernatural turf war.

A vacation in Belgium is the perfect way for an incognito immortal to get in touch with his roots. Former Roman Legionnaire and vampire slayer Luke Irontree is pulled into a supernatural feud when he's offered a job he can't refuse—rescue an innocent woman and child from his ancient enemies. When he goes undercover at an EDM festival, he has everything under control. But when his prey find out he's more than a simple tourist, things take a turn for the deadly.

Suddenly up to his neck in vampires, Luke must play a lethal game of cat and mouse in which his survival is the prize. Can he escape the trap set for him while rescuing the people caught in the middle? Or will the blood of his immortal life trickle down a rusty grate in a basement in Liege?

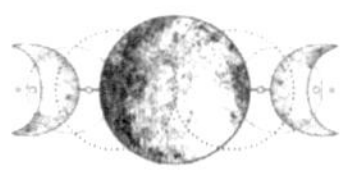

Get a free copy of a Luke Irontree Prequel
The Centurion Immortal here:

www.cthomaslafollette.com

PRONUNCIATION GUIDE & AUTHOR'S NOTES

Pronunciation: Latin names and words are mentioned throughout the book and are intended to be read with the classical Latin pronunciation. For instance, "c" is always pronounced hard, like a "k." "U" is always a short "oo" sound. "V" typically sounds like a "w." There are plenty of resources on the internet if you wish to learn more about Classical Latin pronunciation.

- Lucius – Loo-kih-oos
- Silvanius – Sihl-wahn-ih-oos
- Ferrata – Fehr-rah-tah
- Sol Invictus - Sahl Ihn-vihk-toos

Latin Words: Latin words are used for effect and to add to the "flavor" of the story, not to reflect Latin grammar/declensions/conjugations.

Other Names: The Roman Empire and its legions were multicultural and filled with people from all over the empire. This is the pronunciation I'm using for these names.

- Ariazate - Ahree-ah-Zah-tay

- Tigran - Tee-Grahn
- Syphax - See-fahks
- Mylitos - Mee-lih-tahs
- Tiridat - Teeh-rih-daht
- Venextos - Vehn-nehst-tahs
- Zyraxes - Zihr-raks-sees
- Selene - Seh-lee-nee
- Mithras - Mih-thrahs

Anachronisms: It's nearly impossible to write historical settings without some anachronisms, especially when you're writing scenes set nearly 2,000 years in the past. Those used are done so intentionally for the purpose of story telling and to convey sentiments that would be recognizable to people then and now. Also, there are vampires.

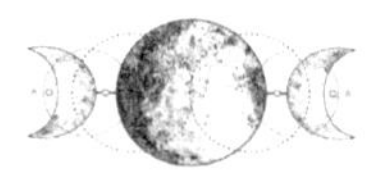

PROLOGUE
109 CE

LUCIUS AMBLED toward his parent's house. He didn't know what to expect during his first trip home after leaving it to join Roma's legions. Freshly returned from the mountains of Dacia, Roma's newest province, the XXX Ulpia Victrix had marched to the Rhenus River to take up its permanent station at Noviomagus, deep in the lowlands of Germania Inferior. He'd spent the last two years after the cessation of combat with the Dacians building roads and other public works with his legion in the newly conquered province. After the long march to Noviomagus, Lucius was tired of seeing nothing but the men he'd served beside for six years.

He took a much needed and earned furlough, deciding to walk the three-day trip home from the fort. As he drew closer to the Roman-style manor house his father had built a few years before Lucius joined the legions, he sped up, eager to see his parents. He crested the hill overlooking his family's home and stopped to take in all that had changed in the last six years.

The gardens that had been in the earliest stages were now established and showing solid growth. There appeared to be another small outbuilding or two he didn't remember as well. When his stomach rumbled, he returned to his journey. At the bottom of the hill was food and family. When he stepped through the door, the delightful scent of food swept over him — he'd arrived during dinner.

"Lu…Lucius?" His mother Verlia pushed away from the table and got up.

When she got close enough, Lucius pulled her into a tight hug. She hadn't felt this tiny when he'd hugged her goodbye before he left to join the legions six years ago.

"I'm glad to see you, mother," Lucius said, voice thick with emotions. He'd missed her while he'd been away. Getting to see her again was all he'd thought about when he'd gotten word that the XXX Ulpia Victrix was being transferred back to the Rhenus River.

His mother pushed back, holding him by the shoulders, tears in her eyes. "You're so big and strong." She pulled him back in for another hug.

Gray streaked her brown hair and more wrinkles than he remembered creased the corners of her eyes and crossed her forehead. Lucius embraced his mother as tears of joy spilled from her eyes. His father limped over and waited for Verlia to finish so he could get a hug of his own. At six four, his father towered over him by a good four inches. The wild red hair that had been streaked with silver when Lucius left for the legions was more white than red these days.

A space was made for him at the table, and soon he was feasting on fresh baked bread and pork stew and catching up on everything that had happened in the last six years. While the food the legions ate was adequate, the taste of home seasoned the simple hearty food, making it seem like an imperial banquet. His father talked about the ways the business had grown since Lucius left.

Lucius steered the conversation away from himself, simply reveling in the domesticity of his family. Even two years after the fighting had ended, he wasn't ready to talk about what he'd seen and done in Dacia. He hadn't known what to expect in his first war. There hadn't been time to think during the fighting, only to react and survive. As he rose through the ranks, his commanders tested him further, sending him to the front ranks. He'd survived and thrived, but the violence and bloodshed stayed with him, haunting his dreams with images of the killing fields.

Lucius slept poorly that night. The nightmares he'd first had during the quiet months after the fighting ended returned to plague him inside what should have been the sanctuary of his home. He woke groggily to a servant knocking lightly and inviting him to break his fast with his mother. Afterwards, he wandered out into the pleasantly warm spring morning. The only dark clouds were those in his mind as he sifted through his feelings about being home, paying no attention to where his feet carried him.

Bluebells, newly bloomed, surrounded Lucius's legs, and a soft breeze tugged at the leaves and branches above him, the scent of the flowers pulling Lucius from his wandering thoughts and back to the present. His feet had carried him to the old haunt of his boyhood. He stood in a sun-dappled meadow, the gently swaying branches adding a shimmer to the interplay of light and shadow. The delicate rustle of leaf on leaf soothed his mind, palpably drawing out the tightness in his shoulders. Lucius inhaled deeply, holding the breath for a few seconds before releasing it slowly along with the tension that had furrowed his brow. He sat in the center of the meadow before sprawling out on his back, his hands behind his head, legs spread out, mimicking the position he'd spent so much of his youth lying in while avoiding chores.

He watched the clouds slowly move across the sky while he tried to spot shapes in them like he'd done as a boy, but the scent of the bluebells and the gentle rustle of the leaves lulled him to sleep. Sometime later, the sound of footsteps and winded breathing pulled him from his dreams and put him on alert. Lucius relaxed when the steps grew closer, and he heard his father, Ambeltrix Gaius, grunting out curses. His father's head blotted out the sky above as he looked down at his son.

"Father."

"Son. Your mother said this is where I'd find you." Ambeltrix wiped a sleeve over a sweaty brow.

"She used to find me here when I was avoiding chores."

"Mind if I join you?" Ambeltrix asked.

Lucius released one of his arms to gesture to a patch of dappled sunlight dancing over bluebells. "Please."

Grunts and curses accompanied his father dropping to the ground next to Lucius. "Don't ever get old, boy. This body isn't what it used to be."

"You're not that old." The words left his mouth before he thought them over and remembered how old his father actually was.

Ambeltrix laughed ruefully. "I'm fifty-six, and a lot of those years were hard years. You're going to have to help your old father off the ground when we're done here."

Lucius nodded even though he knew his father couldn't see it as they both stared up at the clouds. The men's steady breathing joined the gentle symphony of birds singing and squirrels scampering about in the trees above them. It was Ambeltrix who broke the silence.

"What brings you out here, boy?"

Lucius exhaled sharply through his nose. "I don't know. I just needed to take a walk and get some fresh air. This is where I ended up."

"I see."

"It's just—" Lucius tried to organize his feelings and put them into words.

"Not sure how to feel about being home?" Lucius's father interrupted. "After being away at war?"

"I didn't know what to expect when I got home. I don't even know if it's home anymore."

"You'll always have a place under our roof, boy, but I know what you mean. It felt the same way the first time I returned home."

"After Mons Graupius?" Lucius asked, tipping his head to look at his father.

Ambeltrix nodded. "I'm not sure why I came home; my mother and father were no longer alive. I just needed to get out of Britannia for a while. I stayed with a cousin while I was here. I'd been away so long, the village of my birth felt more alien than the foreign land I'd been marching through for fifteen years. That's when I started wandering around the countryside."

"Is that when you met mother?" Lucius asked.

"Yes. Your mother was a fiery little thing when I met her. It wasn't long after meeting her that this place started feeling like home again. Not like my parents' home or my boyhood home, but a home to come back to when I was done with the legions…" He paused for a while as a pleasant breeze shifted through the meadow. "Then I received word of your birth. I'd thought about signing up for another tour before that trip home, but after I met your mother and knew you'd be waiting here with her, the end of my tour couldn't arrive fast enough."

Lucius had never heard his father talk about this aspect of his life and his experience with the auxilia. They'd talked plenty about the day-to-day life of being in the military. Ambeltrix's and his friends' anecdotes filled the years between his father's return and Lucius's departure for the legions. They'd never broached the emotional side of his father's time serving in Roma's war machine, although Lucius knew it had affected his father in profound ways. His father's words now called up the memory of the time he'd walked outside late at night not long after his father returned home. He'd found his father sitting against the wall of their small home, drinking and crying in the moonlight.

They lay in silence, listening to the breeze rustle through the trees and the birds sing their spring songs until Lucius eventually broke the quiet. "It's nothing like I thought it would be…"

"It never is. Nothing can prepare you for the first time you're staring across a patch of dirt at someone who you're about to try to kill. At someone who's about to try to kill you. Neither of you are sure why you're there, just that you're following orders from someone important. He's trying to protect his land. I'm there to earn my pay. I know I'm protecting my home, in a roundabout way. Some other bastard is holding the line here while I'm protecting his home over there."

"I didn't do anything to the Dacians. They didn't do anything to me, but I sure killed a lot of them. They killed a lot of my comrades…" Lucius paused, trying to hold his emotions in check, tears running down his cheeks. "They killed my friend Cassius. He bled out in a cave while I held his hand."

Ambeltrix reached out and squeezed Lucius's arm for a moment. "Do you hate them now? The Dacians?"

Lucius shook his head. "I did for a while, but then we took Sarmizegetusa, and all the men and women we captured were gathered and marched out to the slave markets in Roma. Any hate I had for them died then. Even after, when one of them killed Cassius, I couldn't rekindle that hate. We'd decimated an entire people, removed them from their birthplace, and sent them into slavery. Did you hate the Caledonians?"

"No," Ambeltrix replied.

The men returned to the silence of the spring day. When the sun passed behind the clouds for a few minutes, Lucius shivered, goose flesh rising on his arms. As the sun reemerged and warmed him, he let his mind drift to a question that had been bothering him for a while.

"We were a free people once, weren't we?" Lucius asked.

"We were. Before Caesar came."

"If the Romans took our independence, why do we serve them now?"

Ambeltrix took in a deep breath and let it out as a slow sigh. "How many legions were there in Dacia?"

"About twelve."

"How many auxilia?"

"A lot."

"How many vexillations from other legions?"

"A lot."

"So, 80,000? Maybe over 100,000 men marshaled to execute the will of Roma?" Ambeltrix paused for a moment. "All of Gaul could rise as one and not be able to win against that many professional soldiers. Besides, you could never unite all of Gaul and Belgica. Our men are spread throughout the empire in the legions and auxilia. How many of them will split from their Roman masters? How many units could be raised from all the colonies spread throughout the empire? Each of those colonies is filled with retired legionnaires who can be called up to fight Roma's enemies if needed. Traianus has given Colonia status to Vetera. It's Colonia Ulpia Traiana now."

Lucius nodded. "I know; we saw the work as we marched to Noviomagus."

"You. Me. We're Roman citizens now. We've cast our lot in with Roma. Things are largely peaceful behind the borders. We are Romans for all intents and purposes. That, and the pay is good."

Lucius chuckled, thinking of his share of plunder from Dacia, then he sighed. "I guess so."

The men returned to their silence until it was broken by a third party.

"Lucius? Ambeltrix?" Verlia called out. "Oh, where are you two?"

Lucius looked over at this father. "I suppose it's time to go home. We don't really want her angry at us."

"Smart lad. Now, help your old man up."

Lucius stood and extended his arm down to his father. Grasping it, Ambeltrix used his son's strength to pull himself off the ground.

Verlia crossed her arms and scowled at them, its potency robbed with the smile threatening to tug up the corners of her lips. "There you are! What am I going to do with both of you out here counting clouds?"

Lucius walked over to his mother and clasped the small woman in a tight hug. He released her and held one of her hands. Ambeltrix joined them, taking her other hand, and together, they began the trek home.

"We'd have come in by suppertime," Ambeltrix said.

"Of course, the belly must be fed," Verlia teased. "Can't a woman miss her son and husband?" She emphasized it by squeezing Lucius's hand and leaning her head against his arm as they walked hand in hand through the bluebell covered meadow.

"I've missed you too, mother."

"You were always a good boy, Lucius. But the reason I came looking for you is there's a messenger here for you. A nice boy in armor."

"What does he want?" Lucius asked, brows furrowing.

"He didn't say, and I figured he wouldn't answer if I asked," Verlia replied.

Despite someone waiting for him, Lucius didn't increase the pace of the casual stroll through the wood back to his parents' house. It wasn't his home anymore. The legions were his home. But for now, enjoying a walk through the woods he'd grown up in with his mother and father on a glorious spring day was all he wanted. If a messenger waited, he had no doubt he was being recalled before the end of his furlough. Before that, he wanted to absorb as much of this feeling of domesticity as he could, not knowing how long it would be until his next visit or even if there'd be anyone there to greet him when he returned.

As the trio approached the house, the hive of activity changed from bees flitting about in the bluebells to servants moving about Ambeltrix and Verlia's property. Ambeltrix and Lucius slipped off their caligae and set them by the door, then put on the slippers they wore in the house.

"Where's the messenger?" Lucius asked.

"He's right here, Lucius. Or I guess I should say Optio Ferrata," a man with a familiar voice said, stepping out of the shadows of the kitchen door. He looked slightly ridiculous in his full kit, helmet under his arm, contrasting with a set of spare house slippers on his feet.

"Sego!" Lucius rushed forward and clasped his friend in a robust hug. "It's good to see you. What are you doing here?"

"I ran into Brabo when he was looking for a messenger to send out. I volunteered. Figured it would be worth it to get out of the fort and have a nice ride."

"I didn't know you could ride."

Sego shrugged. "I'm Batavi; my father served with the Ala Gallorum Petriana in Brittania. I grew up on a horse."

"Let me introduce you." Lucius turned to his parents. "This is my friend Segomaros, signifier of the II Centurio, VIII Cohors of the Legio XXX Ulpia Victrix. Sego, this is my father Ambeltrix Gaius Silvanius, Centurio of the I Cohors Tungrorum, retired. And this is my mother, Verlia."

Sego saluted Ambeltrix before clasping the older man's hand. He gave Verlia a respectful bow. Ambeltrix turned to his son.

"Optio Ferrata?"

"You didn't tell your parents?" Sego turned to face Lucius's parents. "Your son has done well. By the end of the war, he'd been promoted to Optio in the V Centuria, I Cohors. He caught the eye of the Imperator who bestowed Ferrata on him and awarded him the Corona Civica."

Lucius blushed as his father caught him up in a crushing hug. "Corona Civica? I'm so proud of you, son."

"Thank you, father."

"Corona Civica?" Verlia asked.

"It's one of the highest honors bestowed on a common legionnaire. We must celebrate!" Ambeltrix stalked off to the kitchens.

"Can you stay, Sego?" Verlia asked. "We'd love to have you as a guest until you have to leave."

"I'd be honored, ma'am. I don't have to go back immediately."

"Excellent. I'll get a bed setup for you and leave you boys to talk." She fondly touched her son's shoulder as she left to find a servant to set up a place for Sego.

"When do you have to go back?" Lucius asked.

"I'm to take you with me. Sorry to cut your furlough short, but you need to be back at Noviomagus in eight days. Rumor is this order came all the way from Roma."

Lucius tipped his head to the side. "Really? Any other rumors along with it?"

"Not that I can interpret. My guess, though, is that Brabo is going to need a new optio."

Lucius's eyebrows shot up before furrowing around his brow in confusion.

Sego grinned at his friend. "Word came in they're returning the I Adiutrix back to full strength. They've been training new recruits up and down the Germania border to send to the staging point in Pannonia Superior. They'll probably need qualified men to lead them. They could be promoting you to Centurio."

Lucius shook his head and pursed his lips. "I'm too young. I'm not even close to thirty yet."

Sego shrugged, the plates of his shoulder armor clanking lightly with the motion. "The Imperator can do what he wants. If he says he wants you to be a centurio, they'll find some men for you to lead."

Lucius snorted and chuckled. "Where do you get all this?"

"I like gossip. You keep your ears open, and you can hear all kinds of interesting things," Sego replied.

"Well, master of ears, why are they refitting the I Adiutrix?" If it were true, he'd miss Sego, guessing the lanky German would most likely be staying with the XXX Ulpia. He wasn't sure if he wanted to leave his friends and the legion he'd been a founding member of, but he had little choice if the orders were indeed coming directly from the imperator. He'd signed the contract, and he'd do his duty.

"Old Man's going after Parthia…"

ONE

117 CE

THE AFTERNOON SEA breeze blew in from the Internum Mare, cooling Antiochia in the stifling heat of high summer. After three years of campaigning in Armenia and Mesopotamia, Trajan had decided it was time to return to Roma, bringing Lucius and his legion along with him for their brief stop in the city founded by Alexander the Great's general Seleucus.

"With Traianus leaving for Roma, we'll lose all our gains. All that fighting, killing, and dying for nothing." Lucius shook his head as he pulled a rag out of his belt pouch and wiped the sweat running down his nose. Lucius's armor shone, the polished phelarae catching bits of sun and reflecting them like he was gemstone. He'd earned a couple more medals during the years serving Trajan in his Parthian War.

"Yeah. It's unfortunate. Parthia is already gobbling up all the territory we took from them. It is what it is," Syphax replied with a half-hearted shrug.

Lucius nodded. "As my old centurio used to say, 'ours is not to question why, but to do and die.'"

"He's not wrong." Syphax pulled out the summons from the emperor as they approached the gates of the palace Trajan used while in Antiochia.

A pair of Praetorians in their shiny, segmented armor and purple cloaks stood sentinel at the palace's entryway, their shields propped against one side of their body, their pila held upright. Lucius and Syphax stopped before the Praetorians, Syphax presenting the orders allowing them entrance into the temporary imperial residence.

"Alright, you're free to proceed." The Praetorian handed the orders back to Syphax while his comrade opened the doors for them.

They stood in the entryway as their eyes adjusted from the bright Syrian midday sun to the darker confines of the palace. Syphax untied his helmet and pulled it off. His short tightly curly hair was damp from sweat. Lucius followed suit. The cool interior of the stone building felt good on his head after being confined inside the metal helmet.

"All this sweat is going to rust my armor, then I'll have to polish it again." Lucius wiped his forehead and neck with the rag, then ran it over his short brown hair.

Syphax laughed. "If you quit wearing that manica, you'd have less armor to polish. It would probably be cooler too. Still not used to the heat after all this time?"

The manica that covered his right arm from shoulder to wrist had only been issued to the legions fighting in Dacia to protect their arms from the deadly falx. A legionnaire without a right hand was a useless soldier, assuming he even survived the encounter.

"Mostly used to it, but walking around inside my own personal oven doesn't help. Not all of us were born in the deserts of Mauretania Tingitana."

Syphax, born of Berber heritage in Africa, was dark brown after the years fighting throughout Mesopotamia. Lucius, at best, managed a red tinted tan, preferring to wear a long-sleeved, light linen tunic to keep the sun off his fair skin.

Lucius, eyes adjusting, spied a small, fussy older man making his way towards them. A moment later, he recognized the emperor's personal chamberlain.

"Ah, if it's not Syphax Quietus and the young Ferrata." Felix bowed before the two legionnaires.

"Not so young anymore, Felix." Syphax turned towards Lucius. "What are you now, thirty?"

"Thirty-one last spring," Lucius replied.

Felix chuckled. "Still younger than either of us, eh, Syphax?"

"That's the truth." Syphax reached up and ran his hand through his hair, the white hairs interspersed with black catching rays of sunlight streaming in from the still open doors. His fingers pulled the hairs and released them, the curls springing back into place. Lucius's centurion wiped his hand across the dark brown skin of his forehead. "Our world is graying, Felix. Fading. Tell me true, how is the old man doing?"

Felix took in a deep breath and let it out slowly, reaching to grasp Syphax's forearm. "He's…" His voice caught. "He is…still himself."

Syphax and Felix made eye contact, an intense understanding exchanged. Lucius, looking between the two older men, turned his thoughts towards his father. Ambeltrix Gaius Silvanus had walked the earth as long as their emperor had and a few years more. His father, the image of robustness and vitality—a larger-than-life figure—had weathered poorly from when Lucius had left to join the legions and when he'd returned six years later. He wondered how his father fared with another eight years on his shoulders. Legionary years were hard years; Ambeltrix had served twenty-five of them.

In many ways, Lucius had felt an affection for his emperor akin to that of a son to his father or a favored uncle. That feeling had become tarnished over the years as Lucius fought in two long wars, but he'd signed the contract and hitched his fortunes to those of the empire. And because of his service, the emperor had recognized him and raised him up, not once, but many times, placing the burden of leadership on his young shoulders and ensuring he was guided to his full potential. Syphax, a member of the Quietus family who was beloved of the emperor and who had served him so well, had been placed above Lucius to guide him and develop him so he could better serve the emperor both men had dedicated their lives to. Syphax had become the older brother he'd never known in his own family.

Watching the exchange between Syphax and Felix confirmed the rumors were true; Trajan, Imperator Caesar Nerva Traianus Divi

Nervae filius Augustus, was dying. The man who'd called Lucius from the forests of Belgic Gaul to the mountains of Dacia and the arid deserts of Mesopotamia, the other looming figure of Lucius's life, was about to pass on from the world.

"How is he *today*, Felix?" Syphax asked.

Felix sagged in on himself. "Tired and spiteful. He wants to challenge the gods who have brought him so low when he was about to do what no Roman had done before him."

"He rages against the coming night?"

Felix nodded, shaking loose tears from his eyes. "He does. When he thinks I'm not listening, he argues with himself about his past failings. Men like him are not suited to die in bed. He should have been struck down with a gladius in his hand and armor on his chest."

Lucius watched his centurion's face droop.

Syphax's eyes grew distant. "Aye…"

Syphax and Felix, after their shared quiet grief, made eye contact and nodded at each other signaling they were ready to greet their ailing imperator.

"Shall we?" Felix asked, turning away from Lucius and Syphax and walking back down the hall whence he'd come. "He wants you to meet with his liaison to the Mithraic leaders before I take you to him."

Although Lucius had been initiated into the secrets of Mithras when he'd been assigned as Quietus's optio and eventually risen to the third rank, he hadn't met the man who stood between the emperor and the various pater patrum of the empire's Mithraic temples. The religion had come out of the east and grown in popularity with the empire's elite, particularly those leading Roma's legions. Lucius had been promoted to third level, Miles, as learned the mysteries of Mithras and its tenets as practiced by the leadership of the empire.

They followed Felix through a series of dark corridors sparsely lit with the occasional oil lamp, passing a few Praetorians standing watch. The corridors felt dry and dusty, as if the imperator's people hadn't taken the time to properly clean the large space before his temporary residence.

and paid honor to local gods when he traveled through their lands. Since he'd been initiated into the mysteries of Mithras, he'd paid the honors due to the god who'd become prominent with the legions. He'd never met a god, nor had he heard of one needing mortals to aid in their defense, but if Trajan ordered them to obey the call of the priests and the auguries, his opinion mattered little.

"If it were only one, it might be suspect, but we've been in contact with several pater patrum of various Mithraeum who've had the same experience," Drusus replied.

"Exactly?"

Nodding seriously, Drusus locked his gaze with Syphax's. "Exactly—to the last image."

Syphax kept silent for a few moments as he nodded to himself. "Right. Lucius, what are your thoughts?"

Lucius shrugged. "If Caesar says go to Armenia and take up mountain climbing, I march to Armenia."

"Your optio has a clear understanding of the situation," Drusus said, looking Lucius over.

"That he does," Syphax replied.

"I need to send a few messages," Drusus said. "Felix will escort you to the imperator. I'll join you soon."

Syphax nodded. Together, Lucius and his centurion followed Felix out of the room. Lucius had wanted to get out of the sun of Syria and Mesopotamia, but into the mountains of Armenia where winter could come on early and violently wasn't exactly the change he'd been looking for. But like he'd said, if Trajan said he needed to go to Armenia, he'd start preparing to be cold instead of hot.

TWO

LUCIUS ASSUMED they were getting closer to the Imperator—the corridors smelled fresher with a hint of sea air. Soon, a tantalizing sound joined the gentle breeze moving through the corridor, teasing at the corner of his awareness. As they got closer, the reedy noise became clearer, the sound simultaneously soaring and sorrowful.

"What is that music?" Lucius asked Felix.

"Ah, the Armenians are entertaining the Imperator," Felix replied. "Let's slide in quietly so as not to interrupt. They've been keeping him company much recently."

"I don't think I've ever heard that instrument before," Lucius commented.

Felix gave Lucius a half smile. "It's native to Armenia. They call it a tsiranapogh."

Felix nodded to the two Praetorians guarding the door and gestured that Syphax and Lucius should step inside. Lucius followed Syphax, stepping aside and taking up a post out of the way but present. After the dark corridors, the airy room felt fresh and lively, the breeze gently waving the diaphanous white curtains. Lucius could just make out the western side of Antiochia and the sea in the far distance through the thin curtains. A dozen more Praetorians were spread about the room, standing at attention near the walls.

Trajan lay on a well-cushioned couch with a nearby slave pulling a rope that led up to a series of cloth panels that swung back and forth over the imperator, moving the air around to cool him. Every once in a while, his hand would dip into a bowl on a low stand next to his side and pull out a date which he'd pop into his mouth.

Two youths sat on cushions in the middle of the room, each playing a small wooden flute-like instrument that looked like it had a reed at the end they blew into. The boy looked twelve or thirteen and was playing a series of droning notes while the older girl sitting next to him carried the melody.

The boy wore a simple green tunic belted at the waist by a band of bronze medallions, his hair shorn short in the current Roman fashion. The girl, who was maybe sixteen, wore her long black hair in braids wound around her head, intermingling with a series of chains and bronze baubles dangling onto her forehead from a diadem. Her traditional Armenian dress shone bright red against the fluttering curtains, delicate patterns of blues and gold interwoven through the red. Their light brown skin bore the olive cast of the people of the region.

The boy's drone kept a steady note for the girl's melody as she at times soared high or settled into a low note, its resonance settling deep in Lucius's heart and filling it with the sorrow of the player and her people. Armenia had once been a mighty empire in the region for a brief time under Tigranes the Great, stretching from Mare Caspium to the Caucasii Montes to the Internum Mare, encompassing Damascus, Antiochia, and Tarsus. Now, it was a border region and pawn in the ongoing power struggle between Roma and the Parthian Empire. For the moment, Armenia was ruled by Trajan and Roma, but Lucius knew that wouldn't last much longer with Trajan reducing the number of legions in the east.

Felix ordered cushioned seats for Syphax and Lucius, then brought them delicate cakes and wine watered with fruit juice, honey, and spice while they waited for the imperator to address his soldiers. The food and drink far surpassed the humble soldiers' rations Lucius was used to, even as a leading officer in the special cohort the imperator had ordered formed. He savored the repast and the music, letting the sea-laden breeze soothe the heat of the day. The honeyed cakes melted in his mouth as he let the transcendent music carry him away from the oppressive heat of Antiochia.

As the music enveloped him, Lucius's eyes drifted nearly shut. The drone of the boy's instrument lulling him, while the girl's delicate notes entwined his senses as he stared into the distance through his eyelashes. He fully relaxed for the first time in ages, not letting the anxiety of waiting for Trajan surface. He knew moments like this were few and far between, so he savored them while he could.

At first, his mind drifted to the cool and shady forest near the home he'd grown up in with his mother and then later his father. He's spent nearly half his life away from the land of his birth, but it was still the place that called to him, the place he thought of as home, especially after three years in the deserts of Mesopotamia. Even if his parents' house had lost that feeling, he still yearned for Belgica. After the comfort of home sank into his soul, the sad sound of the reeded flute brought him back to the mountains of Armenia.

The image of the stark beauty of the rugged mountains and the cool air of the lower passes they'd marched through rose in Lucius's mind. While the mountains they'd crossed when they entered Armenia with Trajan were taller than anything Lucius had seen in Belgica, he could see they were only foothills compared to the rugged mountains of the main Caucasus. After marching through the arid lands skirting the Syrian desert, climbing up into the Armenian plateau had felt like a refreshing cool breeze.

Apparently, the imperator was in no hurry to deal with the men he'd sent for, requesting several more songs. A younger Lucius would have been politely impatient at the delay, keeping his annoyance tightly bottled inside, but eight years serving under the sardonic Syphax with his dry wit had loosened up Lucius, helping him mature into a patient and steady officer. Since he wasn't that naïve younger man, he ate more cakes when they showed up next to his chair and enjoyed the fine wine the imperator offered. He listened intently to the beautifully haunting music that took images of his home and the mountains of Armenia and merged them into a place both familiar and new, enticing Lucius to ignore the heat of Syria and allow the coolness of forest and mountain to sooth him inside and out.

"Felix? Gods, where is that man?" Trajan mumbled.

"Here, Caesar. How may I serve you?" Felix bowed deeply.

Lucius opened his eyes and straightened up, popping a last piece of the honeyed cake in his mouth. Syphax, like Lucius, sat at attention, waiting to be called before the imperator.

"Clear the room save for Syphax and his man, and send for Drusus Gracchus."

"Yes, Caesar." Felix bowed and started to turn.

"Oh, and have the Armenians wait outside until I summon them." Trajan picked up a cup from the table near his couch, his trembling hand and arm sending a small splash of wine to the floor.

"Of course, Caesar." Felix sent the servants scurrying to carry out Felix's orders. Next, he ushered the Armenian children out of the room.

"Syphax, come here," Trajan ordered.

"Aye, Caesar." Syphax stood and gestured for Lucius to follow.

Syphax picked a spot where the imperator could easily look at them from his reclined position. The old man waited until only he and the two legionnaires were left in the large room. Even the Praetorians filed out—no doubt waiting outside the door where they could be easily summoned.

"Don't make me crick my neck up at you, Syphax, my old friend. Bring a chair to sit on and one for your man as well." The imperator picked up a piece of the cake and placed it into his mouth while Syphax and Lucius returned with the chairs they'd been sitting in earlier. "Good."

The imperator seemed to doze for a few moments before covering his eyes with his hand. It looked frail and thin, much like the imperator. Trajan was in severe decline. The man who'd been a robust commander of his legions looked years beyond his sixty-three.

"This headache just won't leave me be. When will the sun go down? Its damned light pierces my eyes," Trajan complained.

"I can request the servants add more shades to the windows," Syphax said.

"No, it doesn't help. Only the darkness does." Trajan sighed. "We'll just have to soldier on, won't we, young Lucius Silvanius Ferrata? We've both come a long way from the mountains and forests of Dacia, haven't we?"

"Aye, Caesar. That was a while ago and far away," Lucius replied.

Trajan made a weak affirmative sound, closing his eyes again. They sat in silence as the imperator rested his hand over his eyes to block the sun's light. A slight frown teased at Lucius's lips. The imperator was twice Lucius's age. He didn't want this to be his future, his strength failing him as he withered into a frail old man fighting off the pain of sunlight. Stealing glances at his friend Syphax, Lucius wondered what the older man was thinking. Syphax was closer in age to the imperator than Lucius. Seeing the imperator, a man Syphax had grown to know intimately over the years, brought low by time had to be hard for him.

A knock drew their attention away from their imperator. Felix poked his head in to check on the room before opening the door and ushering Drusus Gracchus in. The man Lucius had met earlier strode in calmly and confidently. Syphax and Lucius stood. When the man joined them near the imperator, he bowed to Trajan.

"Caesar, how may I serve?" the man asked.

"Ah, is that Drusus?" Trajan asked.

"Yes, Caesar," Drusus Gracchus said.

"Excellent. Drusus, these are the men I mentioned." The old man tipped his head toward Lucius's centurion. "Syphax, it's time for you to detach your cohort from the I Adiutrix and strike out on your own mission. It's time for you to use all you've trained for. You shall be advanced as Tribunus Militum. You'll need to select your replacement as Primus Pilum."

"Thank you, Caesar. You honor me," Syphax said, bowing low.

"You and your family have served me well over the years. It is deserved." Trajan slumped into his couch, looking even wearier. "I grow tired. Syphax, Drusus will give you the rest of your orders. Treat them as if they come directly from me."

"Of course, Caesar," Syphax replied.

"Felix?" Trajan called.

Felix stepped forward. "Yes, Caesar?"

"Do you have the pilei?" Trajan asked.

"Yes, Caesar." Felix pulled felt hats from within his robes and opened them into cones.

Turning his head toward Syphax, Trajan forced his eyes open. "The Armenians who were playing earlier will be your guides. They know the mountains where you're going well. When they get you to your destination, they are each to be given a pileus and freed. Felix also has some coin you will give them."

"Aye, Caesar. It shall be as you say." Syphax looked at Lucius and gestured toward the old servant.

Lucius took the hats that were the symbols of freed slaves and the small bag of coin he'd pulled out with the pileus.

"Now leave me. I wish to rest." Trajan weakly waved them away, closing his eyes.

Felix and Drusus Gracchus bowed, and the two legionnaires saluted. Drusus Gracchus led the group out of the large chamber, the imperator already dozing, though it appeared uncomfortable and troubled to Lucius.

Syphax walked next to Felix. "What are the Armenians called?"

"The girl is Ariazate, and the boy is Tigran," Felix replied.

"Noble names for peasant children from the mountains," Drusus said.

Lucius quirked his head to the side. "I'm not familiar with either name."

"Tigranes Magnus was Armenia's greatest king and briefly made Armenia into an empire. Antiochia was a part of it. Ariazate was one of Tigranes Magnus's daughters, and I believe she was married off to a Parthian king," Drusus Gracchus answered.

Lucius caught up to Drusus Gracchus. "When was that?"

"Oh, about two hundred years ago."

"Old glories die hard," Syphax said, "and the memories live on in the names of children."

Lucius wondered what Gallic hero he could have been named after if his mother hadn't given him a Roman name. The next time he was home, he'd have to ask her why she'd chosen Lucius. Felix stepped ahead and opened the door, then gathered the Armenians and gestured for everyone to follow him.

"When will you be ready to depart?" Drusus Gracchus asked.

"We need to lay in supplies and take care of a few administrative things before we're ready. Three days."

Drusus Gracchus nodded. "Good. You'll need to stop by the Mithraeum to pay your respects before departing on this mission, then you're off to Armenia to fight Mithras's di inferi."

TWO DAYS LATER, Syphax called Lucius to his quarters.

"Sir?" Lucius said, poking his head in the door.

"Ah, Lucius. Come in," Syphax replied.

Lucius saluted and took the camp chair Syphax gestured to. Syphax's tunic now bore the broad stripe of the tribunus laticlavius

"Now that I've sorted out who will take command of the first centuria, I want to make you an offer, but I want you to consider it carefully. You've been my right-hand man and my trusted friend for a while now. You're one of the finest soldiers I've ever served with, both as a fighter and as a leader. Over the last few years, you've also developed into an excellent administrator. You have all the qualities Roma's legions need at the highest levels." Syphax leaned forward, resting his elbows on his knees.

"I will advance you to Centurio if you still wish it, but I would like to offer you the position as my second-in-command. I have a feeling this mission is only the first of many as the imperator's elite force now that we've been detached from I Adiutrix. I need a man beside me who I trust explicitly, especially if there actually are di inferi in the mountains of Armenia." Syphax chuckled and shook his head.

"Di inferi…I can't believe we're chasing after evil undead creatures." Syphax picked up his wine. "If you'd rather lead your own centuria, I'm holding open the position of the fifth centuria. Leading your own men and forming them into your unit is a heady experience. But if you take the position as my assistant, you will only be outranked by the primus pilus and answer to him in my absence."

Being a centurion and leading his own century had been Lucius's next goal in his career. He'd not thought of a position higher than that. He wasn't from a prominent Roman family. His chances of higher leadership were low, but a position as a centurion was one of respect hard earned. However, taking the position as Syphax's second would be a big step. If Syphax's suspicions turned out to be true, the imperator might expand their cohort into a full legion and promote Syphax to Legatus Legionis. Syphax would need a tribunus militum. Trajan had singled out Lucius all those years ago and had taken a personal hand in Lucius's career, seeing something in him that could further the imperator's goals. To hone the new weapon he'd found, he sent him to Syphax Quietus so his old friend could mold and season the young legionnaire. Now it was Lucius's turn to select the direction his career would take.

His ambitions had always been modest, but this presented new possibilities he hadn't previously considered or imagined. He mulled over this new opportunity while thinking about the other option. While it still held appeal, why would he want to mold a century when he could help mold the whole cohort and maybe an entire legion in the future? The opportunity was too good to pass up.

"While the chance to lead my own centuria has been my goal for a while now, I'm more interested in helping you lead this cohort," Lucius replied.

"Good man." Syphax reached out his hand.

Lucius took it.

"Congratulations, Centurio Ferrata. Now, what are your thoughts on the open centurio spot for the fifth?" Syphax asked a smile spreading across his face as he narrowed his eyes shrewdly.

With Lucius getting promoted, there were only four other optios in the cohort, each of them with their own skills and qualities.

"Antoninus is an able administrator and well respected. Zyraxes is tough and an excellent battle leader. He's also good with training. Venextos is well liked and easygoing, though respected still. Micipsa is the most well rounded, though he occasionally has trouble with indecision," Lucius said. He knew this was a test of his judgment, of his worthiness to hold this position. Syphax had tested him often in their eight-year relationship, always pushing Lucius to grow and improve.

"I know you're close with Venextos as a fellow Gaul," Syphax said.

"He's my friend. Now, the fifth has most of our newer and younger men. With that mix, I think Zyraxes is the best choice. The fifth needs to be guided by a firmer hand to finish its development, and Zyraxes's style is the best choice to maximize the fifth's potential."

"Not Micipsa?" Syphax raised an eyebrow.

Lucius shook his head. "While he's your countryman and a Berber like yourself, he's not ready to lead a centuria. He needs more time to develop his confidence."

"Not your friend the Gaul?" Syphax asked, a mischievous twinkle in his eyes.

"He's too easygoing for the fifth. Maybe a different centuria someday. Antoninus, I think, should be moved to the first centuria as optio. He would make an excellent second for Bandua as the new primus pilus and free him up to take care of the bigger responsibilities of the role," Lucius said, finishing his assessment.

"You've put a lot of thought into your answer, and that's why I offered you the position as my second. I think your words are true. Zyraxes it is. Also, I hadn't considered moving Antoninus to the first, but I like your thoughts on him. He'll be a perfect match with Bandua."

"Thank you, sir."

"You can still call me Syphax when we're in private or with the other centuriones."

Lucius chuckled. "Sure, Syphax. Do you wish me to fetch Zyraxes for you?"

"I would. The last of the supplies are arriving later today, so we'll be ready to march out tomorrow. But, before you go fetch Zyraxes, you'll need to change your crest." Syphax reached behind him and grabbed a crest with spiky black horsehair.

"Black?"

"I've decided to change our cohort's colors now that we've been detached from the I Adiutrix." Syphax handed Lucius the crest. "Though, we'll keep our winged horse."

Grinning broadly at his first centurion's crest, Lucius pulled the two optio feathers from their slots over each ear, then removed the front-to-back optio's crest and replaced them with the transverse centurion's crest that went over the top of the helmet from ear to ear.

"The black crest looks excellent, Centurio Ferrata. I've ordered all the scutums to be painted black. They'll look sharp with a white pegasus in the center. They should dry fast enough in this heat so we'll be ready to march. After you find Zyraxes, inform the other centuriones I wish to meet here to discuss our final preparations. We'll also need to arrange a visit to the local Mithraeum to seek Mithras's blessing before we march." Syphax stood.

"Perhaps we can get some clarity on these di manes and di inferi." Lucius joined Syphax on his feet and gave his commander a crisp salute. He was skeptical of their mission, but hopefully their visit to the Mithraeum would bring clarity.

"Again, congratulations, my friend. You've earned it." Syphax clasped Lucius's hand.

"Thank you for your trust, and thank you for guiding me along to this place." Lucius smiled and nodded.

Syphax patted Lucius on the back as the younger man went off to carry out his orders.

THREE

LUCIUS AND ZYRAXES stood respectfully behind the other centurions, even though technically, Lucius outranked them all save for the primus pilus. They were the two newest centurions in the cohort, and Lucius was uncomfortable with his new rank coupled with the responsibility he'd accepted from Syphax. While the older centurions chatted, Lucius and Zyraxes stood awkwardly, listening to their officers speaking with Antiochia's wealthy patrons of Mithras.

He couldn't tell what Zyraxes thought about his new situation, but a part of Lucius felt like he didn't belong there, not in the position he'd been entrusted with. Lucius looked around the wealthy neighborhood, admiring the marble construction and statues. The city's privileged competed in their displays of ostentatious wealth, both in their personal dress and adornment and in the flashy paint and other decorations on their houses, announcing to anyone who saw that they were important and deserved their place among the elite.

Lucius and his fellow centurions waited for admission into Antiochia's Mithraeum as the day's heat dissipated into more comfortable evening temperatures. Drusus Gracchus felt Lucius and Syphax needed to make an appearance to seek the favor of Mithras before departing on the strange mission to fight some otherworldly enemy of Roma, and Syphax agreed. Lucius never minded fulfilling his responsibilities to the gods; it seemed the least he could do to keep them from finding him too interesting and deciding to interfere in his life. If seeking the blessing of Mithras and his priests helped smooth their way through a country about to experience a turbulent change as Roman troops withdrew and Parthians stepped into the power vacuum, he'd be there and pray fervently. Besides, the food served at the end of the service would likely be excellent judging by the wealth of the Mithraeum's location and its attendees.

When the doors opened, Lucius followed the pater patrum down the stairs to the sub ground floor and into the Mithraeum's antechamber. Once they were safely ensconced in the Mithraeum, they pulled on their robes and other accoutrements that accompanied their rank and position within the mysteries of Mithras. The higher one's rank, the more elaborate the embroidery and decoration. Robes of the pater and pater patrum were the most elaborate with metallic threads sew in and covered in jewels. They displayed the symbols of the person's rank. As a miles, the third rank, Lucius's robe was simple, symbols of a soldier embroidered around his chest, shoulders and back—helmets, lances, drums, a cingulum belt as well other symbols sacred to Mars.

Lucius had been introduced to the mysteries of Mithras when he'd been transferred into Syphax's command, later learning that it was part of the orders transferring him from his original legion—XXX Ulpia Victrix—to the new elite cohort nominally attached to the I Adiutrix. Syphax had told Lucius that Trajan had been instructed by Mithras to form the elite force, according to the pater patrum who represented Trajan's interests with the mysteries of Mithras. Lucius was still learning about all the aspects of the god who'd become popular with the soldiers. Though he was a new god in the west, he made appearances under many names in the religions of Persians, Parthians, and Armenians. It was rumored that the worship of Mithras even extended deeper into the east into the mysterious lands even Alexander hadn't conquered.

Like all initiates into the mysteries, Lucius had first joined as a corax, the first level. Now, he entered the Mithraeum as a miles. Syphax held the fifth rank of Perses. As soon as they finished changing, Syphax led his men into the Mithraeum.

Antiochia's Mithraeum was older than the ones in the western parts of the empire. The mysteries of Mithras had spread out of the east, out of Persia and India and had stopped off in Antiochia before making their way west and into the legions and upper echelons of Roma's elite.

Rows of benches jutted out from the white marble walls painted with elaborate frescoes depicting scenes of Mithras's adventures and legends. As they strolled two abreast down the central aisle with Lucius bringing up the rear, people stood and bowed to them. Lucius had never had this happen before. Perhaps word of their mission to defend Mithras had spread through the Mithraeum's ranks. But when he looked down, the symbols on his robes glowed with a silvery gold light. As they approached the front, the occupants in the first rows stood, bowed, and moved to different benches. After Syphax and the other five centurions sat, Lucius joined them, taking the edge of the bench to the left.

With the seven legionnaires seated, the rest of the room took their benches. As if that were his cue, the pater patrum stepped in front of the altar. The marble bull scene, the legend of Mithras's slaying of the great world bull, was one of the most magnificent Lucius had ever seen. Mithras looked resplendent in a bright red coat and blue Phrygian hat as he hauled back on the head of a muscular black bull, using the bull's nostrils for leverage. Both god and the bull were covered in gems and precious metals that caught the flickering light of oil lamps, creating a dancing effect.

The background was painted on one side to reflect the bright blue sky of day, while the other represented the dark night and where they met, the blending twilight of day and night. Sol Invictus, the unconquered sun, flew through the day sky in his sun chariot pulled by four white horses. In the night sky, Luna drove her moon chariot across the starry night fields, her chariot pulled by two great oxen.

He'd always preferred to finish his inspection of Mithras slaying the bull with Luna's corner, though he'd adopted her Hellenic name of Selene as his preferred means of address to the goddess. In his time away from his family, he'd grown fond of the moon and her goddess. Selene driving her moon chariot across the night sky brought a constancy to his life. No matter what province's sky he looked upon, Selene watched over him with her gentle silvery light.

The pater patrum spoke, "Brothers, we are most blessed to see off our fine warriors on a mission from divine Mithras. Blessed is their bravery as they seek to protect Mithras from his enemies. Join me as we raise them up in Mithras's honor." He raised his arms. "Syphax Quietus, rise and proceed to the altar," the pater patrum called out.

Syphax stood and stepped up to the altar, placing his hand on the blade of Mithras's sword where it plunged into the neck of the bull.

"Perses Quietus…" The pater patrum asked Syphax a series of liturgical questions, which he answered with the ritual words. When they finished, Syphax turned to the room as the pater patrum raised his arms again. "Now go forth, Heliodromus Quietus, and do Mithras's bidding."

One by one, the pater patrum raised each of the remaining centurions one rank each. The first three centurions were all raised to Leo. Bamilcar was raised to Miles, and Zyraxes was raised to the second rank of Nymphus.

"Miles Lucius Silvanius Ferrata," called the pater patrum.

When Lucius rose and stepped to the altar, he collapsed onto his knees, the weight of divine notice falling heavy on his shoulders. Closing his eyes, he reached out and touched the spot where the others had before him.

"Raise your head, brave soldier," a gentle feminine voice said.

When Lucius lifted his head and opened his eyes, Selene looked down at him, eyes brimming with kindness. The goddess was tall, nearly rising to the ceiling of the barrel-vaulted Mithraeum. Upon her brow, she wore a crescent moon that glowed so brightly Lucius had to squint to see her beautiful, dark hair. Pale arms reached out from the shimmering silver-gray folds of the silky himation she wore.

His heart opened in wonder. He'd always paid the gods the honor they were due, but more out of casual respect than true devotion. When one had to travel through the lands of so many gods, it made no sense to draw their ire, but this was the first time Lucius had ever truly felt a divine presence.

Selene's delicate moonlight suffused him, leaching out his fears and insecurities and filling him with love and appreciation.

Lucius bowed his head respectfully. "My Mistress."

"I have observed you as you've watched me cross the night sky. I wished to see the soldier whose loyal devotion has reached me even in the heavens. You are already strong and brave, my loyal soldier, but if you seek wisdom and are thoughtful, we shall meet again in the days to come. Know that I have marked you as mine. Rise with my blessing upon your heart." The light around Selene faded as she receded into the corner representing night.

Selene had commanded his complete attention; he hadn't heard a thing the pater patrum had said, which meant he hadn't answered his liturgical questions. He expected to have to repeat them.

"Rise, Perses Ferrata, servant of Luna, and serve Mithras's will." The pater patrum's voice shook as he spoke.

When Lucius rose from his knees, he turned and stopped. Everyone in the room was on their knees, a look of wonderment in their eyes. The pater patrum's face had paled in shock. Lucius's eyes darted about the room nervously, as every set of eyes followed his movements. His audience with the goddess hadn't been private.

Syphax cleared his throat, drawing the attention away from Lucius—something for which he was deeply grateful—and stood. Lucius's comrades followed suit. Soon, the rest of the room joined them in ones and twos until everyone was on their feet. The pater patrum stood still until Syphax nudged him in the side with his elbow.

"Ah, yes." The pater patrum stepped toward Lucius and extended his hand.

Lucius took his hand, and they shook, completing the ancient ritual in honor of Mithras and Sol Invictus, sealing their bond in the same manner.

Leaning over to the pater patrum, Syphax mumbled, "Let's move this along to the banquet before things get out of hand."

Finally recovering, the pater patrum nodded, lifted his arms, and addressed the room, "Please, move the benches to the walls and summon the servants with the banquet so we may honor Mithras's servants with the blessings of food and drink."

Syphax took his friend by the elbow and led him to an out-of-the-way corner, the other centurions following and forming a protective barrier between the rest of the adherents and their leader and Lucius.

Lucius leaned toward Syphax, placing his lips close to the older man's ears. "Why is everyone acting so oddly?"

"You fell to your knees, then glowed as if you were lit from within by the light of the moon. Everything went silent, then we heard Luna claim you as hers and put her blessing upon you—'Know that I have marked you as mine. Rise with my blessing upon your heart.' It was by her power and grace you were raised two grades instead of the one that was planned. You have been touched by the divine, and everyone here was a witness to it." Syphax chuckled nervously. "Her presence was overwhelming, and I was just a bystander. Damn it, man, she even changed the symbols on your robe to her crescent moon."

Lucius looked down. A silver crescent moon covered the cloth over his heart. She'd changed the entire robe. The cloth shimmered, shot through with silver threading. Besides her crescent moon, stars dappled the surface. He lifted the robe to inspect it closer. Syphax's eyes went wide.

"Gods above and below, she's even marked your armor." Syphax ran a finger over one of the steel plates of Lucius's lorica. "A goddess has noticed you, my friend, and for good or ill, you've been marked. Let's hope it brings us luck instead of bringing unwanted eyes down upon us. We're going to have enough trouble with Parthians and Armenians with unknown loyalties."

Lucius, robbed of speech, nodded. As the words Syphax had repeated moved through his mind, he realized that most of his audience with the goddess had been private. She'd only appeared to him, but she'd let the room know her presence through the glow and her blessing. Too overwhelmed to comprehend the magnitude of his meeting, he closed his eyes and tried to cement every image into his memory, though he doubted he'd forget any bit of it, even to his dying day.

Responding to an urge, he reached down to pull his gladius free so he could inspect it. When he found his right hip empty, he chuckled and shook his head. It now resided on his left hip, as befit a centurion. He held the scabbard and pulled the gladius out a few inches. The one side was blank and unmarked as it had been when it was purchased. When he moved the sword so he could look at the other side, he gasped. It too had been transformed. Near the hilt guard, a crescent moon adorned the steel, etched into the blade with both points of the moon pointing toward the tip. Stylized stars were scattered about the rest of that side of the blade.

He pulled the sword the rest of the way from the scabbard and held it flat in his hands so Syphax could look at it. Syphax shook his head, an inscrutable expression on his face.

"Treasure this, Lucius, but put it away before anyone else wants to see it." Syphax slid over to help block the view while Lucius resheathed the weapon.

The wall of centurions kept the civilians away while the servants set up the banquet. The scent of food drifted to Lucius's nose, making his mouth water as servants carried in platters of food. The aroma of roast meats, probably beef, lamb, and goat, competed with the spicy scents of dishes he couldn't name. Though he rarely got the opportunity, he sought the heavily spiced food of Syria that was so different from the cuisine of his youth. He peeked around the shoulders of his comrades to see what all was being brought in. His stomach rumbled.

"Well, gentlemen," Syphax said. "At least we'll get to eat well before it's nothing but marching rations."

The centurions mumbled their acknowledgments, eyeing the piles of food.

"Let's tuck in." Syphax reached out and took a wine cup offered by a servant with a jug of wine watered down with fruit juice, spices, and fruit.

Lucius took a deep drink from his cup, savoring the rich flavors of the quality wine—berries, exotic fruits he didn't know the name of, honey, and more of the tantalizing spices of the east. Tomorrow, he'd return to life as a legionnaire, but tonight he'd celebrate with wine and food provided by Antiochia's rich patrons of Mithras.

FOUR

"IS THAT IT?" Lucius asked.

"Aye, Centurio. Across that hill should be the town of Tigra-nocerta," the legionnaire replied.

"Thank you, Decanus." Lucius stared over the hills. After a hot summer, the greens had turned to golds and browns, especially in the terraces and valleys where farms and farmers were harvesting their crops. Raising his hand, he brought it down toward the hill the decanus had pointed to and nudged his pony forward.

His men fell in behind him. Patting the neck of his pony, Lucius smiled, glad the horse's legs would be the ones doing most of the hill climbing, because Armenia had more than its share of hills. The farmers and workers eyed Lucius's fifty-man scouting party wearing obvious Roman equipment and dress. Anyone close to the road drifted away from it, not interested enough in watching the Romans pass to stick around in case they might want to talk. Unless they were the archers promised by Trajan's Armenian puppet, Lucius had no interest in bothering the Armenians going about their lives.

When they crested the hill overlooking Tigranocerta, Lucius didn't see a camp anywhere. A unit of two hundred or more archers and support personnel should make for a noticeable bivouac unless it was tucked back in one of the many valleys.

"I don't see our loaned archers, do you, Decanus?" Lucius asked.

"I do not," the decanus replied. "What now, Centurio?"

"They were supposed to be right outside the city walls." Lucius scratched his chin under the leather strap holding his helmet on. "I'm not particularly interested in standing around out in the open. Let's turn around. We'll meet the rest of the cohort and report to the Tribunus." Lucius turned to the man wearing the black crest and white feathers of an optio. "Optio Venextos turn us around. Send out scouts front, back, and sides."

"Aye, Centurio." Venextos saluted and yelled out the orders, swinging their vexillation around.

A couple hours later, Lucius and his vexillation road through the gates of the cohort's road fort. Handing off his pony to a groom, Lucius marched to Syphax's tent, stepping through the flap when Syphax called his name. He saluted and sat in the camp chair his leader gestured to.

"Where are my archers, Lucius?" Syphax asked, looking up from the wax tablet he'd been scribbling on.

"Either they're camouflage specialists, or they're not where they're supposed to be. We scouted the area but didn't enter the town."

"We'll pay a visit to the town administrator, see which way the wind blows." He mumbled a curse. "Half the damned nobles of Armenia are related to the damned Parthians. I hope we finish this damned mission before this whole country reverts to Parthian control. Three fucking years of fighting, and we're already handing it all back."

"Do you think Hadrianus will try to reconquer it?" Lucius took the wine Syphax's servant brought over.

"Gnaius, can you find the Armenians, please?" After his servant left, Syphax relaxed back into his chair, stretching his legs in front of him. "I doubt it. Hadrianus isn't the type."

"You think the old man will actually name him his successor?" Lucius sipped the watered-down wine.

"I don't know if he'll do it or not, but unless something I don't foresee happens, Hadrianus will be the next imperator." Syphax shrugged. "As long as he keeps the pay regular, I could do without dragging my old ass across whatever border the empire wants to push back. I wouldn't mind finding a little patch of dirt and train up the rest of this legion."

Lucius chuckled. "Yeah, we're not much of a legion with only one cohort."

Gnaius popped his head back in "Sir? I have Ariazate."

"Thank you, Gnaius. You're free for the evening."

Gnaius bowed, said, "Thank you, sir," and left.

"Would you like some wine, Ariazate? It's watered." Syphax gestured toward a jug.

Ariazate nodded. Lucius fetched a cup and poured a splash into it, handing it to her as she sat in the other chair.

"What do you know about the town ahead of us? Tigranocerta?" Syphax asked.

"Not much, sir. I haven't spent much time in this part of Armenia, not since I was small." The young woman wore her road clothes—a black tunic and a pair of green trousers—and had her thick, black hair gathered at her nape.

Syphax pursed his lips. "Damn. Please, call me Syphax when we're here. I was hoping you might know what we're riding into."

"Are you going into Tigranocerta tomorrow?" she asked.

"I'd planned to have a chat with the local officials," Syphax replied.

"Can you give me a couple days? March around Tigranocerta and set up to the northeast?" Ariazate took a small sip, making a face that said the flavor wasn't to her taste.

Syphax leaned forward, resting his elbows on his camp desk. "What do you have in mind?"

"Let me and my brother slip into town. As musicians, we can go unnoticed, play on the street, earn a meal at a tavern. We can find out if the wind blows east or west."

Syphax rubbed the stubble on his cheek. "What do you think, Lucius?"

"She's probably right. If we march into town, I'm sure we'll be welcomed and hear nothing but meaningless apologies. We can wait a few days for the local potentate to kiss your ass before he passes on information about us to whoever's paying or pulling the strings."

Tenting his hands in front of his face, Syphax stared into the space between Lucius and Ariazate, eventually nodding lightly. "Since you agree with our young friend here, you'll go in with them to keep them safe."

"I don't know the local language," Lucius replied. "Not sure I'll be of much use."

"They'll speak the Hellenic tongue well enough, and probably a few will know enough Latin for you to get by," Syphax said, a smirk spreading over his face.

"It's probably better that we pose as your slaves. You won't be able to go in with full armor though, you'll be too conspicuous." Ariazate sized him up, her eyes seizing on the arrow scar through his left forearm. "You can be a wounded soldier mustering out, trying to sell your slaves to someone who can profit off a couple Armenian tsiranapogh players before retiring to your homeland far to the west."

"It's a plausible story." Syphax's eyes dropped to the scar on Lucius's forearm. "You'll have to fake a weak hand for the ploy to work, but you're a resourceful fellow. With our black tunics and cloaks, you won't look too official since no other legion uses the color. Pull a pair of trousers from the winter stores, and you'll look a right proper barbarian discharged from the legions."

Lucius pursed his lips. "If you insist…" He turned to Ariazate. "When do you want to depart?"

"After your cohort marches out. We can hide in one of these groves and then make our way later in the afternoon." She took another sip of her wine before setting it down and pushing it away.

Syphax chuckled silently before settling his gaze on Lucius. "What do you think, Centurio?"

He took a drink of his wine, thinking about the girl's plan while enjoying the fine vintage Syphax kept around no matter where they were. He always managed to find the best merchant and lay in a stock of premium wine. It always made time with Syphax more enjoyable, though he liked his commanding officer and considered him a close friend. The wine was just a tasty bonus.

Lucius was a front-line soldier. He'd been responsible for solo missions, but never in espionage. Looking over at the girl, he sized her up. She seemed confident enough, and her plan was solid. But none of his previous missions had put him in charge of children, though he wasn't sure Ariazate fit that description, hovering on the line between childhood and adulthood. If she was positive she could play her part, Lucius could do his.

"It's workable—better than going in blind and getting nothing useful," Lucius said.

Nodding, Syphax dismissed Ariazate, refilling his cup and adding some to Lucius's. "She's a bold one for a slave."

"Not everyone is born a slave, and she won't be when we're done with this mission," Lucius replied.

"And we'll just turn her and her brother loose into a power vacuum? No one to look out for them?"

Lucius, brows furrowing, looked down and sighed.

"Not so straight forward, is it? But then, that's a problem for a later date and ultimately, for the young lady and her brother, if they get their wish."

They sat in silence for a while, enjoying their wine. He didn't know what Ariazate and Tigran would do once they received their freedman caps and their papers, but at least they had a generous stipend from the imperator. Since he'd be spending some time with them, he'd be able to get to know them, find out if they had people to go to or a family to return to. Other than their names and their musical talent, he knew little about them. Though they'd stayed near him and Syphax on the march from Antiochia, they hadn't spoken much, and Lucius had focused on keeping the march moving. He yawned, shaking his head.

"Why don't you go to bed? We'll have another early morning. You've got to keep some kids out of trouble and see what we're up against. Should be an easy job," Syphax teased.

Lucius tossed back the last of his wine and stood up. "Goodnight, Syphax."

"Sleep well, Lucius."

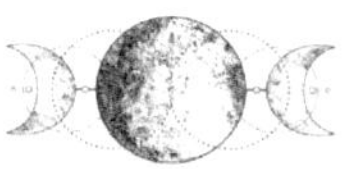

LUCIUS, Ariazate, and Tigran rode through the gates of Tigranocerta late the next afternoon, the youngsters in the lead and a packhorse hiding Lucius's gear bringing up the rear. Even though his armor was close at hand, he felt naked without its steely protection. After Ariazate stopped a few people, peppering them with questions, they headed toward the market district to find something to eat. It would also give Ariazate a chance to nose around, find out what was going on in this part of Armenia, and maybe find a tavern looking for music.

While Lucius and the boy dove into their bowls of spiced rice and chicken with chucks of a delightful tangy fruit, Ariazate chatted up the old woman who'd sold them their bowls. The boy scooped the food into his mouth like he was afraid it might run away if he set his bowl down. Lucius chuckled and shook his head. After a month of eating legion rations and however long they'd been in Trajan's service before that, the food of his homeland probably tasted like the best thing he'd had in ages. He wasn't wrong. The bowl of spiced rice and chicken was the best thing Lucius'd eaten since leaving Antiochia.

When the boy's spoon scraped the bottom of the bowl forlornly, Lucius caught the eye of the old woman and nodded to his young companion. She smiled warmly at the boy and refilled his bowl. When Ariazate finished questioning the old lady, she brought her bowl over to the table and scooped some into her mouth, the bite bringing a small, contented smile to her serious face.

While she ate, Lucius followed Tigran around the food stalls, picking up a couple sweets the boy kept eyeing and a few of the fabled Armenia plums for himself. Biting into the small, golden fuzzy fruit, Lucius savored the tangy sweetness.

"That's the same fruit that was in our bowl," Lucius said.

"Mhm," Tigran mumbled around a mouthful of the pastry Lucius had bought him. "You can get them everywhere in Armenia. Our tsiranapogh are made from their wood. That tree is part of who we are as Armenians."

By the time they made the circuit around the market and returned to their table, Ariazate had finished her food. After accepting a plum from Lucius, she gestured toward the exit and walked ahead of Lucius and Tigran. They wove their way through the crowd, moving about their day as people returned to their homes or headed to the markets. Once they found a quiet alleyway, Ariazate slipped in and waited out of the way behind a turn in the wall.

"What did she say, Zati?" Tigran asked quietly as soon as he joined her in their sheltered nook.

Looking up at Lucius briefly, she wiped a crumb off the boy's cheek. "She suggested we play by the bridge. We should be able to make a bit of coin. She suggested a couple taverns that might pay for a night or two of music."

Cautiously looking around to make sure they weren't being eavesdropped on, Lucius bent down so he was closer to their height. "Did she give you any kind of indication what's going on here?"

"She looked a bit nervous. Said to stick to the roads when traveling," Ariazate replied.

"Bandits?" Lucius asked.

"Maybe, but she implied they might be a bit more heavily armed than common brigands. Told me to keep my nose out of partisan issues if I wanted to stay out of trouble."

"Partisan?"

Ariazate snorted in annoyance. "Romans or Parthians and those looking to make a name or fortune on either or both." She made a sign against evil and spat on the ground.

Tigran looked scared. "What are we going to do, Zati?"

"I don't know, Tigi." She looked at Lucius with her stern gaze. "What do you want to do, Roman? This is your operation."

Lucius looked at the faces of the two kids he'd been saddled with on this mission. The boy looked rightfully scared at being mixed up in politics between two warring empires. Ariazate, however, betrayed nothing beyond the general annoyance and stoic calmness that was her everyday expression.

"How old are you two?" Lucius finally asked.

"Twelve," Tigran replied, standing taller and puffing out his chest. "Zati is sixteen."

She scowled at her younger brother and shook her head, huffing. Tigran was a child just entering adolescence while Ariazate neared adulthood. She was only a bit younger than he was when he signed his contract with the legions.

Exhaling through his nose while trying to avoid displaying his exasperation, he nodded between the two of them. "Let's blend in and do what the old lady recommended. You two play by the bridge, then we'll see about finding a tavern. While you're playing, where would you like me?"

"Give us a few moments' head start and then mingle with the crowd and watch." Ariazate looked him up and down. "Try to slouch some. You look like you're on parade, Roman."

Lucius smiled and relaxed into a slouch. "Get going. I'll be along shortly."

He watched as they left the alley, counting in his head so he didn't follow too closely. Without his armor, he felt naked. Although he wore the black tunic of his legion, he looked like nearly anyone else in his trousers and cloak. He didn't even wear the cingulum militare, missing the belt with its leather and brass dangling from his waist. His caligae were the only thing that marked him as being a legionnaire, or former as the charade dictated, but they were a comfortable boot made for walking, a solid choice for any traveler. Besides, he didn't have any other footwear with him.

When he'd counted high enough, he left the alley, the hobnails of his caligae clicking on the cobblestones as he entered the roadway and slipped into the flow of foot traffic. Every person bumping into him increased the tension between his shoulder blades, creating an itch he couldn't reach. Without steel wrapped around his body, a dagger could find its way into his back, and he'd have no protection beyond a few layers of cloth.

As he approached the bridge running over a stream low from the summer's heat, he heard the reedy sounds of the siblings' tsiranapoghs as they warmed up. They'd set up in a nook next to the bridge out of the way of the traffic but easily accessible so people could drop coins on the cloth they'd set in front of them. The rich and practiced tones of the players had already enticed a small crowd.

Once they'd determined they were ready, Ariazate signaled to her brother, lifted her tsiranapogh, and played the opening notes of the first song. When she touched back around to the melody, Tigran joined, accompanying her with a drone. The upbeat song had the audience tapping their feet and humming along. After they finished, a few people threw coins on the cloth and continued on their way, though the crowd didn't suffer from their departure as far more had stopped to listen to the talented youths. After a few moments, they launched into another song. This time, Tigran started, playing a simple melody, but instead of joining with the drone, Ariazate added a complex counter melody that soared like a hawk riding the wind.

Lucius shook himself out of the musical trance and focused his attention on watching the crowd to ensure the safety of his charges. He didn't recognize anyone that looked Parthian, though he doubted they'd be standing about in full armor with a banner flying above their heads. And after the long association between Armenia and Parthia and the intermarriage of their nobles, the differences were slight between the two peoples, far too slight for Lucius to distinguish.

The anxiety from earlier returned as he realized how out of his depth he was as a spy. After rising quickly through the ranks of the legions to make centurion by the time he turned thirty-one, he didn't like the feeling of not having the needed skills and competence to carry out the mission, nor did he like relying on two children with unknown loyalties and goals. He'd have to trust his instincts.

FIVE

THE OLD WOMAN'S plan had worked. Ariazate and Tigran had earned a respectable pile of coins by the time they called it quits, although Lucius didn't see anyone who looked particularly martial. The big victory, though, was a tavern owner offering them a job playing later that night. If the crowd responded well, there was a possibility of more.

When the listeners dissipated, the siblings rejoined Lucius, and together they looked for a place to stay for the evening. Ariazate asked around and found them a quiet, reasonably priced inn, though they'd have to share a room.

Once they had their lodging secured, they proceeded to the tavern to get some dinner before the siblings would be called on to play. The first night went smoothly, though they didn't pick up much that they didn't know already. The locals worried about the transition of power amid rumors the Romans would be pulling out. Some whispered about Parthian agents filtering into the countryside, even this far west. A few even mentioned sightings of larger forces. All this was translated by Ariazate or Tigran as they listened to the talk in between songs or when they moved through the room, chatting for tips. Since things went so well, they took the offer from the tavern's owner to return the next night.

Fortunately for Lucius and his stomach, the tavern served good food. Along with vegetable soup and a hearty loaf, diners could order a chunk of fresh venison which Lucius did, wanting to keep his strength up for the coming march into the mountains. He'd need the extra fat stores when things got tight on the trail.

They showed up on time the second night started with dinner. Once their empty bowls were cleared, the siblings set up in the corner, taking out their instruments, and warmed up. Soon they broke into a few simple but lively melodies that seemed to draw people in off the streets, or maybe it was just time for the evening crowd to roll in for their drinks and food.

Lucius found a quiet corner where he could nurse his wine and monitor the crowd. Every few songs, Tigran would work his way through the crowd with his hat out to collect tips. The longer the patrons drank, the more generous they became.

After a long set, the Ariazate and Tigran took a break, rejoining Lucius at his table. The innkeeper brought over a bit of watered-down wine. When they returned to the corner that had been set aside as their stage, a quartet of armed men stepped into the tavern.

In a moment, Lucius identified them as fighting men. These weren't farmers with old swords, but sharp-eyed lean warriors assessing any dangers in the crowd with a quick glance. They didn't wear anything that announced who they fought for other than a few pieces of equipment that marked them as not Roman, though it was possible they could be an auxilia unit from the eastern part of the empire. They sat at a table near the entrance.

Lucius tried to relax and look casual, but he struggled to keep his eyes on the performance and not on the four men. Every time one of them shifted, his eyes flicked over to their table and lingered longer than was wise. He adjusted his seat to make it harder to stare their way. He must have been too aggressive and not casual enough; all four gazes drifted toward him after a whispered comment from one of them. The leader stood and moved through the small tavern to sit across from Lucius at his small table.

"Is there a problem here, Roman soldier?" the man asked in halting Latin.

"No, problem. Just curious." Lucius kept his surprise contained at the man's accurate identification and opted to reply in Hellene because it had been spoken widely throughout the region since Alexander the Great.

"This tongue is better than your Latin," the man replied in Hellene. "Curiosity can be dangerous."

Lucius shrugged. "I'm not looking for trouble. I'm retired. Took a Parthian arrow in the arm." He lifted his left hand from under the table and set it on the table, letting his hand flop uselessly onto the wooden surface.

The man looked smugly at the pink scar on both sides of Lucius's left forearm where the arrow had pierced it while fighting across a bridge on the Tigris River for his imperator.

"Hard to hold a scutum when you can't use your hand," Lucius added.

The man laughed, then stood up. "Keep your eyes to yourself, Roman, if you want to keep those working." Then, he turned and returned to his friends. A few moments later, they all looked at Lucius and laughed before picking up their conversation.

After that, they seemed entirely disinterested in Lucius. Forcing himself to appear relaxed, he focused on Ariazate and Tigran's music, letting their melodies soothe his agitation. Earlier, they'd played more upbeat songs, as upbeat as a tsiranapogh could sound, but now, the sadness of the haunting instrument took center stage as they poured their hearts into their songs. Breathing deeply, he exhaled the tension he held in his shoulders and back and let the music take him.

When the brother and sister finished their last set, they joined Lucius at his table, taking their free drinks from the tavern keeper.

Ariazate leaned in close, brows furrowed in annoyance. "What were you doing antagonizing those Parthians?"

Lucius had guessed who they might be after their interaction, but it was good to have confirmation. "Sorry. I'm not exactly a spy."

"Well, at least you defused it before blades were drawn."

It amused Lucius how much annoyance she could infuse into her voice for one so young, though he kept it off his face, not wanting to offend his companion. "At least we confirmed there are Parthians in the area. Did you pick up anything from the crowd?"

"About the same as last night, until those four walked in. Then I got nothing." She scowled.

Lucius raised an eyebrow. "That in itself is a lot of information."

Tigran looked confused. Ariazate narrowed her eyes, puzzling over the idea.

"I see," she said.

"What?" Tigran looked back and forth between them. "I don't get it."

"Everyone here recognized those men as Parthians as soon as they walked in, so they stopped talking about politics," Ariazate explained.

Tigran nodded.

"Did you collect your pay? I think it's time we make an exit," Lucius said.

Ariazate nodded. Lucius stood up and pulled his cloak around himself, letting his lame left hand rest on the pommel of his gladius. Ushering his young companions out the door, he followed them into the darkness of Tigranocerta.

"QUICK, THROUGH HERE," Ariazate whispered after looking down the narrow alley.

Lucius took the lead, looking for anything out of the ordinary. Almost immediately after leaving the tavern, they encountered small groups of Parthians wandering around the city, though it felt far more like an active patrol sweeping Tigranocerta than random groups moving about. Any pretense of being civilians ended when they stopped several people, questioning them loudly. Ariazate, who knew some Parthian, was able to pick up a phrase or two. They were looking for Romans or anyone suspicious.

When the moon ducked out from behind a cloud, Selene's light bathed Tigranocerta, setting the stone of the buildings aglow.

While they waited for another patrol to pass by, Lucius cast his gaze to the sky. *"Please watch over us…"*

Looking to Ariazate, he whispered, "Are we clear?"

She nodded and waved them forward. Opting for bold, they strode across the wider road into the shadows of another alley, then ducked into the darkness, the buildings blocking the light. Even though Tigranocerta wasn't a large city, they couldn't get close to their inn and its stables. The Parthians idly strolling around were too well armed and organized to be coincidental.

Lucius whipped around as someone shouted behind them. The men from the tavern pointed at them. Behind him, he heard stone against stone, but couldn't turn to see what it was with four men pelting down the alley toward them. Lucius let his left hand settle onto the pommel of the sword strapped to his left hip, resuming the character he'd played earlier.

"What do you want?" Lucius called out, holding his right hand up so they could see nothing was in it. Ariazate and Tigran stepped behind him.

"Keep your hands where we can see them, Roman," the man said as he slowed, stopping a few steps away from Lucius.

"The left isn't going anywhere," Lucius replied, keeping his right arm up. "Not with this injury. What do you want?"

"You're going back to camp with us. Someone wants to have a chat with you." The same man who'd accosted him at the table earlier took another step closer.

"I don't know why. I don't know anyone around here, and I'm a nobody. What would anyone want with a common soldier discharged with a wound? I'm just trying to sell these slaves and go home." Lucius indicated Ariazate and Tigran.

"We'll just let our boss sort you out." The man stepped closer. "Get some rope so we can bind their hands."

"Look. You've got the wrong people. I'm just passing through," Lucius protested.

"Then you have nothing to worry about if you come with us. But if you don't shut up and let us bind you, we'll take you by force. Either way, you're going with us."

Lucius slumped, defeated. As the Parthian stepped closer, slowly raising his arm to take Lucius's wrist, Lucius let his left hand slip off the pommel as he wrapped his fingers around the hilt in a reverse grip. Yanking the sword out of its scabbard, Lucius brought it up, slamming the end of the pommel up and into the Parthian's chin, then dragged the edge of the blade along the Parthian's neck, cutting his throat.

Lucius tried to turn the blade so the flat would catch most of the blood spray, but still felt the warm spatter of blood on his face. As the Parthian reached for his throat, he choked and gagged on his own blood, stumbling backwards into his companions. Flipping the sword into a standard grip, Lucius charged after him, shoving the wounded man to trip up the other three. The first was caught completely off-guard as Lucius plunged the gladius into his guts. Lucius twisted and yanked the blade free in time to block a hasty swing at his body. Though he wasn't as good of a sword fighter with his left hand, he was more than capable of taking out these men who were probably more practiced with bow and lance.

With his sword out of position, Lucius lashed out and punched the next Parthian, shattering his nose. By the time he cleared his blade, the last of the quartet had turned and fled back down the alley and out onto the street. Lucius only caught a brief glimpse of his back as he turned right and disappeared. Before Lucius could catch his breath, Ariazate screamed behind him.

Spinning around, he saw the young boy and his sister trying to fight off a trio of Parthians. Lucius charged forward. Leaping between the two Armenian adolescents, he knocked over the closest Parthian, stomping down hard with his hobnailed caligae. A scream and the crack of bones brought a smile to his face as he raised his gladius to block a sword thrust at his head. Shoving the blade aside, he whipped a backhanded slash, catching the third Parthian in the face. As the second Parthian grabbed at him, he turned in time to see the Parthian drop his blade, his back arching.

He fell to the ground, a dagger in his back. Zati stood behind him, a horrified look on her face. Before he could scramble off, Lucius slashed the throat of the Parthian he'd stomped on earlier, then looked down both ends of the alley. It was clear. He grabbed the nearest Parthian and dragged him behind a pile of debris. By the time he was done, Tigran and Zati had moved deeper into the shadows where they couldn't see the bodies.

Wiping the sweat from his forehead, he grabbed the two Armenians and prepared to go. Again, the sound of stone on stone drew his attention. Without the distraction of the Parthians, he found the noise. A shiny bald head poked out of a secret stone door in the middle of the alley wall.

As Lucius raised his sword toward the new threat, the little man waved them closer. "Roman, I can hide you and your companions."

"Who are you?" Lucius didn't lower his sword.

"I'm the pater of the local Mithraeum. I was told to look out for you. Hurry. Before more Parthians show up." The little man looked nervously up and down the alley.

"Who sent you?"

The little man's eyes drifted up toward the moon. "She did."

Lucius nodded, placing his hand over the crescent moon Selene had carved in his armor over his heart and casting a prayer of thanks to the night sky. He ushered Ariazate and Tigran toward the man. As soon they stepped inside the door, a larger, muscular man pushed it closed, barring it. Putting himself between the doorman and the pater and the two Armenian youths, Lucius lowered his sword some, but kept it ready.

"Please, follow me." The little bald man waved them deeper into the building.

"Send your man in first, then you, then I'll follow," Lucius ordered. If this was a trap, he wanted the strangers in front of his sword and the siblings behind his back. He didn't like this, but it was better than running into gangs of Parthians.

The man nodded and sent the large man ahead, stepping in behind him. Lucius caught the eyes of the two Armenians and gave them a faint nod before turning to follow the men deeper into the stone corridor. It matched the basic gray stone of the alleyway as they wound through more halls before descending a set of stairs. When they reached the bottom, they stood in the antechamber of Tigranocerta's Mithraeum.

The man spoke rapidly in Armenian, sending his large companion away. Though he tried to follow along, his grasp of Armenian was far too rudimentary to catch more than a word or two, though he'd been trying to learn. He'd have to rely on Ariazate to translate. She didn't seem bothered by what was said, though she looked distracted, a wide-eyed look of horror on her wan face as she stared into the distance. A motion caught Lucius's eye—Ariazate's hands trembled.

"My man is fetching a bucket of water and a rag so you can clean up. If you tell me where your horses and belongings are, I'll see them brought to a safe stable nearby," the pater said, returning to his rough but adequate Latin.

"Thank you, Pater. But you'll have to forgive me if I'm not exactly feeling terribly trusting right now. If you don't mind, I need to speak with someone..." Lucius nodded toward the main chamber of the Mithraeum.

The little man nodded, gesturing toward the door with an open hand. Lucius nodded and stepped into the Mithraeum, stopping just before the large painted scene of Mithras slaying the bull. He's spent the weeks since leaving Antiochia thinking about his brush with the divine. Marching allowed for a lot of time to ponder such weighty topics. Though he'd come to terms with catching the eye of Selene, he was about to reach out to her directly, something he wasn't sure was a wise idea. Dropping to his knees, he laid out the gladius before him, the side marked by Selene facing up. He closed his eyes.

"*Blessed Selene, I thank you for your aid.*"

"*Of course, my brave soldier. I'm glad I was able to help in your time of need,*" the goddess replied in the vault of Lucius's mind, her voice warm and gentle.

"*Can this man, he who claims to be the pater of this Mithraeum, be trusted?*" Lucius asked.

"*I've looked into his heart. You are safe while you are with him. He commands respect among the local adherents of Mithras. He will aid you in getting back to your men because I have so ordered it with the backing of The Wanderer himself."*

"Thank you, My Mistress, for watching over me and my friends."

"Be well, Lucius Silvanius Ferrata, and look you toward the temple of Gorneae on your way to The Wanderer's temple. The pater will provide a guide for you."

"I am in your humble debt."

"Go with my blessing, Lucius."

Lucius opened his eyes but blinked as the silvery glow surrounding his body dissipated. As with his first interaction with the goddess of the moon, warmth and serenity infused him. He stood, picked up his sword, and rejoined Ariazate, Tigran, and the pater in the antechamber. They stared at him wide-eyed, their mouths hanging open. The pater bowed deeply before Lucius.

"Selene says I can trust you."

The small man nodded jerkily as he stared at Lucius, his eyes flicking about a bit wildly. Lucius told him where their horses were billeted and what room they'd been staying in. Once the doorman returned with water, the pater sent him to get food and drink, then left to take care of procuring their horses and the rest of their belongings. Lucius offered the rag and bucket to Ariazate first who eagerly washed the blood from her hands until they looked pink and raw from scrubbing. Lucius took her hands and dried them, then helped her to a nearby bench to sit down. Her eyes were having trouble focusing. He'd seen the look in soldiers suffering shock and would address it as soon as he got himself cleaned up.

Tigran had managed to stay free from blood and left the water for Lucius to use. He couldn't do anything about the blood on his tunic, but he washed his hands and face as best as he could, finishing with his gladius. With that stowed, he sent Tigran to look at the murals and statues inside the Mithraeum with the order not to touch anything.

Sitting next to Ariazate, he left a foot between himself and the young woman while remaining quiet. After a while, she broke the silence.

"I killed that man..." she scooted over, resting her head on

Lucius's shoulder. "I keep hearing his scream over and over as my knife plunges into his back."

Lucius wrapped his arm around her shoulders and gave it a squeeze, letting the girl cry quietly on his shoulder. When she finished, she sniffed and sat up, wiping her sleeve across her nose.

"I've never killed anyone before," she said quietly. "I can see every detail in his face when he turned around. Does it ever go away?"

Lucius thought back to the Dacians he'd killed in his first battle. After the intense fight to survive the ambush in the mountains of Dacia, he hadn't had time to think about what he'd just done, but the faces were still present in his mind. He'd killed many people in battles since then, but those first stuck with him.

"Not appreciably." He sighed.

"I hope it goes away."

"The intensity of the imagery will decrease, but at times it'll flash back just as bright and clear as right now." Lucius squeezed the bridge of his nose. "I'm sorry you had to do that. It was my job to protect you and your brother."

Lucius was about to speak more but clacked his jaw closed when he heard the scrape of leather on stone. His hand drifted toward the grip of his gladius. When he saw the pater reemerge, he relaxed.

"I have food and drink for you, as well as blankets. It's probably best that you stay here for the night. In the morning, we'll sneak you out of town and back to your people." The pater directed a few servants to set up their beds along the wall.

"Thank you, Pater. You probably saved our lives." Lucius bowed his head in respect.

"You are most welcome, Perses Ferrata. Is there anything else I can do for you?"

"I've been informed you can provide me with a guide to get us to Gorneae."

The pater bowed. "I have been instructed by holy Selene to aid you in this manner. We'll leave at first light. I'll send someone to wake you."

Lucius nodded. "We'll be ready."

"I know there aren't many hours before dawn, but sleep well."

Lucius stood and clasped hands with the pater. After the old man left, Lucius gathered his charges and inspected the food the pater had brought. Ariazate looked at, looking a bit green, and rolled up in her blanket instead. Lucius and Tigran dug into the food, then crawled into their blankets. The last thing he did before lying down was pull his gladius so he could sleep next to the naked blade in case they were discovered.

SIX

FOOTFALLS SCRAPING on stone startled Lucius awake. He lunged for his sword, pointing it toward the sound.

A man squeaked and backed away. "Easy, Perses."

The voice sounded familiar. Once he'd rubbed the sleep from his eyes, he recognized the pater. Forcing his fingers to unwind from his sword, he sat up, then sheathed the blade.

"Sorry. Just a little jumpy," Lucius said before yawning.

The pater chuckled nervously. "Understandable, Perses. Nervous times."

Lucius reached over and gently shook Ariazate. "It's time to wake up."

The young woman sighed and sat up, wiping her eyes. While the pater directed Lucius to a chamber pot, Ariazate woke her brother. He returned to a small meal the pater provided to break their fast. As soon as they'd finished their quick meal, the pater gave them new clothes to aid in their surreptitious escape from Tigranocerta, then led them out of the building the Mithraeum was hidden under. They blended into the early morning flow of people.

A few people nodded or greeted the pater as they passed. He replied casually, but Lucius could see the man's underlying anxiety.

He'd spent fourteen years learning to read men going into action—understanding how his comrades would react to battle and how to best mold them into reliable soldiers who could face any challenge.

Wrapping his cloak tightly around him, the crisp mountain morning aiding the ruse, he longed to put his hand on his gladius and feel the familiar and comforting texture of the bone grip. He resisted the urge, not wanting to draw attention to himself or to their little party as they worked their way toward the wealthier part of town. Every eye that lingered on Lucius could have been a Parthian, up early to hunt down the man who'd killed several of their comrades only a few hours ago in the alleys of the small city.

When the pater finally waved them into a walled estate and toward the stables near the back, Lucius kept his guard up, ready for either betrayal or discovery. As they approached the stables, the pater stopped and called out in Armenian. A response came immediately; he smiled and stepped into the stable.

"These are my people. They'll escort us out of town," he said to Lucius. Turning to the men inside the stables, he asked, "Are the horses ready?"

"Aye, Pater. We've got the Roman's horses and their belongings from the inn. They've been fed, watered, and saddled," the man in the lead replied.

"Excellent. We'll walk them out, then mount up once we clear the gate." The pater shook hands with the leader of his men.

Three men brought out Lucius's horse and the two the cohort had lent to Ariazate and Tigran. The packhorse Lucius kept his gear on was tethered to his saddle. Lucius rubbed the cheek of his short war pony. It was several hands shorter than the horses the pater and his men favored, but the Roman pony was bred and trained for war. Its small size made it an efficient mount—it required less food and water than a taller horse—but it could still eat up the miles. Before they left the stable, Lucius pulled his lorica from a bag on the packhorse and slipped it on. He put on his black cloak, then layered on the ratty gray one the pater had loaned him for their disguise. The steel was well enough concealed, but he'd rather risk the bulk than not have it when needed. He left the rest of his gear stowed, since it was harder to conceal and would be a dead giveaway he was a Roman.

Lucius longed to put his back to Tigranocerta and return to his cohort, where he'd have the strength of the elite unit to protect his back and help him watch over his young charges. They were his guides, putting their lives in danger to earn the freedom Trajan had dangled over their heads. Lucius meant to see that they actually lived to enjoy it.

Once they cleared the gate after the pater spoke to the guards, they mounted up at a signal from the small man. Lucius fought the urge to nudge the horse's speed up beyond the gentle trot the pater and his men set. The pater took the central position, his men surrounding him.

"Zati, I want you and your brother to move up next to the pater. You're out of place," Lucius said just loud enough for the girl to hear.

She nodded and caught her brother's attention, directing him to follow her. Once they were safely in the inner circle, Lucius drifted back to join the men in the rear, his eyes sweeping around them looking for any threats. He tried to keep from turning in his saddle to look back at the city too many times. Once they'd passed beyond the sight line to the city, Lucius didn't relax, keeping his surveillance up.

The pater firmly kept his eyes forward but twitched every time a noise intruded on his consciousness. The pater's skittishness rippled out to his men. Or Lucius's nervousness was the source of their anxiety. Either way, the constantly shifting bodies and swiveling heads spoke louder than any words that they were hiding something.

Not even stopping for a midday meal, they only dismounted long enough to walk and keep their mounts fresh. As they got closer to the spot on the map Syphax had designated as their rendezvous, Lucius moved to the front of their little band, letting his armor shine in the sun so any of their patrols would know it was one of theirs coming in. As jumpy as he was, the rest of the cohort had to be nearly as anxious as they sat unmoving in what was clearly becoming hostile territory.

When they neared a section of road running through a thick grove, Lucius ordered the rest of the group to hold up as he rode in alone, sword drawn but held low against his horse's damp shoulder. As he breached the shadows, he let his eyes adjust for a moment before proceeding. Something wasn't right. He couldn't place his finger on what it was until he realized it wasn't an issue of what it was but what it was lacking—sound.

The grove should have been alive with the sound of birds singing and small animals scurrying about, but all that greeted him was the eerie silence of a forest with its breath held. Why, Lucius couldn't guess.

His only warning was the snapping of a branch and a grunt that sounded vaguely like a curse. In an instant, he'd kicked his horse into action and raised his sword, ready for whatever might emerge. When he saw two riders burst out of the trees, he aimed for the nearest, angling so he'd put that rider between himself and the other one. Just as he was about to bring his slash down, he recognized the color of the cloaks and the gear and diverted his swing, finishing with his sword pointed at the neck of the rider.

Lucius recognized the face of one of his legionnaires. Sighing, he took a moment to get control of his body as adrenaline pumped through it before giving the pass code he'd setup with Syphax and getting the proper response, then lowered his sword. "Damn, Mylitos, I nearly took your head off."

"I noticed that, Centurio." Mylitos breathed heavily, his eyes wide and darting erratically.

Lucius nodded at the other legionnaire, a newer man, unable to place his name at the moment. "Come with me. We need to gather up the rest of our group."

He turned his horse and rode back. Trying to calm himself after the near brush with fatal action, he breathed deeply and steadily, matching the rhythmic stride of his gelding. By the time they made it back to the Armenians, he'd reasserted his control and combined his two parties, turning over the lead to Mylitos, who'd take them into the camp.

Lucius had never been happier to see the wooden walls of their fort. If the cohort had been allowed the full time of Lucius's planned absence, they'd have dug in more trenches and made it even more formidable. As it was, it was a sight for sore eyes.

After Mylitos gave the day's password to the guards holding the gate, Lucius ordered Mylitos to take care of the pater's attendants, waving the young Armenians and the pater to follow him. He walked down the central lane into the center of the camp to Syphax's tent. Before Lucius had even opened his mouth, one of the men standing guard out front poked his head in and announced that Centurio Ferrata had returned. Lucius turned and asked the three Armenians to wait outside a few tents down, then stepped toward Syphax's tent.

The two guards held the flaps open for him as Lucius stepped in and saluted. "Tribunus Quietus."

"Lucius, you're back early." Syphax stood up and reached across the camp desk to shake Lucius's hand.

"We ran into a bit of trouble and had to move up our schedule," Lucius replied.

Syphax handed Lucius a cup of water. Lucius drank it down in a single gulp, exhaling happily after the cool water slid down his parched throat.

"You look tired and sweaty, my friend." Syphax sat back down.

"Then I look how I feel." Lucius refilled the cup and took another swig. "We slipped in easily enough and found a tavern for Ariazate and Tigran to play. Seemed like the pickings were good as they worked the crowd for information, but everyone got really quiet when a quartet of poorly disguised Parthian soldiers walked in and found a table. They saw I was a former legionnaire and tried to start something with me. We slipped out of the tavern, but the streets were swarming with patrols. Eventually we ran into trouble, and I had to act."

Syphax raised a sardonic eyebrow. "How many did you take out?"

"Seven." Lucius left out that one of them had been finished off by Ariazate, not wanting to reveal that the young Armenian slave had a sting. He also didn't want to subject her to Syphax's questioning and force her to relive the incident.

"How'd you make it out?" Syphax leaned back, tapping a finger on his desk.

"The local pater found and hid us. I brought him with us."

"How did he know to look for you?" Syphax looked relaxed, but Lucius could tell he was on full alert from the steady, sharp gaze the older man gave him.

Lucius lifted his right hand and tapped the crescent moon of Selene that she'd engraved on his armor over his heart. "She sent him."

Syphax shook his head and chuckled. "You've made a powerful and dangerous ally, my young friend. I'll be sure to give her my thanks for bringing you back alive. Let's meet this pater who risked his life to help you escape."

Lucius nodded and stood up. Poking his head out of the tent, he waved the pater and the two Armenian youths over, making room for them to enter. Turning to the pater. "Tribunus Militum Syphax Quietus, this is the pater of the Tigranocerta's Mithraeum…" Lucius paused for a moment. "I didn't get his name, but he helped us escape."

The pater stepped forward and shook Syphax's hand. "Tiridat Aruseak, Tribunus."

"Please sit." Syphax gestured toward one of the camp chairs. "Thank you for helping my wayward centurio escape Tigranocerta."

"You're most welcome, but the duty was placed on me by one who I could not deny," Tiridat replied. "She also bid me lead you through the mountains to the temple at Garni, or Gorneae as you Romans call it."

Syphax's eyes drifted toward Lucius. Nodding, Lucius confirmed the pater's words. Pursing his lips, Syphax took a moment to mull over the information, then turned and rummaged through his maps. When he found the one he was looking for, he stood and rolled it out on the camp desk, orienting it so Tiridat stood at the south side of the map.

"We'd planned on taking the main road through to Vagharshap-at…" Syphax trailed off as he ran his finger on the line that indicated the road.

Tiridat set his finger on the map at the spot where their fort was situated. "While the road is easier, it'll be lined with Parthian agents. Armenia is awash in them. There are lesser-known paths through the mountains along the skirts of Ararat that will bring you north of Arxata. From there, it's a short march north to Garni."

"Pater Tiridat," Lucius interjected diffidently, "what is Garni?"

Tiridat smiled and turned to Lucius. "It's a temple dedicated to Mihr, the sun god of our people. Sometimes he bears the face of your Mithras."

SEVEN

NEVER ONE TO RIDE IN the center of his own column, Syphax and the primus pilus took the I Centuria, along with the pater and his men, and scouted ahead. They kept a watchful eye out for any potential resistance, and if they made it through the day without finding any, they'd look for their next night's campsite. While they were up and out of the fort before first light, Lucius followed with the rest of the cohort at a more reasonable pace, ensuring a strong rearguard to alert them of enemies.

The first day out, they met no resistance. Neither did they on the second or the third, though the scouts reported occasional sightings of potential Parthians. Despite Lucius's desire to swivel his head around or to lead one of the small scouting parties, his place was in the center of the column, leading the rest of the elite cohort while Syphax ranged out with the scouts.

Each day as they advanced into the wilder parts of Armenia, they made it to their camp with nothing more than glimpses of people through the thickening forests as they approached the turn in the road that would take them into the highlands. The few Armenians they saw quickly hid from the marching Romans. At night, their watch reported distant flickers of light in areas where there were no villages. It could have easily been a farmstead, but the constant reports of potential watchers set Lucius on edge, though he did his best to keep a resolute exterior around the men. Only in the presence of Syphax did he let his guard down, complaining about his irritation.

"There's little we can do." Syphax, as always, was as calm as a windless lake. "Until they decide to make their presence fully known, we have to keep moving. Tiridat says we're nearing the spot when we can leave the road and get lost in the mountains."

Lucius snorted. "I hope it's the Parthians who get lost. I don't fancy losing my way in these mountains come winter. I don't imagine you got much snow in the deserts of Mauretania Tingitana."

Syphax laughed. "You'd be wrong. Though you'd have to ride south of the border Roma controls, the Atlas Mons get quite a bit of snow in the winter." His face sank slightly. "It's been too long since I've been home, and here I am about as far away as one can be on the opposite side of the entire empire."

Lucius thought back to the forests and lowlands of Belgica. He wasn't as far from the land of his birth as they were from Syphax's home at the western edge of Roma's African provinces, but they were still a long way from the northwestern frontier of the empire. The men sat in silence, thinking about their homelands. Lucius marveled at the series of events that had taken him from his home in Belgica to Dacia and to the western reaches of the Parthian Empire. Now he sat with his friend about to go even higher into Armenia's mountains. Off in the distance, the sound of the Armenian youths and their tsiranapogh filtered into Lucius's consciousness.

Syphax smiled and poured himself some more wine. "Go listen to your young friends play."

"I'm fine," Lucius replied.

"Go. Enjoy. I've never seen you as calm and relaxed as you are when you listen to their music. You need it; you're wound up tighter than a ballista." Syphax made a shooing motion before picking up his wine cup.

Lucius refilled his cup with Syphax's excellent wine and heeded his commander's advice. As he worked his way through camp toward the haunting melody, he nodded as his men greeted him, calling out a name if he recognized the voice or face. He walked with purpose, plastering an occupied look on his face so people wouldn't stop him to talk. When he found Ariazate and Tigran, they were seated next to a fire playing for Tiridat and the other Armenians. Lucius stood just out of the light, not wanting to invite himself into their circle.

"Centurio Ferrata. Please, join us." Tiridat gestured toward the fire.

"Thank you, Pater." Lucius sat in an empty camp chair next to Tiridat.

"Your young friends are quite talented."

Lucius slouched in the chair, trying to find a comfortable position. "They make beautiful music."

"I might go as far as to say they're more than talented. I've not heard such good playing in a while."

Lucius nodded, losing the sound of Tiridat's voice as he immersed himself in the music. Tonight, playing for her countrymen, Ariazate's playing soared. Or perhaps it was enhanced in Lucius's mind as they sat around a fire in the shadow of the mountains they were about to navigate. All of Armenia was highlands, but the Montes Caucasii reached up into the sky. With the fire in his eyes and the dark of the night, the distant peaks were only visible as a darker smudge across the horizon. He'd get to know them soon, probably more intimately than he wanted. Instead of focusing on their upcoming struggles, he closed his eyes and let his mind drift along with Ariazate's melodies while allowing Tigran's droning notes to keep him grounded. Unlike in Tigranocerta where she let her younger brother take his turn with a melody, tonight she took the lead, serenading the mountains of her home.

ONCE THEY SLIPPED into the mountains, the scouts reported no more sightings of Parthian scouts. Syphax and the other centurions relaxed visibly, their shoulders sinking. Lucius, however, had an itch on the back of his neck he couldn't scratch away.

Syphax's brows narrowed as he eyed Lucius. "It's your feeling, Centurio Ferrata. Take some men and drift behind the rearguard, but keep in contact."

Lucius saluted. "Thank you. Please keep an eye on Ariazate and Tigran."

"You've grown close to them," Syphax commented, raising an eyebrow.

Lucius nodded. "They're good kids, and I intend to see they live long enough to enjoy their freedom when we're done with this mission."

"I see." Pursing his lips, he nodded slightly. "I'll keep an eye on them. Be careful, Lucius."

Lucius shrugged. "I'm always careful."

Syphax laughed. "Except when you're not."

"That's because sometimes you get in a situation where careful isn't good enough to keep you alive, and I very much intend to get through this one alive."

Once they settled into camp for the night, Lucius organized the scouts he wanted to take and the supplies they'd need. After he'd finalized his plans, he sought out Ariazate and her brother.

Lucius took the siblings aside and looked around to make sure no one was close enough to listen. "I'm going to be gone for a few days. Stick close to Tribunus Quietus. Syphax will make sure no one bothers you."

Ariazate bristled. "We can take care of ourselves."

"I know you can, but I'd rather you not have to kill again if it can be avoided."

Ariazate nodded, acknowledging the point. "Be well, Roman, and good luck."

"I'll see you two later." He smiled at them and tousled Tigran's black hair before returning to Syphax to receive any final instructions.

When they left before dawn the next morning, their party numbered sixteen legionnaires, three men to wrangle the spare mounts and pack animals and one of Pater Tiridat's men to guide them should they need it. As they walked their mounts through camp, Ariazate emerged from her tent, hair disheveled, and waved to Lucius before returning to sleep.

Mylitos, walking beside Lucius, looked at his centurio, brows raised.

"Yes, Miles Mylitos?" Lucius asked pointedly around a yawn.

The short man of Illyrian origin studiously returned his gaze straight ahead. "Nothing, Centurio."

As soon as they cleared the gates, they mounted up, though they kept their pace measured until they had more daylight. They made good time, despite trading speed for a certain amount of quiet and stealth. Tiridat's man led them down the path they'd been on the day before until he found the side trails that were inaccessible to a full cohort but were ideal for a small scouting party. By the end of the day, they saw no tails save for those on the occasional deer wandering about the wooded mountains. They stopped at a secluded place to camp for the night, then started fresh the next morning, breaking camp just after first light.

"You expect to find anything, Centurio?" Mylitos asked, joining Lucius near the front of the small party.

Lucius rode in silence as he watched their Armenian guide, Varghat, slip into the woods as he worked ahead of their main party. "I hope not. But I'd rather find nothing and be thought over-cautious than the other way round."

"True."

Lucius patted his pony's neck, their breath steaming in the cold mountain morning air. "I don't like this cold though. Snow's an enemy we can't fight."

"No, Centurio, not unless you're owed favors from powerful gods."

Lucius chuckled. "I don't think I've accrued those kinds of favors. We'll have to hope for a bit of luck to keep us from freezing our asses off."

"That and a few good sets of woolens," Mylitos replied.

"DAMN IT, where has that man gone?" Lucius hissed just above a whisper.

No one answered the rhetorical question. Varghat had disappeared with only a brief word to one of Lucius's legionnaires about wanting to drift ahead to check out something he'd heard in the distance. He'd been gone too long, and Lucius was reluctant to break cover to search for him, especially if the man had actually found something worth inspecting.

A frigid splatter of rain bounced off his nose. Looking up, he closed his eyes and shook his head, his jaw clenching. "Of course."

"At least it's not snow, Centurio," Mylitos whispered just loud enough for Lucius to hear.

"Shut up, Miles." Lucius was usually better at absorbing the good-natured banter some of his men liked to use to stave off nerves, but right now he wasn't in the mood for anything but silence. And the return of their wayward scout.

A snapping branch drew Lucius's attention. He held his breath, turning his head so he could point his ear down the narrow trail in front of them. When the bird call Varghat liked to use sounded, Lucius heaved a sigh of relief. Mylitos whistled the counter sign. Lucius never could get the knack of whistling more than an off-tune shrill note. He could whistle loudly when he needed to, but he couldn't make notes let alone realistic bird calls.

Varghat emerged around a distant bend in the trail and raised a gloved hand in greeting. Lucius, waving his men to hold back, nudged his gelding forward to meet Varghat.

"You were gone for a while," Lucius said by way of greeting.

"Sorry about that, Centurio. I was curious about something," Varghat replied in his Armenian accented Hellenic.

"Did you find anything?"

Varghat nodded. "I found a Parthian scout, at least from the few glimpses I saw. He was working his way west and south."

"The way we just came from. Care to show me?" Lucius asked.

"If we keep it small. You and maybe two or three other men." Varghat scratched at his thick beard.

Lucius nodded and turned around, picking the three best scouts. "The rest of you wait here. No fires, keep out of sight, and be ready to move out quickly."

He didn't wait to hear responses before turning around. They were professional and knew the stakes. Rejoining the Armenian, the party of five disappeared down the path into the steadily thickening drizzle. Lucius hoped the weather stayed wet instead of shifting to snow. It would be easier to disappear and rejoin the rest of the cohort as their trail blended into the muddied mess of nearly a thousand passing men and horses. If it snowed, they'd leave a clear trail through the fresh snow alerting anyone following them they'd been spied.

The five men wound their way over the game path, ducking under branches laden with rain. By the time they'd ridden an hour, Lucius was nearly soaked through. The only thing keeping him warm was the quality woolens Syphax had procured for their venture. Riding in silence, they halted when Varghat raised a hand to stop them, then dismounted.

Lucius joined him on the ground and signaled for the three scouts to step down as well. "Josephus, you stay with the horses," Lucius whispered.

The legionnaire nodded and gathered the reins of the horses, stepping under a particularly large pine to shelter from the rain. Varghat looked them over, then tapped his head. Removing his helmet, Lucius set it on his saddle, then ran a hand through his shortly cropped hair. With their helmets left behind, there wouldn't be any shiny metal to give them away. Their black cloaks would blend well enough into the shadows of the forest made gloomy with gray clouds.

In single file, Lucius and his two scouts followed Varghat as he wove his way through the trees. The thick carpet of pine needles kept their footsteps silent. They carefully set their feet, doing their best to avoid rocks that might click with contact under their hobnailed caligae. When the Armenian guiding them hunched and slowed down, they followed suit until he stopped, waving Lucius forward.

Varghat held a branch down so they could look over it. Inhaling sharply, Lucius bit off the curse he wanted to air. They looked over a ridge to the main track they'd passed over several days ago. Below them, hundreds of Parthians rode, filling the trail. Inspecting the rows and columns and how they were organized, he did some quick math and estimated there were over a thousand riders—maybe closer to fifteen hundred—probably mixed kataphraktoi and lighter lancers and archers. This was far more than a few Parthian spies. Roma's enemy was sending an army to fill the power vacuum Trajan's withdrawal had left.

Their cohort was cavalry heavy compared to most other Roman legions and cohorts, giving extensive training to everyone in the unit, but they weren't extra heavy kataphraktois—both horse and rider covered in armor. They could probably hold their own and defeat the Parthians, barring any more troops joining them, but they'd spend too much of their strength and leave too many bodies in the mud to be able to successfully carry out their mission.

Committing as much information as he could to memory, Lucius let the other scouts move up next to him so Syphax would have more than just his perspective to analyze when they got their information back to camp. Clenching his jaw in frustration, he waited while his men inspected the Parthian column. For all the satisfaction he should have felt at being right, he wished for all the world he'd been wrong. He could have returned to camp and shared a laugh with Syphax at his overzealous caution. Instead, he had to get his men back to their cohort while outracing some of the finest horse soldiers he'd ever faced.

Lucius gave them a couple minutes then tapped them on the shoulders, heading back to where their mounts waited. He wanted to jump on his horse and kick it into a run but knew that would be dangerous and noisy on the heavily wooded trail. The Parthians were bound to have scouts of their own moving through the woods. Lucius's priority was to get the information back to Syphax.

When they returned to their mounts, they rode out without

speaking, picking their path carefully until they rejoined the rest of the small squad Lucius had assembled for this mission. Before they could pepper him with questions, he signaled them to stay silent. Lucius had their saddles switched to rested mounts while they attended to their personal needs and grabbed food they could eat while riding.

While his feet were on the ground, Lucius's mind focused on the lines of Parthian cavalry, but as soon as he climbed up onto his fresh mount, a smart mare he rode when his gelding needed a break, he focused entirely on their next mission—living to deliver their news. He used every bit of horse craft he'd learned from Syphax and his Berber heritage along with the wood craft he'd learned in Belgica and Dacia to move as quickly and as quietly as possible.

If they rode near a spot where he could look down to the main trail, he sent his men ahead so he could sneak to the edge to survey the progress of the Parthians. So far, Lucius and his men were moving much faster than the bigger column. As long as disaster didn't strike, they'd be able to increase their lead and give their people the warning they needed. It would be long days in the saddle and cold camps once there wasn't enough daylight to safely ride before they rejoined their comrades.

Lucius slept little, his mind fixated on getting his men to safety and on the superior number of enemies pursuing them. Forced to keep a facade of calm as befit his position, he let his turmoil churn under the surface. In all his years serving Roma, he'd never been so far from the aid of the other legions.

After three days traveling the opposite direction from the rest of the cohort, he figured it would take them five until they made contact with their rearguard. He just hoped they didn't encounter a large Parthian vanguard. If they ran into any resistance, they'd have to rely on speed of horse. A handful more than a dozen men wasn't enough for any kind of fight. Lucius would have to trust to his skills and cunning to get them back to their cohort.

EIGHT

LUCIUS HAD NEVER BEEN SO relieved to be challenged for his identity as when they finally found the rearguard. Once Lucius acknowledged the passcode, he took a fresher horse from the rearguard and brought the optio along to speed his entrance into the main force with today's codes.

Syphax had halted their march for the day and was setting up their road fort. Cutting his way through their men erecting tents, walls, and fortifications, Lucius dismounted outside of the command tent and was ushered inside by the men standing guard. He gave a quick salute, then sat in the leather camp chair Syphax gestured toward.

"You look a little worse for wear, Lucius." Syphax picked up a jug of wine and filled a cup for Lucius. "I take it we have company of the uninvited sort?"

Lucius nodded, taking a swig of the wine. "Yeah. We're looking at close to fifteen hundred horsemen—mixed heavy and light."

Syphax's eyebrows shot up close to his tightly coiled curls. "One thousand five hundred?"

"Approximately. I got as good of a count as I could, but I didn't want to hang around and get caught." Lucius rubbed the stubble on his jaw that threatened to turn into a beard if left unattended for much longer.

"How fast are they traveling?" Syphax took a drink of wine, keeping his eyes firmly locked on his aide-de-camp.

"We lost sight of them about two days ago. With this rain, the trail's got to be slowing them down. It won't do them much good to get here with half their horses breaking legs." Lucius scooted his chair closer to the brazier.

"Two days? That's not much time. We'll have to pick up our march a bit. I don't relish trying to hit Caesarian speed in this muck, but the men are in fine condition; we can push them some." Syphax refilled his wine and leaned back in his chair, staring at the tent wall above Lucius's head as he mulled over his options.

Lucius scooted even closer to the heat source, enjoying the warming feeling of the wine as it unknotted some of the muscle tension in his shoulders and neck.

When Syphax's eyes drifted back to Lucius, he sat up. "I'm sorry. I don't need to keep you here. Go attend to your needs and get some food. Have someone find the pater and send him in. I want to see how well he knows this territory he's marching us through."

Lucius nodded and got up.

"Good job, Lucius. I'm thankful for your instincts. Keep listening to them."

"Thank you, Syphax. I'll check in after I get cleaned up and find a bite to eat." He paused for a moment, reluctant to head back into the frigid drizzle, then plunged outside into the growing twilight.

"Roman. It's good to see you back safe." Ariazate stepped out from behind a tent and joined him as he walked toward his tent.

"It's good to be back. Did you and Tigran manage to stay out of trouble?"

"Aye. Syphax had us pitch our tent near his. When you're ready, stop by our tent. I'll have some food ready for you." A bit of her usual harsh tone had receded some.

Stopping, Lucius smiled warmly at her. "Thank you, Zati. I'll stop by after I clean up and put some dry clothes on."

Zati nodded, the barest of smiles tipping up the corners of her mouth, then turned toward Syphax's tent.

Lucius found a fire and some warm water, procuring a bucket to take with him so he could give himself a quick bath. Staring at his grooming kit, he decided to skip the razor. The beard would keep his face warm, and the itching gave his hands something to idly scratch. With dry clothes and the grime of the ride washed off, he headed back into the rain toward Syphax's tent. When he drew nearer, he heard the soft tone of a tsiranapogh—judging by the playing, it was likely Tigran. He was an excellent player, but he wasn't as good as his sister.

He followed his ears to their tent, stopping outside. Ariazate hummed and sang a sad melody, though he couldn't understand the words.

"Ariazate?" Lucius called lightly.

"Around back, Roman," she replied.

Stepping around the tent, he found Ariazate working over a pot hanging over a small fire. She'd rigged an awning over her to keep the rain off while she worked. Tigran sat cross legged in the tent, quietly practicing.

"You're just in time," she said without looking up. She scooped something from the pot into a wooden bowl, handing it to Lucius, then handed him a second one. "Tigi, your dinner is ready. You can sit inside and eat, Roman."

Lucius handed Tigran the second bowl, then found a spot to sit down, fishing out his spoon from his belt pouch. "You know, I'm not an actual Roman. I'm a Gaul, from Belgica."

Ariazate shrugged. "You wear the uniform and march under the eagle, Roman." She filled a bowl for herself, then sat across from Lucius, her knee touching his in the tight confines of their small tent. "I apologize. It's not as good as what you had in Tigranocerta. The facilities aren't as complete, and I've had to make do with what ingredients were available."

Lucius inhaled deeply, the steam carrying savory aromas of meat and a light spicing. "It smells wonderful, especially after a week of nothing but mostly cold rations."

Stomach growling, he resisted the urge to pile a piping-hot spoonful into his mouth. He was hungry but not burn his mouth hungry. Tigran wasn't as wise and cursed as he fanned air into his mouth to cool the hot rice and salt pork scalding his tongue. Lucius tried to keep his laugh from escaping, not wanting to bruise the boy's ego, but the corners of his lips twitched erratically, sparking a snigger from Ariazate that caused his guffaw to finally slip out. Tigran tried to pout, but the laughter was too much for him, and he joined in sheepishly.

The brief silliness eased some of the tension from his shoulders and allowed for his bowl to cool enough so he could dive in. He finished it quickly. When Ariazate offered him a second bowl, he refused at first, not wanting to take any of their food despite his hunger. However, she insisted, and he didn't wish to insult her or damage the first delicate notes of friendship he could sense growing between the three of them.

While they ate, Ariazate and Tigran continued Lucius's lesson in Armenian. He enjoyed his time with the siblings. He'd had none of his own and spent most of his later adolescence in the company of military veterans until he left for the legions. It felt nice to develop a relationship with someone who wasn't a commanding officer or a subordinate. After he finished his second bowl, he thanked Ariazate and dismissed himself so he could check in on Syphax and whatever news he might have regarding their plans.

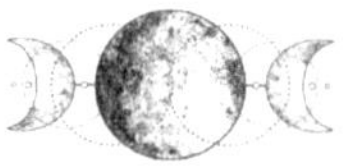

THEY'D MARCHED HARD the next three days, going late into the night and risking a quick camp in favor of increasing the distance between themselves and the large force of Parthians trailing them. By the time they reached the narrow pass Tiridat had suggested, they'd gained another day, possibly a day and a half of extra time.

Three days was more than enough time for the Romans to establish a fort and the surrounding defense works. There were few militaries who could build forts as quickly as the Romans could. They'd used every minute of the extra time, preparing to meet their enemy. The narrow gap in the trail was ideal for their needs. The legionnaires worked feverishly, chopping down trees for walls and stakes and digging trenches. By the time they'd finished, they had thick walls with platforms for the legionnaires, a trio of ballistae, and rows of deep trenches lined with sharpened stakes. They were outnumbered, but Parthian cavalry wasn't an ideal force for attacking Roman fortifications.

The Parthians had to know something lurked ahead of them, but as best as Lucius and Syphax figured, none of their advanced scouting parties were returning to reveal a heavily fortified force, dug in and ready to do battle.

After making his final inspections the night before the coming battle, Lucius joined the Armenians for another simple meal and language lessons. This time, the siblings played for a while after they'd emptied their bowls. Lucius, laying on his back and smiling, let their songs and melodies push his cares aside until it was time for the last meeting with Syphax.

Lucius woke to the sound of the cornicen blowing the signal to wake and ready for battle. In a matter of minutes, Lucius was fully dressed, armored, armed, and out the tent when he overheard Ariazate and Tigran arguing.

"Tigran, you can't…fight. You're…young. You'll get killed!" Ariazate said in Armenian.

Lucius, picking up enough of the words, changed direction and found them outside their tent. Tigran had a scabbarded sword in his hand; he tried to hold it away from his sister who was grabbing for it.

"How can I be a king…if I…in a tent with my sister?" he replied, his voice cracking.

"Tigi, hush," Zati hissed, looking around frantically. As Lucius turned the corner, her eyes went wide with shock as she was temporarily robbed of words.

At the sudden change, Tigi stopped struggling and followed her gaze, his face going pale when he saw Lucius. Before he could respond, Ariazate stepped around her brother and placed herself between him and Lucius. Her dark brown eyes, vulnerable and pleading, bored into Lucius.

Lucius clenched his jaw and flexed his cheek muscles. Licking his lips, he took a step forward.

"I don't know what you were arguing about. I didn't hear the details." He ensured he held Ariazate's gaze. "But this is not the time or place for such arguments." Turning to Tigran, he added, "No one here is doubting your bravery, Tigran, but this isn't the kind of battle you're ready for yet. It's going to be harsh and bloody, and it's going to take the discipline of hardened professionals to get out of this alive. When your time comes to stand in battle, I'll fight by your side, but today, I need you to stay with your sister and protect her."

Ariazate turned to face her brother. "Please, Tigran. I'd be too scared without you here to watch over me."

The three of them knew Ariazate was tough and could take care of herself, but it was a fiction that let Tigran withdraw from his belli-cose offer with dignity intact.

"Please, Tigran," Zati pleaded.

He nodded slowly then looked up to Lucius. "If that's where you think I'll do the most good, then I'll do my duty."

Lucius smiled and squeezed his shoulder. "Ariazate, would you walk with me for a minute?"

In answer, she fell in behind him as they walked away from her brother and their tent. Lucius kept silent as he moved away from the bulk of the activity. Ariazate started to speak several times, stopping before she even managed a full syllable. When Lucius finally felt they'd gone far enough for a bit of privacy, he stopped and turned around.

Finding her courage, she straightened her spine and held her head regally. "I don't know what you heard—"

Lucius held up a hand to interrupt her. He'd vowed to protect them, even if that meant from themselves. He had no idea if what the boy had let slip was true, but it didn't matter. Accusations like that needed little evidence when a dagger and a few spades of dirt would solve the problem of inconvenient rivals. "I didn't hear anything that needs repeating to anyone else. Understand? But I suggest you counsel your brother to be more careful with his words. There are a lot of ears, and not all of them here are friendly."

She nodded hesitantly then with more force as she took in his words.

"Now listen, I want you and your brother to break down your tent and pack your things. You can stay in my tent. I think we're in a strong position, and we should be able to hold the Parthians off, but I don't want to gamble with your lives." He explained where their pileus hats were and the gold that had been entrusted into Lucius's care for the siblings. "I don't know if you were told you'd get your freedom, but you will. If things go bad, hide in the mountains until the Parthians move on. If they found you, your association with us would spell your doom. If any of the legionnaires question you, tell them you are under my protection and are obeying my orders."

Ariazate stood in silence for a moment then threw her arms around Lucius. Shocked by the sudden display, it took Lucius a moment to respond and fold her into the hug.

"Thank you, Lucius," she said.

"Hey, you didn't call me 'Roman.' Does that mean you actually like me?" Lucius teased.

"Don't push your luck, Roman." She smiled up at him and stepped back. "May fortune watch over you."

"Ariazate. It has been a pleasure getting to know you. If I don't see you again, good luck."

She gave him a half-smile filled with the nerves they both felt about the coming battle and potential repercussions. He watched as she returned to her tent and her brother, not looking back at Lucius. It was the best he could do for them right now, even if it felt inadequate. Two Armenian children couldn't balance the scales against all the lives he'd taken in service to his empire, but it was something he could do—give them a plan and chance. Though he hoped they didn't need the plan, it settled his mind to not have their dubious safety niggling at the back of his mind, not when he was about to go into battle against the dangerous Parthians.

NINE

LUCIUS STARED over the trail approaching their fort, waiting for the Parthians to come into range. The scouts had reported sightings of their advanced force all morning. The Parthians knew the Romans had blocked the narrow pass, leaving only steep wooded hills and mountainsides on one side and a cliff on the other. Unless they turned around, Lucius would be called on to draw his blade to defend himself and his comrades.

A faint sound drifted on the breeze. Quirking his ear to the side, he heard the far-off note of a horn. A few moments later, a steady drumbeat joined it.

"Finally," someone down the line said.

Silently, Lucius agreed with them. The anticipation was almost worse than the actual fighting. Leaning forward, he squinted, using his hand to block the low glare from the gray sky. A pair of riders flew around the corner side by side. Once they approached the designated lane, they moved into single file.

"Gates," Lucius called.

Below him, the legionnaires operating the gates swung them open in time for the two riders to make it through, then closed and barred them once again. Lucius made it down the ladder just as they dismounted. They saluted.

"Centurio!" Mylitos, breathing heavily, stepped forward.

"Report."

"Our scouts say they're only sending in about a third of their force. Mixed cavalry, mostly archers, and foot with scaling ladders," Mylitos said.

"Where are the rest?"

"Waiting in reserve. They've got scouts out working the hills, but Tribunus Syphax and the I Centuria are ensuring they don't make it back to report."

Lucius had tried to talk Syphax out of leading the century they'd sent into the hills to hunt scouts and to harry their flanks, but his friend had insisted on leading the operation instead of staying inside the fort and leading the defense. Roma didn't like her war leaders to develop rusty blades, he'd said. Syphax's cousin was second only to Trajan in military matters and, in essence, commanded all the legions in the east. Lucius wondered at times if Syphax was jealous he'd not risen as high, though forming an elite unit surpassing all other legions in training wasn't without its glories. Syphax would never admit to it, and Lucius would never ask. Syphax might be a friend, but he was also his commander, and although they were close, their friendship didn't rise to that level of intimacy.

"Grab a quick breather. I'll have fresh horses brought up." Lucius waved at a nearby legionnaire, who went to fetch a pair of horses that were already saddled and ready to go.

Mylitos and the other scout saluted and jogged off to visit the latrine. He shimmied back up the ladder. The first row of horse and rider could be seen. With lances held high, they were packed in tightly. A cavalry charge wouldn't do much against their walls, but it worked well to screen the infantry behind them. Another minute and the first lines would be within range of their ballistae. They'd tested the ranges and had set up landmarks so they knew what trajectories were needed for which ranges.

Lucius nodded to the signalman who waved to the ballistae crews. Working as a team, they cranked the winch levelers, pulling back the swing arms and loading the skeins with tension. Once they had it fully cocked, they loaded in the rounded stone balls. He wanted to wait until the Parthians were fully committed before unleashing the ballistae.

Their cohort was meant to be traveling fast, and they lacked the heavier siege equipment a full legion would have. Their three ballistae would get a heavy workout. Every legionnaire that could shoot a bow was on the walls, ready to do their part. And when the Parthians got in close, the rest of the men would fill the sky with their javelins. Then, when the ladders were on the walls, it would come down to bloody work with gladius and scutum.

"Loose!" Lucius shouted.

The ballistae crews pulled the release pins and the swing arms flung their stones down their chutes and into the sky. Squinting, Lucius tried to find the approximate spots where the stones were aimed. One snapped a lance on its downward path before disappearing into the crowd. Lucius didn't see it hit, but he heard the scream of man and animal. Another smashed through, striking flesh. The third one came in lower, pulping the helmet-covered head of one of the riders in the front row. Lucius winced.

The crews rearmed their ballistae and shot again; they'd keep firing until new orders and ranges were given to them.

"Archers, nock," Lucius called. "Light. Loose!"

Flaming arrows streaked across the sky between the fort and the Parthians, plunging indiscriminatingly into flesh. More screams filled the space. A few horses, driven past endurance, broke and trampled through their own ranks. One toppled over the edge and off the edge of the trail into the open air and rugged rocks of the cliff.

"Again," he called.

It didn't matter how many times he'd heard the screams of pain and terror coming from beast and human, it still made him cringe and fight back a wave of nausea until it all blurred and became numb. Another wave of flaming arrows arced across the sky. It was brutal, but they were outnumbered. If they could force the Parthians to retreat, great, but if not, they had to ruthlessly reduce their numbers any way possible before they met face to face, hand to hand.

The front lines of Parthian cavalry burst into action, dropping their lances and pulling their bows.

"Shields ready!"

The legionnaires who'd been waiting snapped into alertness, bringing their scutum up to form a protective layer of leather and wood between their archers and the incoming arrows. Lucius ducked behind the stout timber at the top of their wall as arrows thudded into the wood below. Some made it over to plunge into scutums, raising a few screams of pain from his people. Flexing his left hand, he felt sympathy pangs. Peeking over the edge, the cavalry continued their dash forward, firing at will.

The Parthians were some of the finest horse archers in the world. After fighting them for years, he was still amazed at how many arrows they could put into the air while at a full gallop and still maintain accuracy. Unfortunately, horse archers weren't the best against fortified walls. They were nearly within range for their next tactic.

When horses tumbled to the ground, spilling riders, he closed his eyes, but he couldn't stop the sound from assaulting his ears. They'd found the field of shallowly buried stakes hidden by loosely filled dirt. The torn-up ground soaked with rain couldn't hold the weight of the horses. The muddy slop tripped the horses, breaking legs, and dragged horse and rider onto the stakes.

The lines not currently mired in the muck ground to a halt, bunching up as commanding officers tried to organize something from the chaos. Before they could, Syphax and the bulk of I Centuria burst out of the woods, the momentum of coming off the hill plunging them deep into the back lines of the Parthians. When their lances broke, they freed their spathas and went to work with the longer swords. However, their trap hadn't gone entirely unnoticed.

"Centurio…" someone nearby said.

"I see it." He turned, looking for the signal officer. "Cornicen, blow immediate withdrawal."

The cornicen answered by putting the large, curved horn to his lips and blew the orders out over the wall. Stopping for a few moments, he repeated the horn call. Lucius found Syphax in the scrum and watched, waiting. On the third blow of the signal, the Tribune barked out the orders and got the cavalry retreating in an orderly fashion.

With the century disengaging, Lucius returned his attention to the incoming Parthians. The kataphraktoi had entered the engagement. With horses covered in armor and their riders totally encased, a wall of steel bore down on Syphax. If they were caught between both forces of Parthians, they might as well be in a meat grinder. When the last of the Romans disappeared back into the woods, Lucius breathed a sigh of relief.

Their cavalry wasn't as heavily armored, but they were quick and had spent the days exploring the area and knew it well enough to avoid contact with the extra heavy cavalry who'd have been unable to easily move through the dense trees, not without abandoning their long lances.

"Ballistae! Marker range one, shoot at will!" Lucius yelled. He looked down the wall. "Archers, don't waste shots on the downed horses and riders. Aim at the infantry."

Once the stone balls started falling among the kataphraktoi, they turned around since they no longer had a target to charge at. Soon, in dribs and drabs, then in an increasing flood, the infantry and remaining horse archers broke and ran toward their own lines.

"Ballistae, cease shooting," Lucius called. "Cornicen, sound advance for the I Centuria."

After the horn call sounded over the battlefield, Lucius gave the archers a few more moments to take shots at the fleeing Parthians before calling them off, unwilling to risk hitting his own men as they returned to the battlefield.

Syphax swept out of the trees and plowed into the retreating Parthians, cutting them down in huge swaths. At the far end, the kataphraktoi were trying to reform to provide cover but couldn't keep a line moving through the disorderly retreat of their countrymen.

"Call out withdrawal." Lucius saw movement in the back of the

Parthian line and didn't want to risk his friends if the enemy moved up archers to screen their retreat.

The cornicen played the retreat. On the second call, their cavalry spun around and made for the trees again.

"Blow advance for the II Centuria and then bring the I back inside." Squatting down at the edge of the walkway along the top of the wall, he cupped his hand next to his mouth. "Zyraxes, you feel like getting muddy?"

"No," the centurion of the V Century replied, a ripple of chuckles from his century following the pronouncement.

"Too bad. If you see anyone that looks like a nobleman, bring them in for questioning. Put the rest down."

Zyraxes saluted and relayed the orders as the gates swung open to let them out. At the side gate, Syphax, the primus pilus, and his century filed in. Sliding off his horse, Syphax tossed the reigns to a nearby legionnaire, grabbed an offered waterskin, and joined Lucius on top of the walls.

Syphax took a deep drink from the skin, before wiping the dribbles from his beard. "How are things looking up here?"

"The Parthians don't appear to be interested in advancing at the moment. I haven't heard from the scouting party we sent east. I have Zyraxes cleaning up out front."

"Yeah, I can hear." He pursed his lips and furrowed his brows. Looking into the sky, he tried to find the slightly brighter gray spot that would indicate the sun's presence. "It's only a couple more hours until the sun starts fading."

They faced out over the wall, the V Century working its way through the Parthians, and stared toward the other side of the pass they straddled. A line of heavy cavalry sat astride the trail as small squads worked to assist any wounded they felt were close enough to collect without engaging the Romans. While they watched each other across the distance, the gates opened and men went out to butcher a few of the horses for fresh meat while the V Century formed a line blocking the trail.

"So we wait," Syphax said.

Together, they leaned against the top edge of the wall and looked west. Every few minutes, Lucius's eyes slipped up to find the sun, hoping it was magically further in its progress than it normally would be. However, it seemed to have slowed down, dragging on interminably.

When the sun finally progressed too far for any further attacks, Lucius exhaled explosively, letting his shoulders sink. Syphax barked out the signals to recall the two centuries outside the fort. Once both units rejoined their comrades inside the fort, Lucius and Syphax organized the night's watch and sent out the evening's first scouting parties to ensure the Parthians didn't attempt a dangerous night assault. Lucius doubted they would, not with the drubbing they'd taken earlier and not with the current conditions, though he'd been wrong before. After Syphax dismissed him for the evening, he retired for a meal with his young Armenian friends and then turned in early. Tomorrow would come entirely too quickly, and this time, the Parthians would be more serious about digging out the entrenched Romans.

LUCIUS'S LANCE had long ago broken as he laid about him with his spatha from the back of his mare, giving the gelding a rest after leading several sorties on him the second morning of the siege. As Sol moved toward midafternoon in his sun chariot, he tried to ignore the ache in his muscles and the fact he had several more hours of fighting if he wanted to see another night.

When the tough pony lashed out behind them, Lucius spun around and brought his blade down into the junction where the Parthian's neck met his shoulder. The mare's kick had probably saved his life and knocked the Parthian off balance. Nudging the horse away, he let the weight of the animal drag the blade out of the man's neck as he sloughed off his saddle to fall in the mud. He wished he could be behind the walls and safe with the gelding, giving his arm a rest, but there was more sword work to be done.

All day, he'd been playing cat and mouse with Parthian squads trying to sneak around their position and bring the battle to two fronts. After yesterday's failed assault, they'd resorted to the heavy work of assaulting the walls, dismounting their useless cavalry, and sending their warriors in on foot with hastily constructed siege engines.

Looking around in a momentary pocket of calm, Lucius nudged his mare toward a couple Parthians assaulting one of his men. Deflecting an axe with his shield, he shifted his aim, coming in low, and slashed toward the juncture where the Parthian's lower armor joined his chest armor. He found the seam and drew blood but hadn't cut deep enough to get the kill. That came as the Parthian cringed around the wound, opening a spot in his defenses. Lucius rammed the tip of his sword into the face mask of the Parthian's helmet, the tip scraping across steel until it slipped into the seam between the helmet's rim and crunched into skull. With a twist of the blade, he backed his mare up, then used the pony to shoulder aside the now riderless horse to carry the assault to the next rider. At the loss of his companion, the other Parthian panicked and left an opening for Lucius's comrade. The Parthian tumbled from his saddle, dead.

Lucius nodded at his legionnaire, then spun his mare to meet the next Parthian. He didn't have time to think about the burning in his arm. He'd rest it later. With that attacker downed, he looked around. The last few Parthians were being dealt with. Taking a moment to catch his breath, he waited until the last was downed, then pulled his centurion's whistle to his lips and blew the signal to regroup and withdraw back to the reset point. Once they reassembled, he took an accounting of the wounded and dead, sending those who needed care back to the fort and having their field medic patch up those who could stay. At some point during the last sortie, he'd put a few nicks in his blade. He'd have to spend extra time with the sharpening stone that evening to return it to ready status.

At the sound of a horse riding hard through the woods, he spun around, his sword at the ready. He relaxed somewhat when he recognized one of their messengers. After he was cleared with the passcode, he rode directly to Lucius.

"Centurio, you need to get back to the fort. It's the Tribunus…" the messenger gasped out between labored breaths.

Closing his eyes, his body sank in on itself, a hollow pit opening in his stomach. "How bad is it?"

"I don't know first-hand, but bad enough to send for you."

"Fuck." Lucius shook his head. "Zyraxes, you're in charge. Don't get too aggressive. Just protect this flank."

He spun his horse back toward the camp and nudged her into a trot. The messenger joined him, then they picked up the pace to race back to the fort. Seeing Lucius coming, the gates swung open to let him in. He slowed to work his way to the field hospital they'd set up to handle the wounded who seemed to be too numerous for the small space.

Moans and screams assaulted his ears as he stepped inside the tent. The surgeon and his assistants had their hands full, leaving the overflow to be handled by the field medics. They'd already had to make a lot of tough decisions, using painkillers to ease the agony of those who were waiting at the banks of the River Styx but hadn't yet purchased their crossing.

"Centurio, he's over here," someone called to him.

Lucius slipped between the hornets' nest of activity, meeting one of the optios before he could get to Syphax.

"What happened, Quintus?" Lucius asked.

"He took an axe to the lower back, right into his spine. I don't know how he's still alive, but he's hanging on." Quintus ran his dirty hand through his wet hair.

As the surgeon passed by Lucius, he waved him over. "Is there…anything…"

The surgeon shook his head. "Ease his passing, that's about all there's left to do. The Parthian axe took care of everything else."

Lucius nodded, the corners of his eyes burning as the pit in his stomach deepened and threatened to suck him in. Not waiting for Lucius to respond, the surgeon found his next patient and went to work.

"Take me to him," Lucius said. His tone sounded brittle and flat even to his own ears.

Quintus nodded and turned, leading Lucius deeper into the tent. The men surrounding Syphax made room for Lucius. The man who'd been like family to him was laid out on his stomach. In the center of his back, a bloody gash rent the silver armor. Syphax, normally dark brown, looked sallow. He scrunched his eyes tightly, his lips pulled back in a grimace as he let out a grunt of pain he tried to control.

Lucius squatted down next to his friend. "I'm here, Syphax."

Once the wave of pain seemed to subside, Syphax's face relaxed somewhat. Opening his eyes, it took them a moment to focus on Lucius's face.

He let out a weak chuckle that ended in a wheezing cough. "What a cruel joke, my friend. Of all the places I could die, why did it have to be in the mud and rain?" He sighed, then tensed up as another wave of pain contorted his face.

From the entrance of the tent, voices raised in argument.

"I have to speak with the tribunus. It's life and death," a familiar voice shouted.

Syphax groaned.

"I'll take care of it, Syphax," Lucius said, standing up.

As he crossed the tightly packed space, people slid out of Lucius's way at the sight of the black clouds in his eyes. When he stepped out, two guards held back Mylitos.

"What is it, Mylitos?"

The scout relaxed seeing Lucius, but hesitated, eyeing the guards. Lucius waved him after him as they stepped away from the hospital tent and found a quiet spot. Once Lucius took a moment to look over the legionnaire, his brows furrowed at the mud and blood on the man.

"What happened to you?"

"We were ambushed on the way back. They knew we were coming. I was the only one to get away."

"How'd they know you were coming?" Lucius dreaded the answer.

"Varghat. He led us along the path, then as soon as the Parthians jumped out at us, he turned on us. He betrayed us, Centurio. There's a second force coming for us, from the east."

Lucius closed his eyes and rubbed his temples with his thumb and middle finger. He wanted to ask Selene why one of Tiridat's men had betrayed them when she said they could… The conversation flashed through his mind. She'd only vouched for Tiridat, not his men. He shook head, biting off a curse. "Start at the beginning."

Mylitos nodded. "He led us through trails that wound up along the south side of the hills. Once we got up to a good hiding spot, he had us wait and disappeared like he did when we found the first Parthian army. When he came back, we followed him on foot to a ridge with a clear view of the pass. I haven't seen that many Parthians since Ctesiphon."

"How many?"

"I estimate twenty-five hundred to three thousand. Infantry, horse, wagons. Once he let us get a good look, we started back, but before we got to our horses, we were jumped. The bastard stabbed Gnaius in the back, then cut Prextos's throat. I ran for it at the point. I had to get the news back. A Parthian tackled me, but I killed him and got away."

"How soon will they be here?" The crisis pushed aside the numbness sliding over Lucius.

"They're not pressing hard, but they'll be here by midday tomorrow at the latest."

The news slapped Lucius. "Gods below." As the wheels turned in his head, he looked closer at Mylitos. "You've got a gash in your arm. Go get it taken care of. Keep this information to yourself and stay nearby in case I have more questions."

Looking into the sky, he found the sun through the thick gray clouds. In the west, Parthian horns sounded.

"What now?" Lucius jogged over to the western wall and climbed to the walkway along the top of the wall. As soon as he cleared the last rung, he looked for an officer. Seeing an optio, he called him over. "Report."

At Lucius's harsh tone, the optio stood straight and saluted crisply. "I don't know what's going on, but it looks like they've called a retreat. The Parthians are disengaging and moving back to their lines."

The Parthians were disengaging, though in a far more orderly fashion than they had yesterday.

"Optio, tell the cornicen to signal hold positions. Do not pursue. All units. Understand?" Lucius turned and started down the ladder.

"Yes, Centurio." The optio grabbed men and barked out the orders.

By the time Lucius had made it down the ladder and halfway back to the hospital tent, the horns were calling out the orders. The Parthians didn't need to keep wasting their men trying to crack the tough nut of the Roman fort. They could pull back and wait until their second force arrived to do the heavy lifting. Unless he and the other centurions could think of something, they were fucked.

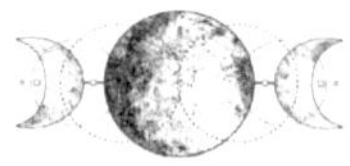

LUCIUS LOOKED up when he heard his name. The primus pilus had made his way inside the walls and found Lucius. The grizzled old veteran from Lusitania was already five years into his second twenty-five-year contract with the legions.

"Rumor is Syphax is wounded," Bandua said without preamble, pulling off his helmet and wiping a rag over his mostly bald head.

Lucius didn't know the man's given name. When he'd signed his contract with the Legions thirty years ago as a brash young man, he'd signed as Bandua—the war god worshiped by the Celts of Gallaecia and Lusitania. The name fit him. There was a reason the man was the first spear of the cohort. He fought with a brutal efficiency coupled with joy in the contest. He'd have been a primus pilus of an entire legion if he hadn't been so loyal to Syphax and wanted to stay with the newly formed elite cohort. He must have been a true terror as a young man.

"I don't know how he's still alive. He took an axe to the back," Lucius replied.

Bandua blinked at him a few times, then exhaled loudly.

"That's not the half of it," Lucius continued. "There's a second army coming towards us. Mylitos counts twenty-five hundred to three thousand."

"Fucking hells. How much time do we have?"

"Tomorrow."

"Does Syphax know?" Bandua asked.

"No."

"We better go tell him. He'd curse us on his deathbed if we didn't." Bandua wrapped his meaty hand around the back of Lucius's neck and squeezed it roughly but affectionately. "Let's go see our friend."

On the way to the hospital tent, they collected Mylitos, and Lucius explained the situation to Syphax. After the tribune thought it over, he issued his final orders to his men.

"Sir…" Lucius protested.

"Centurio." He grimaced and coughed weakly. "Follow your orders."

Lucius nodded, tears slipping over his cheeks. "Yes, Tribunus."

"Now find…" He convulsed and tried to stifle a scream but only partially succeeded. "Give me the poppy tea."

Bandua waved down the surgeon. Lucius squatted down, took Syphax's hand, and squeezed it lightly. Once the surgeon grabbed an assistant to take care of the poppy tea, Bandua rejoined them, squatting next to Lucius, grunting as he gingerly lowered himself.

"Don't ever get old, Lucius," Bandua said.

"Your knees?" Syphax asked weakly.

Bandua laughed. "You worry about your own maladies, Syphax."

"You should have retired at the end of your last contract, my old friend."

"And do what? Die in bed? A horse's knees do well enough for me."

"Listen, Bandua. I left a letter for you and the other officers in case…" He stopped to catch his breath, though he barely managed a few shallow gasps. "The cohort is yours, Bandua. Lucius, stay with me…for a bit."

Bandua laid his hand on Syphax's head for a moment, then

stalked off to see to their disposition for the evening and to lay down the necessary plans. A few minutes later, a medic showed up with the tea of poppy and helped Syphax take it. Once the poppy kicked in, Syphax relaxed some.

"Lucius, you've been a good friend. I'm proud of the officer you've become." His voice was barely audible. "May the gods watch over…"

Syphax's eyes drifted closed and his breathing slowed. No longer able to squat, Lucius slumped onto the ground next to Syphax's pallet. He didn't know how long he sat there holding Syphax's hand after his last rattling breath, but eventually a medic helped him up and ushered him out, needing the space.

When he stumbled back to his tent, Ariazate and Tigran had warm water ready for him to clean up with. After he finished, they returned with warm food he woodenly scooped into his mouth while they played. The mournful sound of the music settled into his heart as he silently grieved the death of his friend, hoping he found his way to the eternal lands of his people.

TEN

LUCIUS FORCED himself to keep his eyes forward, planted on the back of Tiridat as the pater and two of his men led them deeper into the mountains on a narrow trail that probably saw more deer and bears than people. But with a second Parthian force sweeping in on their position from the rear, their only hope of completing their mission meant Lucius had been ordered to flee with a small band of men. The thought of abandoning his friends and comrades behind left a bitter taste in this mouth. They'd trained and fought together for eight years.

The barely audible grumbles and heads turning to look back toward the camp dwindling in the background indicated his men felt the same. Soon the Parthians would throw both of their forces at the fort, choking the narrow mountain road that led from the western reaches of Armenia into the river valley of the Araxes River. There was little hope the remaining cohorts could defeat the massive force of Parthians arrayed against them. Lucius had to keep telling himself that their hundred men would do little to aid the cause other than add more bodies to the carnage.

As they wound their way up the side of the mountain, the rain turned to snow. Looking up at the gray sky, he shook his head, clenching his jaw. The cohort he had helped Syphax raise was the finest in the entire empire, trained to levels far exceeding any other unit, even that of the Praetorians. Now, they were about to spill their lives on a mountainside in Armenia, a territory the empire couldn't hold and didn't entirely want, for a mission he didn't fully understand. And he was ordered to take a century's worth of men and abandon his comrades and friends in the name of completing that mission.

A horse drawing too near coaxed him out of his brooding. When he turned to see who it was, Ariazate held his gaze, sympathy in her eyes. Leaning in her saddle, she reached out and patted his arm just below the elbow.

"I'm sorry you had to leave your friends behind," she said before moving her horse so it wasn't as close.

Not sure what to say and not wanting to say something angrily, he nodded, acknowledging the sentiment. Twisting around in his saddle, he found Tigran riding behind him, his face pointed toward the sky, his tongue out, trying to catch snowflakes on it. Lucius had been a boy that age and probably had spent a snowy day trying to do the same. The memory brought a small smile to his face as his thoughts drifted from snow to his meadow covered in bluebells where he'd spent so much of his youth lying on his back, gathering wool, and watching clouds fly by. Sighing, he longed for those days of innocence when all he had to do was avoid the chores his parents assigned, and his only worries were small, boyish nothings. With every mile further from Belgica he traveled, and with each passing year, that boy faded into a memory that felt like it was a different life and not the one he was living.

Now, he led a hundred men into the mountains and had to get them out alive, if he could, all while moving through increasingly hostile territory with only two Armenian children and and an old man to guide their path. He tried to sit straighter in his saddle, but the weight of it all pushed him back into a slouch. When the faint echoes of horns drifted up to them, he slumped further.

"It has begun," he said quietly to no one.

SIX DAYS LATER, they descended out of the hills south of Artashat. Looking down into the valley of the Araxes River, Lucius raised his hand, signaling a stop.

"Mylitos, fetch Pater Tiridat, please," Lucius ordered.

"Aye, Centurio." Mylitos pulled the reins of his horse and spun around. A couple minutes later, the legionnaire returned with the small man who looked out of place next to the bulk and size of the soldiers surrounding him.

"Do you recognize where we are, Pater?" Lucius stared out over the valley below him.

"We're not far from the temple now, a good day's ride."

"Will the river be a problem?"

"No. It doesn't look like it's picked up much water yet from the rain and snow. There are several places where we can ford it. There's a bridge nearby as well." He looked along the river. "I think just there."

"Is it guarded?" Lucius asked.

"Normally, it's not, but I don't know anymore. I don't even know who's in charge now." He sounded frustrated to Lucius's ear.

"Thank you, Pater."

Optio Venextos, who'd been listening nearby, nudged his mount closer. "What's the plan, Centurio? Do we risk the bridge?"

"We may have to. I don't know how far behind the Parthians are or if they're sweeping up the valley. I don't want to be caught ass deep in a river if they come up on us." He sat in silence, looking up and down the river. "Let's get the men back into the hills and set up camp. The horses could use the rest if we're going to press them hard tomorrow. I want to get out of the open as quickly as possible."

"The men could use the rest too. I'll find us a place to bed down out of the way." The optio turned and barked out orders.

They set a quick camp tucked into a narrow ravine, dousing the cook fires long before twilight set in. After he ensured the watch was set, he made his way to his tent, finding Ariazate and Tigran sitting on the ground quietly playing their instruments outside. Stepping inside, he pulled his armor off and put his cloak back on, then grabbed his blanket and threw it around his shoulders. He grabbed his leather folding camp chair and set it outside so he could listen to the siblings and settle his mind before they made their final run to the temple.

The sad, pensive songs matched his mood, settling deep in his soul. So far, they'd made it through the mountains with only a few minor injuries. None of the scouts he'd sent back along their trail had seen hide nor hair of the Parthians. He almost preferred a distant sighting if for no other reason than to have something to fix his worry on, something he could calculate and plan for. As it was, he had no idea if they'd crushed his friends or if they'd even found the path he'd escaped on. They could be waiting in the valley, anticipating their descent. The not knowing was the hardest part.

The lack of music drew him from his worries. Tigran was gone, and Ariazate stared at Lucius.

"I sent Tigi to check on his horse before we bed down," Ariazate explained.

Lucius nodded.

"What's eating at you, Roman?" she asked.

He sighed. "Nothing. Everything. We're leaving the safety of the mountains and heading into a more populated area. I don't know what's waiting for us or what's chasing us. So far, we've evaded our pursuers, but tomorrow, that could change."

Nodding, she looked down at the ground between them. "That's a lot to have on your shoulders."

"It is, but it's what I accepted when I took the promotion. I shouldn't be complaining." He avoided making eye contact with the young woman.

"Facts aren't complaining, Roman. You're a good man, and you'll do right by everyone. That's all we can do, really, try our best and hope it works out." She stood up and patted his shoulder. "You should get some sleep. We're all going to need it for tomorrow."

"Yeah. I should while I can." He stood up and folded his camp chair as Tigran jogged up, cheeks rosy from the cold.

"It's bedtime, Tigi. Morning for us will come before it does for Mihr." Ariazate held open the flap to Lucius's tent and ushered her brother in. He'd moved them there to save space and ensure their safety.

Lucius chuckled at her statement. They would indeed be awake before the Armenian's sun god made his appearance. Scanning the sky, he found the cloud-shrouded glow of Selene's moon and let the peace he'd felt seeing her in Antiochia fill him. He didn't know why her light had shined especially brightly on him that day, but he was glad it had.

Thank you, My Mistress.

He felt a light touch on his forehead, reminiscent of the kiss she'd laid there all those weeks ago. Letting her subdued light bathe him for one last moment before retiring, he nodded respectfully, then ducked into his tent. Tigran appeared to be already asleep next to his sister, and she didn't look far behind.

Looking fondly at them, he smiled before turning to tuck into his own bed. With fourteen years in the legions, he still had another eleven to go before his contract was completed, assuming he wasn't wounded and discharged or killed. It would be a long time before he could think about starting a family, even if he wanted to. Some of the men had women and children that followed them from base to base when they weren't making war. Signing the contract with the legions didn't stop one from starting a family, just from a contractual marriage. Some had taken lovers among their comrades. He'd not been interested in either option, not while he was fully focused on his career, but caring for the Armenians filled a hole inside he hadn't known was empty.

He was an only child, and his cousins had moved away when his aunt remarried. Since Ariazate and Tigran had been placed in his care, he found his concern and affection for them growing until he spent nearly as much time worrying about them as he did the legionnaires under his command. Tomorrow would be another day to be put to the test. If he did well, he'd get those under his care through it to another night of sleep. If he didn't...

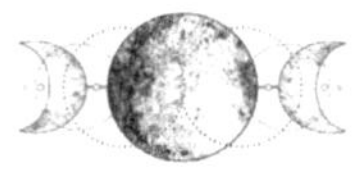

LUCIUS WATCHED their small scouting party return to the grove of trees where they hid. Off in the distance was the bridge Tiridat had mentioned the day before. While they'd waited for the scouts to return, Lucius had ordered a quick meal of cold rations. Shoving the stopper back into his waterskin, he returned it to its place. The scouts had passed their outer line and were jogging toward Lucius, having handed off their sweaty mounts.

"Centurio," Optio Venextos said, saluting.

"Optio. What's the word?"

"The bridge looks clear, no unusual traffic. No guards."

"Good. Grab a quick bite and some water. Then take a fresh mount and lead an advanced party ahead to secure the far side." Lucius patted the optio on the shoulder, the steel bands of his lorica clanking lightly, and went to see if any of the other scouts he'd sent in other directions were back yet.

He hadn't known what to expect at the bridge, but even now that he knew, it didn't settle his nerves. There were too many things that could go wrong.

After Lucius got the all clear from the other scouting parties, he organized his column of a hundred men, two children, and over half again as many horses and got them moving toward the bridge at a ground-eating canter. The optio and the men he'd taken with him had kept the bridge clear of any incidental traffic, so that when Lucius and the rest of the cohort blasted across the bridge, they swept out in advance to continue scouting. Lucius gave them another ten minutes before ordering the cohort to slow. The horses were still fresh and ready, and he didn't want to tire them out in case they really needed their speed later.

He looked to the east, eyeing the nearby mountains. Now that they'd made it over the bridge, they could melt into the mountains again if they needed to. After a couple hours, Lucius ordered a dismount so they could walk their mounts. In a couple hours, they'd approach the Temple of Gorneae, and he wanted his horses ready to run.

"Zati, have you ever seen the temple before?" Lucius asked.

She nodded. "We passed through about five years ago."

He raised his eyebrows. "What's it look like?"

"Tall and colorful, columns. It looks like the temples Hellenes build. It's pretty." She shrugged. "It's not a proper place for Mihr."

He didn't ask why. Mihr was a god of her people; he didn't need to pry into her feelings.

"You should face Mihr in the mountains with his golden rays falling on your face and air so thin your lungs hurt." A flash of serenity passed over her face before it returned to her normal sightly perturbed expression. "What do you believe in, Roman? Your Roman gods taking up space on a Hellene mountain?"

He shook his head and smirked at the young Armenian woman's taunt. She knew he wasn't Roman. "I've paid honors to my gods in their hills and groves, in the high places of light in Albios where I hope to go when I die and in the dark depths of Dubnos whence I came. But I try to be respectful of all gods when I'm passing through their lands."

"No. What do you *believe* in?" Her eyes bored into him.

Instead of answering glibly, he thought about it as they walked their horses. The first image that formed in his mind when he went looking was the divine face of Selene and the calmness that accompanied it. Then he saw the faces of his mother and father, then the men marching with him, then his own face. Furrowing his brows, he opened his mouth to speak but clacked it shut. There was a reason he'd been selected for this post and why'd he'd earned the promotion he had.

"I believe in the goddess of the moon, Selene. I believe in my parents. I believe in my men, and I believe in myself." He risked a look over, catching Ariazate's face with her eyebrows raised high on her forehead.

"Why the Hellene's goddess of the moon and not your Roman or Gaulish gods?" Her tone had drifted to curiosity instead of her normal sardonic voice.

"I've met her. The others I haven't. That's not to say I don't believe in the others, but when you're confronted with the reality of a goddess in close personal proximity, it has an effect."

She looked like she was about to say something sarcastic, but the earnestness in his face must have stopped her. Instead, she nodded respectfully. "Anyway, it's a nice enough temple, but I did not feel my gods are in it."

"We'll see soon, I guess." He turned his head toward the optio. "Let's mount up. I think they've had enough of a breather."

"Aye, Centurio. Legionnaires! Mount up." The optio leapt into his saddle.

He was curious to see Gorneae and who he might or might not meet inside. Syphax had told him to be wary when mixing up with gods, but here he was riding to a temple as directed by a goddess. Oh, he was mixed up with gods alright, right up to his neck.

ELEVEN

"I HOPE the priests have a place for us to stay. That sun is too close to the horizon without a camp set up and ready," the optio said, looking optimistically at the fortress appearing on the horizon as they rode up the valley winding into the east.

"I'll see what I can do," Lucius replied. "Give me two tents worth of men and send for Pater Tiridat. Hold the rest of the men ready."

"Usual watch?"

Lucius nodded. "No sense being stupid." He turned to the two Armenians youths and waved them forward. "You two are with me."

Once he had his sixteen and the three Armenians, he rode forward, leaving the optio in charge of the rest of the cohort. The pater claimed he could get them entrance to the fort if it was shut to them.

When they approached the gates, they found them wide open and unguarded. Holding his fist up, Lucius halted his party and listened. The absence of noise chilled more than the mountain wind whipping around him. Under him, his horse must have picked up on his nervousness and danced. He reached down and stroked her neck, though it didn't seem to help either of them.

He pointed to one of the men. "Get Venextos and tell him to leave a party to hold the gate, then follow us in with the rest of the men. We'll be heading straight to the temple." Lucius nudged his mare forward, though she pranced to the side, not interested in going through the gates.

The fortress had been destroyed sixty years ago by the Romans, then rebuilt with Roman gold, but the streets were abandoned as they rode through. In the growing shadows of the sun as it threatened to set, Lucius saw ominous smudges on the ground and along walls. He couldn't tell if they were shadows or something else. The rest of the horses picked up on the nervousness of Lucius's mount and danced, snorted, and occasionally threw their heads. His men weren't immune to it either, and hands drifted closer to their weapons. The eerie lack of sound caused any disturbance in the silence to draw hasty looks and narrowed gazes. When the shadow of the temple loomed in front of them, Lucius wanted to feel relief, but instead, his dread grew.

Narrowing his eyes, he scanned the area around the temple and its impressive painted basalt columns. It wasn't the largest such structure he'd seen, but it was lovely and majestic and entirely too dark and silent.

He set his left hand on the end of the spatha strapped to his saddle, squeezing the round pommel tightly. Seeing the direction of his hand, his men gripped the hilts of their weapons, their alertness taking another step into the hyper range. Tigran seemed to be the only one not paying attention to the increase in tension as he gawked at the temple he might barely remember from his distant early childhood. Ariazate, who'd slid to the outside of Tigran, noticed and used her horse to herd her brother away from the edge of the group in toward Lucius.

"Zati," Tigran pointed to the top of the temple, "look —"

"Tigran, hush up," she hissed.

"What?"

She gave him a sharp look and covered her mouth with her hand. Tigran's eyes went wide as his head snapped to attention, eyes darting around to tense men gripping their weapons. Assured that Ariazate had her brother in check, Lucius turned his attention back to the temple and his legionnaires. With a couple quick hand signals, he sent three men each to the left and the right and a pair back to rest of the cohort to update them and ensure they were on the way. Sliding off his saddle, he tugged the tall and narrow hexagonal cavalry shield around. Looking at his spatha, he pulled it and handed it over to Ariazate, hilt first. She took it and rested the blade across the two front saddle horns holding her thighs into the saddle.

Lucius left three men to watch the Armenians and hold the horses until the rest of their unit could join them. He waved the remaining four men to follow. Finally, he drew his gladius from its scabbard. A quick glance over the side with Selene's moon and stars engraved in it settled him as he took his first step toward the temple.

If he wanted to get to the stairs, he'd have to step off the grassy ground onto the paved path leading up to the main entrance of the temple. When he set his foot down on the stone, the hobnails in his caligae would sound loud and crisp. Sneaking wouldn't work.

He signaled his plan, then took off at a low run until he reached the stairs and stormed up, sliding around a column and up to the wall near the door, his back flat against the cold basalt. The sun, halfway behind the mountains on the other side of the temple cast long shadows and rich oranges and pinks. Eyes flicking to the door, he saw a dark spot. Unsure of what it might be, he leaned his sword against the stone frame of the door, point down.

Poking his tongue out to wet his lips, he rubbed his hand over the shadow, then held his fingers in front of his face. Shadows didn't wipe off stone. Blood. Wiping his fingers off on his tunic, he snatched the gladius up and lifted his shield. He made eye contact with each of his men, then nodded.

In pairs, the four men swept through the door, Lucius hot on their tail. They formed a five-man wedge with each side scanning the walls while he covered the front. The lack of motion or visible enemies didn't inspire him to lower his arms, and what he saw caused him to tighten his grip as he clenched his fists around the handle of the shield and the handle of the sword.

Blood was smeared across the walls and floor, and a well-dressed man, likely a priest, sprawled motionless in the center of the aisle.

The metallic scent of blood saturated the air. When they swept through to the back of the small temple, only finding blood and bodies, he sent his men to the front to hold the door while he looked for something he could light. With the temple facing to the north-west, the setting sun had nearly rendered it pitch black. He reached into his belt pouch and pulled out his steel and flint.

When he found an unbroken oil lamp, he set it clear of any spilled oil and attempted to light its wick. Once he got it lit, he lifted it above his head to cast as much light as he could with the poor, underpowered flame.

Even with that, the carnage became far more graphic. The priests had been slaughtered. The bright reds of the frescoes contrasted against the shiny, almost black of the congealing blood. Squatting down, he stuck his fingers into a pool of blood. Cold. It hadn't happened in the last few hours.

A young woman's scream startled him. He whipped around. Ariazate stared in horror at the blood and bodies strewn about. At the sound, a couple of Lucius's men poked their heads in. Why hadn't the fools stopped her? Lucius, careful not to spill the oil from the lamp, stepped in front of Ariazate, blocking the view with his body, and wrapped his other arm around her. He rubbed her back while making soothing sounds as she shook and cried. A few minutes later, the optio and a couple other men stepped into the temple.

The optio stopped nearby. "What happened here, Centurio?"

"I don't know. I haven't had much of a chance to figure it out yet." Lucius gestured with his head toward Ariazate.

She pushed back from Lucius, wiping her eyes. "I'll be fine now."

"You should wait outside."

She shook her head tightly. "No. We need to find out what happened."

He raised an eyebrow but didn't push. "Optio, please have someone ensure the boy stays outside, and tell Pater Tiridat what happened in here. He can join us if he wishes, though I don't know if he'll be able to do anything except comfort the dead."

"Right, I'll be right back." The optio turned to leave.

"Centurio! This one's still alive," a legionnaire called.

"Better grab a medic too," Lucius said, closing the distance to the legionnaire squatting next to a body.

The man, probably in his late fifties or early sixties, wore blood-soaked robes. His thick silvery beard was stained pink in spots while in others, thicker black blood had coagulated, matting the hair in clumps. His chest rose and fell shallowly. As his head lolled to the side, Lucius saw it—the grievous wound in his neck—teeth marks.

Lucius's vision darkened around the edges as his breathing grew quick and hoarse. He'd seen a similar wound just over ten years ago in the hills outside of Sarmizegetusa. The face of his best friend Cassius, pale from blood loss, filled his mind as Lucius relived his friend's final moments, gasping out his life, a teeth marks in his neck. Pressure on his shoulder brought him back into the room. Looking up, he nodded at Ariazate in thanks.

"Grah…"

The sudden sound accompanied by a weak jerk from the wounded man startled Lucius, sending him tumbling onto his butt. The old man appeared to be trying to form words, though they weren't familiar to Lucius.

"Can you understand what he's trying to say, Ariazate?" Lucius asked, getting back to his feet.

The hand Ariazate had returned to his shoulder shook. He checked on his young friend. Her eyes had gone wide, her face pale as the blood drained from it.

"What is it, Zati?"

"He keeps repeating the same name. Nhang. Nhang. Nhang." She took a step back, placing Lucius between herself and the old man.

"What does it mean?" Lucius looked back and forth between Ariazate and the old man as he mumbled the same word repeatedly.

She shook her head but kept her stare locked on the old man's lips as he repeated the sound, each time getting weaker. "We…we must go. We won't find anything here but evil."

"We can't go yet. He needs our help." Lucius stood up.

"He's beyond help. We have to go." She pleaded with Lucius, trying to pour her urgency into her eyes. "Please."

He reached out and put a comforting hand on her shoulder, the lamp light flicking shadows around her face. "What is a Nhang? I can't protect everyone if I don't know what I'm fighting."

"They're monsters. Sometimes they look like a serpent or a seal. Sometimes they pose as a woman to lure men in, then drink their blood. Though I don't know what they're doing this far from water… They're foul, evil demons."

Lucius's mouth dropped open as his eyes widened. "The di inferi…"

"Do you know what she's talking about, Centurio?" Venextos asked.

Lucius, still staring at Ariazate, nodded. "Yes. When Syphax and I received our mission from the imperator, his pater patrum said there were evil spirits assaulting a temple of Mithras, but I can't imagine they meant this one…" He finally pulled his eyes away from Ariazate's frightened face and looked around. "It doesn't make sense. We weren't told to go to Gorneae by the priests."

"What do priests know of accurate predictions?" the optio replied.

Lucius held his hand up to halt the optio. "Let me think, Venextos." He brooded, the hobnails on the soles of his caligae clicking crisply as he paced back and forth. They'd been sent here by Selene, but could she have seen into the future to the death of these priests? Or were her directions merely a path to take on the way to their destination in the eastern mountains? For whatever reason, they'd been sent here, and he'd found the monsters. He stopped to look out the door into the growing darkness as true night set in. "Where's that cursed medic?"

"It's too late for the medic, Centurio. He's gone." The optio set down the dead man's head gently, laying his hands on his chest.

A series of screams shattered the silence outside.

"What now…" Lucius's hand drifted down to his gladius.

As he got closer, he realized the screams weren't entirely human. Whinnying horses joined the growing disturbances outside. When he broached the door, sword in hand, he was met with a scene of pure chaos. Several of his men had been dragged from their mounts, a few of the horses taken down with them, thrashing weakly on the ground as they bled out. His men were trying to find order from the chaos but were struggling with their attackers, who in most cases didn't have weapons and were dragging the men down with their hands.

He blinked hard, trying to make the scene make sense. They moved too fast, pulled too hard, lifted too easily. They were overwhelming his men.

"Zati, stay behind me."

She nodded, her head wobbly from the terror of her monsters coming alive.

"To me!" Lucius bellowed, hefting his shield.

The men who'd been with him in the temple snapped into position, providing a line of flesh, steel, and shield to protect the young woman. Noticing a new threat, a couple of the... He could only call them monsters, even though they looked human enough. Regular humans didn't move the way they did.

He almost missed his first strike, underestimating the speed and power of the creature. Plunging his gladius in deep, he did his best to keep the creature from getting to his vitals while Venextos came to his aid and helped him hack the thing to pieces. Before they could recover, they leaped after one who'd brought one of their comrades to the ground. As the creature tried to claw through the legionnaire's shield, they shoved their blades through its back. Lucius hacked its head off before kicking the body off the man on the ground. His face was covered in blood from a couple of deep gashes. They helped him to his feet and let him wipe the blood from his eyes, then advanced forward.

"Form ranks on the temple!" Lucius yelled, trying to cut through the cacophony.

The men who could, made for the temple. One of them brought Lucius's horse on a lead. Leaping into the saddle, he reached down and pulled Ariazate up behind him. With more men around him, he advanced. His horse, despite the terror, responded to his commands.

Wading in, he cut and slashed and stabbed, the pony kicking and biting while Ariazate held on tightly around his waist. The rest of his men had formed a ring and were doing their best to protect the pater and Tigran. He couldn't see the pater's men, but he had bigger concerns. He wished he'd left the gladius instead of the spatha—Ariazate had given it to Tigran before she came in. The reach of the spatha would be welcome. Once Lucius merged his group with the other, the creatures broke off and sprinted into the night nearly faster than his eye could track until only he and his men were left, along with the three Armenians.

"What the fuck happened out here?" Lucius barked.

"I don't know, Centurio. One moment we were waiting here quietly, then they flew out of the darkness," Tesserarius Ramses said, his chest heaving from the intense fight.

"Why didn't our scouts give us any warning?" Lucius turned his horse around, trying to keep an eye out in every direction.

"As fast they came up on us… Centurio, they're probably dead," Venextos said. "Should I send someone to check the men we left at the gates?"

"No, we'll be leaving shortly, and I don't want to split our men." Lucius looked around at the carnage of wounded and dead men and horses. They'd have to be careful leaving the fort. The creatures could be hiding in ambush anywhere.

Ariazate slipped off the horse and ran to her brother, making sure he was OK.

"Check for wounded and dead," Lucius ordered then pointed his sword toward the pater. "This is your country, Pater. What were those things? The priest inside called them Nhang before he died."

The old man shivered in his saddle, his eyes wide in terror. His mouth worked like a fish out of water. Once he regained his composure, he addressed the Centurion. "I don't know. I've never seen anything like it before. They're horrors."

"Centurio," Venextos interrupted, waving Lucius closer.

Lowering his ear toward his friend, he waited for the news bad enough it had to be kept quiet.

"Of the men downed, most are dead. Five are still clinging to life, but I doubt they have any chance at pulling through." Venextos exhaled heavily, frowning.

They both looked up at the distant sound of an unholy screech.

"Fuck, they're gathering again," Venextos mumbled.

"No chance of surviving?" Lucius asked.

The optio shook his head.

Lucius closed his eyes and nodded. "Ease their passing and grab their signaculum. Organize a party to put down the wounded horses and strip what we can of the gear. Prioritize food and survival equipment."

Venextos, his eyes matching the sadness and terror in Lucius's, nodded and started barking orders. Lucius turned back to Tiridat, looking for his men.

"Pater, what happened to your men?"

The pater shook himself out of his stupor. "Dead. All dead…"

"Mylitos, stick with the pater and do what you can to keep him moving," Lucius ordered, nudging his horse toward Ariazate and Tigran.

The boy had tear streaks smudging his face, though he seemed alert and ready. His sister hovered near him.

"You two, find weapons. Take whatever you can use from the dead. Their armor will be too big for either of you. Take a couple packs and load up on food, then stick close to me. I don't know what's going to happen, but don't get lost." He held eye contact with Ariazate.

She nodded. "Tigi, go find a pair of swords, then see if you can find arrows and a couple bows."

Tigran slid out of his saddle and walked reluctantly toward where the men were stripping the usable supplies from the bodies of the men and horses. One of the legionnaires handed him two swords, which he brought back to Ariazate. When Tigran turned back, the legionnaire had found a couple of bow and arrow cases. Sliding down from her horse, Ariazate took the sword and bow case and arranged them to her liking, then helped her brother settle the sword's baldric under his belt. As soon as they remounted, Lucius saw to the organization of the rest of his men. They'd be leaving the temple with just over sixty men. The horses, though they were as terrified as the legionnaires, had fared better, leaving plenty of spares if they had to ride hard and switch mounts.

Sidling up close to Ariazate, Lucius leaned into her ear. "Where are we going? You were supposed to be our guide."

She nodded nervously. "We need to ride east and then ride around the south side of the lake. The mountains we need to go to are on the southeastern corner of the lake. There's a peak, high in the clouds, where people don't go for any reason. I believe that's where we're supposed to go."

"OK." He stared at her for a moment, then reached out and patted her leg. "Alright, we're in your hands. Point me in the direction, and we'll go."

Lucius's men made quick work of their tasks, driven by terror of the monsters that had torn apart their comrades and decimated their numbers, thoughts of Parthians temporarily forgotten. After his men had the horses repacked, he ordered the pack animals and spare mounts forward with an escort. He and the remaining men would screen their advance from the rear and keep the monsters off them as best as they could while they worked their way out of the fortress.

After they cleared the gates—the men he left to guard the gates were dead—they rode hard, switching horses frequently and using every trick Syphax had taught him about horse care. Every strange sound caused hands to clench weapons and heads to swivel around. When the creatures made an attempt on the rear of Lucius's line, he wheeled a detachment around and charged the monsters, churning several of them under the hooves of their tired ponies.

After that, the nhang, or whatever they were, merely trailed them as if waiting for stragglers to fall by the wayside to be collected and consumed. Whatever the reason they stayed so close behind, the result was exhaustion for both people and beasts. Only the terror of what had happened that night and the constant tails kept them men alert. He had no idea how the di inferi traveled so long and fast on foot, but it only added to the terror of their predicament.

When the eastern horizon began to lighten with the approach of dawn, the creatures disappeared like mist before the wind. By the time the sun was visible, no one had heard or seen any of the monsters in a while. As soon as the sun climbed above their heads, Lucius breathed a sigh of relief and issued orders to find a place to camp. They'd been moving for nearly thirty-six hours straight, and they had to stop.

Tucked into a narrow ravine, they quickly erected stakes across the entrance, leaving a minimal watch while everyone else bedded down. Ariazate and Tigran had already found a nook out of the way and had curled up in their blankets, swords resting by their hands. Stripping out of his armor quickly, he rolled up nearby and fell into exhausted oblivion.

TWELVE

AFTER A FEW HOURS, they woke, bleary-eyed and sleep deprived, and continued their journey. Lucius had no idea what waited for them the next night, but he wanted as much distance as possible between his people and the monsters as he could before the sun abandoned them for the day.

By the time evening approached, the scouts Lucius had sent back down their trail were reporting armed men in the distance. They couldn't tell if they were Parthians or Armenians investigating the deaths at Gorneae, but it didn't matter. At this point, Armenian troops were probably reporting to the puppets set in place by the Parthian king. His sixty Romans would quickly find their cadavers stripped of possessions and tossed into a ravine to feed the carrion animals.

With armed men trailing them during the day and monsters at night, it was only a matter of time until one or the other—maybe both—caught them, and they'd be too tired to put up any kind of fight. He couldn't bet on the creatures giving up after only the first night of pursuit. He didn't know if they were intelligent or simply following their base instincts.

Lucius nudged his horse toward Ariazate and her mount. "Zati, can you answer some questions?"

The young woman shook herself out of the stupor she rode in and yawned. "What? Yes."

"What are nhang? They look like men." Though, he'd never seen a man with fangs or claws like that or the burning hatred and hunger in their eyes. It was the eyes that haunted him the most.

"I don't know. They're vile, evil beings. I don't know if they're spirits or a physical monster created by the gods. In some tales, it's only one monster, in others, it's a race of them. They're tricky, false. They befuddle the mind and senses to lure in their victims." She made a gesture against the evil.

He narrowed his eyes and leaned closer. "Do the creatures that attacked us last night match up with the tales of the nhang?"

"I don't know. Maybe in some ways. The blood feeding definitely, but the nhang is supposed to use the shape of a woman to lure in its victims or take the shape of serpent-monster so it can live in the river." She shivered.

"Huh." Lucius didn't know what to make of it.

Monsters were supposed to be the provision of children's tales and priests. Now he lived a monster story and had to find a way to get those under his command and protection out of it alive. Monsters and Parthians. When he left Antiochia, he'd thought they'd been given a reasonable mission—one far safer than the years of war he'd just survived, though not without injury. He flexed his left hand. The tug of the wound still pulled a bit in his forearm between elbow and wrist.

Making it out alive and without lasting injury, he'd counted himself lucky. Perhaps he'd have been luckier to have lost the ability to hold his shield. He'd have been honorably discharged and sent home. With thoughts of home, he wondered what his parents were doing. They were probably preparing for the fall harvests and all the commerce that entailed. He'd be helping his father organize the freight to the legionary forts that sat on the Rhenus separating the empire from Germania Magna. Now, he wasn't sure if he'd even make it out of these mountains.

The minimal sleep they'd crammed into the morning was already wearing off as everybody, human and animal, dragged their feet, heads dipping low with fatigue. They couldn't make it through another night like the previous. If he asked it of them, they'd try to push through, but what shape would they be in by the morning? He knew his men's conditioning. Moving hard and fast as the Parthians pursued them had burned off a lot of fat they'd layered on during the easy march escorting Trajan back toward Roma. They were tough bastards, but he couldn't burn them out for nothing.

"We need to find somewhere to hole up for the night," Lucius mumbled.

"What, Centurio?" Mylitos asked.

"Go find Venextos for me, Mylitos." Embarrassed to be caught talking to himself, he needed to consult with his second-in-command.

Venextos raised a hand in greeting as he rode up. "You called, Centurio?"

Lucius nodded. "Ariazate, would you join us?"

He pulled his horse out of the procession and rode away from the trail, his second and the Armenian behind him. Settling at the edge of the tree line, he turned and watched his tired men trudge on.

"We have to get under cover for the night. The men need rest. I don't know if those things will be back or not, and we need to get defenses set up." He turned to Ariazate. "I don't suppose you know about a handy fortress that might scare those creatures away?"

She shook her head. "I know where we're going, but not about the land between. I'm not a guide. I've been away from my home for too many years."

He'd never asked her when she'd been forced to leave her home, or if she'd ever known life as a free person. Even if she'd been free, she would have been a child and not free to roam about a dangerous country. He sometimes forgot how very young she was.

"Fair enough. Venextos, let's double the number of our forward scouts and send them out wide looking for a place we can hole up for the night." He scratched the growing beard on his chin. At nearly two weeks old, it itched and irritated his skin. But it was a minor annoyance, and it felt nice to have a mundane annoyance to distract his mind from the terrible burden of leadership with two enemies stalking them night and day.

"Right. I'll lead them myself." Venextos saluted and turned his horse, riding back toward the column.

"Ariazate, if you see any of your countrymen, wave me down so we can speak with them. We need local intelligence."

She nodded. "If they don't just hide…"

"We'll offer to pay. I have a fair bit of coin with me for such occasions." He nudged his back toward the line, picking up his pace so he could return to his position in the center of the line. The sound of Ariazate's horse trailed him until it melded into the sound of feet and hooves marching.

THE WORK TO set up their fortifications for the night had been intense. The scouting parties had found a small creek running through a ravine with rock shelves hanging over it in places. Finding a wide enough spot after a bend in the ravine, they set a forest of stakes on both sides of their encampment.

As Lucius sat by his fire, trying to warm some water so he could wash off the grime of two days of hard riding and any remainders of the blood from the temple, one of his men approached, waiting to be called forward.

"What is it?" Lucius didn't mean to sound rude, but exhaustion and stress were warring for dominance.

"Sir, one of the men found a path running up the rock face that leads to the top of the ravine."

He groaned as he stood up. "Show me."

Lucius followed the man to the wall near the back edge of the camp. A legionnaire from Aegyptia waited for them.

"Ramses. I hear you found a back way in," Lucius said.

The man shrugged. "Not really. We haven't found a way it can be used. It leads up to the top from here, but as far as we can tell, there's no way up from the other side, at least not without coming from further up the mountain."

Lucius nodded, gesturing toward the trail. "You better show me, Ramses. Josephus, let Venextos know where I am."

He followed Ramses up the narrow and often dangerous path until they crested the wall. Wiping a hand across his brow, he huffed and puffed from the hard climb. The view the climb afforded nearly robbed him of his breath once he regained it. In the west, the edge of Sol Invictus's chariot had nearly finished its journey for the day, leaving brilliants oranges and pinks edging into purple.

After thanking Sol for another day, he turned to find Selene, letting her silvery light bath over him as he raised his face to the sky, and closed his eyes. He wasn't sure if it was wishful thinking or if he could actually feel Selene's presence in the light as it caressed his face. Opening his eyes, the corners of his lips tipped up, the tension leaching out of his body under the goddess's gentle embrace. He thanked her for watching over him and asked for a peaceful night if it was in her power to provide.

He didn't know Ramses well enough to know if he was a nervous man or if he needed something that prompted his feet to shuffle noisily on the rocky ground. Once Lucius turned and nodded at the man, he pointed into the distance.

"Sir, I think I see something."

Lucius squinted, holding up a hand to block out the light of the moon. It looked like the telltale flickering light of campfires, quite a lot of them. He couldn't be sure, but they appeared to be on the same trail as them, though still a ways back.

"I wonder if that is our Parthian friends, Ramses."

"That's not a small encampment," the legionnaire said.

Lucius nodded absentmindedly. "I don't fancy finding out how many Parthians it would take to need that much space."

"No, sir."

They stared at the flickering flames for a while. Lucius was nearly ready to head back down when the flames went from orderly and contained to something closer to a conflagration. Something had caught on fire. Soon, something else went up.

"The tents..." Lucius said quietly. "Shit. What's... Oh! Oh, no..."

"What is it, sir?"

Lucius stared into the distance as the fires grew, his mouth hanging open. "The monsters... They're attacking the Parthian camp."

"I can't say it hurts my feelings much."

Lucius looked at Ramses. "I'm not sure even our enemy deserves to be ripped to shreds by creatures like that, but at the same time, I have to hope they keep each other occupied long enough for us to get a safe lead."

He continued to watch for a while as the fires leapt to more tents. Others dimmed as they burned out, leaving lower glows of smoldering debris and ashes. "I think I've seen enough." He turned, stopping at the edge of the trail. Down in the dark wasn't the best idea he'd had, but his hot water and some food waited at the bottom of the hill. As hungry as he was, he had no desire to take the fast way down.

THIRTEEN

THE PEACEFUL NIGHT Lucius had hoped for graced them with its presence. When he stirred from his bedding, he felt a modicum more rested, nearly feeling fully human again. Outside his tent, he could hear the activity of the camp waking and packing. He'd ordered a quick but hearty hot breakfast before they hit the roads. The cooks had it ready. The scent of porridge and salt pork drifted into his tent.

What he didn't like was the steam clouding from his mouth as he exhaled into the crisp morning. Pulling on his woolens, he gently shook the two Armenians awake, telling them he'd bring a couple bowls back for them while they got ready. When he returned, he broke his fast with his young friends as the morning's earliest rays slipped over the edge of the horizon to fall in their sheltered ravine.

They'd broken down their camp and were on the move by an hour after sunrise. Though he was curious about what had happened last night, he had no intentions of sending any of his limited number of men to find out. He didn't want to risk them being caught, nor did he want to provide anyone for enemy scouts to follow back. Their best defense was in speed and stealth.

A full night of decent sleep did them all wonders. The horses stepped a bit more crisply, and the men rode straighter in their saddles. Despite what he'd seen in the distance, he kept up the hard pace, taking advantage of whatever had happened.

"Do you know how far we are from your mountain?" Lucius asked Ariazate as they rode next to each other.

"We're maybe six days if we can make up some ground. If we're hiding day and night, it'll take forever."

"What's the land around the lake like?"

"Beautiful in the summer when it's lush and green all around. Stunning if she's frozen in winter. The land is high and the air thin for those who aren't used to the elevations. If the timing is right, the steppe eagles can be seen making their way north or south, soaring high and free. I spent a lot of time near her eastern shores as a child when we weren't in the mountains." Her face was serene as her half-closed eyes focused on images somewhere and somewhen else.

They made it three more nights without seeing either of the enemies trailing them, but at the end of the fourth day as they rose out of the highlands surrounding the lake and into even more serious mountains, their rearguard spied a column in the distance. Trailing back to the end of their own line, Lucius rode out with the scouts to inspect the distant smudge crawling across the highlands they'd just passed through.

"Hmm, maybe a day?" Lucius mused.

"I'd say so, Centurio," the lead scout said.

"We'll just have to rely on our lead and our local guides." He stared into the west for a few minutes before pulling his thoughts in. "Keep an eye on them. Let me know if anything changes."

"Aye, Centurio." The man saluted as Lucius turned his horse and nudged the gelding into a canter so he could rejoin the main force.

"We need to pick up the pace?" Venextos asked by way of greeting.

"Not yet. We have maybe a day's lead on them. I'm not ready to spend our horses quite yet…" Lucius trailed off at the sound of raised voices coming from the north.

A moment later, one of the scouts he'd sent to watch their northern flank skidded to a halt, his horse lathered. Sliding onto the ground, someone took the horse to be stripped down and cared for quickly.

Lucius answered the scout's hastily given salute. "Report, Mylitos."

"There's another column coming from north, along the eastern shore of the lake."

"Shit." He shook his head in frustration, the earlier confidence at the lead they'd amassed dissolving. "How far away?"

Mylitos pulled his helmet off and wiped the sweat from his brow. "Maybe half a day, maybe less. They're riding hard."

"How many do you make?" Lucius tried to relax his jaw from the clench it wanted to be in.

"Five hundred, all mounted with spares."

Lucius nodded curtly. "Get some water and some food. Then when you've caught your breath, I want you to grab a few men and keep an eye on our new friends. Don't do anything risky. Stay hidden and communicate often."

Mylitos saluted and disappeared to carry out his orders.

"Well that's going to make things interesting," Venextos said, breaking into Lucius's brooding.

"We don't have the numbers to put up any kind of fight and that would just give time for the other column to join their friends. Gods above and below, Venextos, nothing about this mission has gone right." He shook his head, catching Venextos's gaze. "Never get mixed up in the business of gods and priests."

"I just take the orders and pass them on, Centurio." The Gaul seemed unsure of how to respond to his countryman and commanding officer.

"So did I, Venextos, so did I." He spat onto the ground. "It's going to be a race, and there's no prize for second place."

"No, sir. To the race." Venextos jumped into the saddle and barked orders, getting their people up from the rest Lucius had called.

His men were highly trained and decently rested, all things considered. He'd have to rely on their professionalism to ensure they made it to their destination, though he had no idea what he'd do if they made it that far.

THEY MAINTAINED their lead over both columns by the time they had to halt for the night. With a short night, they were up and marching as soon as the light permitted, but by the time midday rolled around, the scouts had reported the northern column had made up ground, either pulling a dangerous night march or finding a path that cut the terrain.

"At the rate they're gaining, they'll be on us by tomorrow," Venextos said, eyeing the men around him.

Lucius pursed his lips. "I know. We're going to have to push, switch mounts regularly and keep moving fast. Eat in the saddle."

"I'll get the mounts changed, and we'll see if we can get a little of that distance back."

"Are we going to make it?" Ariazate asked. She cast a look toward her brother, who was currently getting some sword lessons from one of the legionnaires who'd adopted the boy as a bit of a mascot.

"We're running out of lead, and we don't have any allies. Things aren't looking great, but we'll do the best we can to get out of this alive somehow." He wasn't ready to give up yet; he wasn't ready to give up on his promise to Ariazate and Tigran.

By the time they halted for the day, horses and riders were exhausted. They did what they could to erect a rudimentary defense and set guards. After shoving some food down his mouth, Lucius fell into his bed and passed out.

Screams, both human and unnatural, rent Lucius from his sleep. Bolting upright, he grabbed his sword and looked around. He thought he saw shadows running outside his tent.

"What is it, Roman?" Ariazate asked, clutching her blankets to her chest with one arm while the other was wrapped around her frightened brother.

"I don't know." He slid out of bed and started putting his armor on. "I want you to get dressed and packed. Grab the gold out of my baggage. All of it. No matter what happens, you'll need it. I want you to ready a few horses in case you need to get out of here fast. Your manumission papers are also in my baggage, not that they'll be needed up here…"

By the time he'd dressed in his warm woolens and pulled on his armor, he'd run through his directions for his young friends. Stopping in front of them, he tousled Tigran's hair, then leaned down and briefly kissed Ariazate's forehead.

"If I don't see you again, it was a pleasure knowing you both. May the gods' blessings be upon you." He didn't give them time to say anything or argue.

The words had to be said. If it was either of the columns pulling a forced march, they were likely about to die or be captured and sold into slavery. If it was the creatures come back to feast on them, they'd end up as monster shit on the side of the mountain. He didn't want Ariazate and Tigran to end their young lives here when they were so close to freedom and their home.

He'd blocked out the sounds around him while he armed himself and carried out his duty to his friends, but now that he'd stepped out and it was time to engage, the sounds flared in intensity. Men formed lines behind their pickets and stakes. He yanked his gladius free and ran toward the action.

"Venextos," he shouted. "What's going on?"

"Those creatures… They're back. Shit!"

One monster broke through the line, aiming for them. Lucius went high and Venextos went low. Together, they took the creature's head and spilled its guts.

"How many?" Lucius asked.

"Too many. There's no way we're getting out of this…"

"Fuck!" Lucius knocked one of the creatures aside with his shield, following with a stab to the chest.

Venextos sliced its head off. "Take the head. It's the only way to keep them down."

Lucius took a second to inspect the body and head. They looked enough like men, except for the sharp claws at the end of their fingers and the needle-like fangs growing from the top and bottom of their jaws.

"What kind of monster is this?" Lucius had trouble pulling his gaze away.

Venextos dragged him away from the creatures. "Centurio. Lucius, you need to flee. Take the children and complete the mission."

"I can't abandon my men, my command. Not in the middle of battle."

Venextos shook him. "Look at the line. Our men are going down. It's only a matter of time." He shoved a bag of something metallic into Lucius's chest. "We've all known it was you who was meant to finish this mission. Ever since the goddess put her mark on you."

Lucius set down his shield, resting it against his side, and took the bag, stowing it in his pouch for later.

"Go. We can buy you a little time to get away. Ride until sunlight and don't let these monsters from the deepest, darkest places of Dubnos catch you."

"But…"

Venextos raised his sword, poking Lucius in the chest. "For the love of the gods, go. Let us perform our duty to Roma and the gods. We can delay them so you can escape and complete the mission."

Lucius opened his mouth, but the pleading in his friend's eyes changed the argument to a single nod. Stepping back, he saluted his friend. "Venextos. Fight well."

"My friend," Venextos addressed him in their shared Gaulish dialect, "it's been an honor to serve under you. Mylitos and the pater are at the horses. He'll have the mounts ready for you all." He turned and charged into the line, bellowing to announce his presence with authority.

Lucius gave one last look to his command as they struggled valiantly but in vain to push back the onslaught of monsters shredding their defenses. They were the very best of comrades, brave and loyal to the last. Forcing his body to turn, he dashed off to the back of the camp and their horses. As he drew toward the end of the tents, he saw the silhouettes of people on horses. Once he drew close enough, he saw Mylitos, Pater Tiridat, Ariazate, Tigran and another legionnaire Lucius didn't recognize in the dark already mounted up. Mylitos threw the reins of a horse to Lucius then turned and led their small party with a line of six spare mounts and three pack horses.

As soon as they cleared the back picket line, Mylitos kicked his horse into a trot to sweep out in front to scout their way. The other legionnaire brought up the rear to handle the horses. In areas where they could risk it, they nudged up their speed. As he rode, trying to split attention between the trail and the struggle they'd just left, the sound of screams and fighting finally faded to nothing.

Sighing, he hung his head, shaking it. He'd remember their sacrifice and ensure they got the honors they deserved, but now was the time to focus. They needed to survive until the rising of the sun and the protection of Sol Invictus. But now, they were in the domain of Selene, and her light was needed more than anything. He didn't like calling on the gods, but survival was more important than etiquette and becoming more deeply entangled with gods. He was far beyond that point by now.

"My Mistress, I am in desperate straits, pursued by the monsters assaulting the Wanderer's holy temple." He wasn't sure if they were the same creatures but figured it would be better to err on that side of things to ensure they survived to find out if it was indeed true.

"I shall do what I can to assist you, my brave soldier."

With that, the surroundings seemed to brighten. He wasn't sure if she lit their path or enhanced his vision, but with the added light, they could risk more speed. The creatures hunting them could move fast like a horse and had the endurance to follow all night. Opening more distance while they were busy fighting was vital.

They rode for several hours, Selene in her moon chariot riding through the sky above them. When they approached the last couple of hours before sunrise, Lucius thought he heard scrabbling claws on the rocks and bodies moving through the brush behind them in the distance. Risking the time, he ordered a quick swap to fresh horses and led a last run from the creatures, hoping their horses wouldn't break a leg or play out before the sun's light met them.

The tension in the air turned the muscles in Lucius's back to brittle knots as his head twitched toward every sound that might be one of the di inferi. Time stretched out to impossibly long moments that seemed to encapsulate infinity. No matter how many times he asked for it, staring into the eastern sky as they rose higher into the mountains, the sun didn't want to arrive early.

As the sun failed to heed his wishes to rise early, the monsters, like coursing hounds on the trail, gained on them. The noises behind them became too crisp, too close. Looking over his shoulder, he thought he saw a pair of glowing eyes looking back. He shook his head to chase away the illusion, only to see several more pairs blink into existence behind them. He pulled the spatha from its scabbard on his saddle and drifted toward the back of the horse line. If they lost the spare mounts and supplies, the mountains would finish the monsters' work for them, even if the sun chased them away.

"Gods above and below," came a voice from the front of their line.

He saw it. The gentle and nearly imperceptible lightening of the dark horizon. The sun was on his way. Just a little more. They just had to hold on…

FOURTEEN

THEY FOUND a sheltered indent in the rocks that wasn't deep enough to call a cave to shelter in for a few stolen hours of sleep after the sun came up. They needed rest, as did the horses, if they were going to make it to Mithras's temple. After a few hours, they returned to their saddles despite their weariness.

Since Mylitos was an experienced scout, Lucius sent him back to keep an eye out for any unwanted company. So far, he'd reported their trail clear. Lucius thought they might have escaped their pursuers for the moment until Mylitos came barreling up behind them.

"Parthians coming. Riding hard. Maybe a hundred or so about a couple hours behind, maybe a bit more." He leapt off his horse to saddle a fresher mount before remounting.

Ariazate jumped down and unsaddled her horse, moving her saddle to one of the remounts. "Roman, give me a spare horse and some supplies and I'll bring back help."

Lucius couldn't believe what he was hearing. "What help, Zati? We're on the side of a mountain with Parthians breathing down our necks and blood-thirsty monsters trying to rip our throats out."

"There are villages in these mountains, fierce fighters. I can raise enough people to save your skin." She didn't make eye contact as she finished prepping the new horse.

"How?"

The pater narrowed his eyes as he stared at her. Lucius wasn't sure he liked the calculation in his eyes.

Finished, she walked over to Lucius and squeezed his hand while looking deep into his eyes. "Lucius. Trust me. I can bring help."

He couldn't look away from the intensity in her gaze as the mountain narrowed to just the two of them. He nodded once. "Mylitos, help her pack some supplies. Josephus, rig a lead line for her second horse. Everyone grab a bite and some water. We're going hard."

"Zati, what are you doing?" Tigran finally figured out what was going on.

"Tigi, you have to lead the Roman up the mountain. Stay safe and listen to him." She held up her hand to stall more argument. "There's no time, Tigi, and we're running out of options. Do you understand?"

He nodded, his chin quivering. She took his head in both of her hands and kissed him on both cheeks, then on the tip of his nose. "I love you, Tigran. I'll see you in a few days. Be brave, be smart."

"Bye, Zati." A couple tears spilled down his cheeks.

She gave Lucius a nod and the whisper of a nervous smile before leaping into her saddle. Pater Tiridat's eyes moved back and forth between the girl and her brother. As soon as she was ready, she rode ahead, angling toward the north.

"Josephus, take Tigran and get moving. I want to consult with the pater and Mylitos." Lucius's left hand drifted down to rest on the pommel of his gladius. Once the boy and the legionnaire with the pack train moved off toward the east, Lucius nodded toward Mylitos. "Take a spare horse and drift back for a last check on their position. Don't give yourself away."

"Aye, Centurio." Mylitos jumped into his saddle and trotted away.

Once they were alone, Lucius gave his full attention to Pater Tiridat.

"Who are those children, Centurio?" Tiridat asked.

"Just some peasant slaves who grew up in these mountains." Lucius fixed his steely gaze on the pater.

He shuffled nervously, taking a half step away from Lucius. "A peasant who can raise armies? There have been rumors for years—"

Lucius narrowed his eyes and filled his gaze with all the steel and barely contained rage he had boiling under the surface. "I'm going to stop you right there. I didn't like the way you were looking at my friends earlier."

"If we give them to the Parthians, they might—"

Lucius half drew his gladius, interrupting the pater. "You have two choices. You can come with us and risk a Parthian arrow in the back, or you can continue this line of thought and die right here, right now with Roman steel in your guts. Only one is guaranteed."

Tiridat stood up straighter, steeling himself. "Perses Ferrata, as pater, I ord—"

Lucius pulled the sword the rest of the way out of its scabbard and flipped it around, shoving it into the pater's neck just hard enough to dimple the skin. The little man quaked and blubbered, steam rising from his crotch. Lucius looked at him in disgust.

"On this mountain, I give the orders. You say one more thing, and I put this through your throat." He gave a little push to emphasize the point, drawing a bead of blood. "If you understand me, nod."

The pater gave a wobbly nod.

Withdrawing the point of his sword, Lucius wiped the drop of blood off on the pater's shoulder. "I'm glad we understand each other. And just so we're clear, if you so much as give Tigran or Ariazate a glance I don't like or speak their names to anyone, I will kill you and leave your body for the buzzards."

Lucius received another shaky nod. He held the pater's gaze for a few moments more, disgust plain on his face, then sheathed his sword and mounted up, leaving the little man standing. The pater could betray his god's will and use Lucius's friends to endanger their mission, but the fear of Lucius's sword weighed heavier. The pater caught up to Lucius, but ensured he stayed behind the centurion and out of reach of his sword.

Lucius caught up with Josephus and Tigran. Josephus opened his mouth to speak but clacked his jaw closed when he saw the stormy look on Lucius's face. After they rode for a while, Lucius picked up the pace when they found a decent stretch of trail to safely gain some ground on. Once the trail got too steep, they dismounted and continued.

When they heard hooves beating on stone, Lucius yanked his gladius and stepped to their rear, Josephus joining him. Seeing it was Mylitos, Lucius lowered his sword, though kept it out in case he had company behind him. The scout yanked back on his reins, drawing his horse to a skidding stop.

"What's the word with our friends?" Lucius asked.

"They're stopping. It looks like they're setting up camp," the Illyrian scout replied.

"That doesn't make sense."

Tigran cleared his throat. "Lucius, I think we might have something else to worry about." He pointed toward the dark clouds roiling around the peak of the mountain.

The thick, black clouds already appeared to be adding more snow as they wrapped around the upper reaches of the rugged behemoth looming over them. The rain they'd fought through in the central mountains had already given the mountain its wintry start.

"Well, that's just fucking great." Lucius stared at the clouds. He'd been too worried about what was behind them. "Let's find shelter. Quickly."

They hadn't risen above the tree line yet. The wind picked up, and they scrambled up the trail, looking for any combination of features that would work to keep the impending weather off them. As the clouds covered the sky above them, the first spits of moisture slapped into their faces, driven by the wind. Growing desperate, they set up the largest tent over a leeward nook in the rocks that had enough trees to give solid shelter and used the other tents to set up a windbreak for the horses.

With the Parthians already hunkered down, Lucius built a fire while Mylitos and Josephus assembled food they could heat up in a pot. The pater sat out of the way, sulking and casting sullen glances at Lucius, though he kept his eyes from Tigran.

"I hope your sister stays out of this mess," Lucius said.

Tigran scooted closer to the fire, sticking out his hands to warm them. "Zati knows how to deal with the weather. We grew up in these mountains."

Though his words were confident, the tone conveyed the boy's concern for his sister. Once Lucius got the fire going, he sat back and let his two legionnaires work over the fire to prepare their meal. Tigran, staying close to the fire, took out his tsiranapogh and provided music.

With their meal finished, Lucius set up their watch. Mylitos took the first watch, Josephus the second, and Lucius the last. Curling up in his blanket and cloak, Lucius heard Mylitos grumble about snow before he fell asleep.

LUCIUS BOLTED AWAKE to the sound of a cut-off scream and horses whinnying. Scrabbling into his caligae, he grabbed his sword and sprinted out into the dark, snowy night to hooves clattering on stone as the horses ran away. Mylitos joined him a moment later.

"You go left, I'll go right," Lucius instructed.

Not waiting for an affirmation, he swept to the right. The tent they'd set up as a wind block was trampled into the ground.

"Centurio, over here!" Mylitos cried out.

Running over to the scout, he found the Illyrian crouched over Josephus.

"His throat is cut."

Lucius looked around, trying to figure out where the danger might be coming from. After a few moments, Mylitos joined him, pulling himself away from their dead comrade.

"Tigran?" Lucius called, not remembering seeing the boy after he bolted out of bed. He heaved a sigh of relief when the young Armenian poked his head out of the tent. "Are you OK?"

The boy nodded, his eyes flicking about. "The pater is gone."

Lucius cursed. "I should have killed him when I had the chance."

"What? Why?" Mylitos asked.

"He tried to talk me into turning in the boy to the Parthians to save our necks." Lucius looked at the body of Josephus, steam rising from the blood around the gash in his neck. "I didn't think he'd resort to murder."

"We've got to get the horses, or we're as good as dead," Mylitos said.

"Right. Let's grab a couple torches." When they had lit torches, Lucius set a hand on Tigran's shoulder. "You stay here inside the tent. Keep your sword in your hand."

The boy nodded nervously.

"Stay close, Mylitos. We don't want to get lost."

They swept out into the dark, intermittent flurries of snow dancing across the mountainside and reducing their vision. Ensuring they kept within sight of either other's torchlight or the light from their campfire, they searched. Lucius was about to give up when he stumbled on his mare milling about. A few minutes later, Mylitos snagged one of the pack horses. With the wind picking up, and the snow coming down in a thick blanket, Lucius called it quits before it became a white out. With the horses secured, they moved Josephus's body out of sight of the camp after Lucius pulled Josephus's signaculum and added it to the bag with the rest. One more man dead, one more piece of lead to turn in, one more name to strike from the records. Lucius sent Mylitos to bed and took the long watch before the sun came up.

Despite the short night's sleep, the cold kept him awake, and his fury at being betrayed kept him warm, that and piling plenty of wood onto their fire. When the sun first peeked over the horizon, adding a dim glow to the steady snowfall, he decided to let the others sleep. With the snow coming down this hard, it would be foolish to attempt the ascent up the windy path that lay ahead.

When Mylitos woke, he relieved Lucius, who retired to his bed to get a few hours of sleep. The Parthians wouldn't risk this weather any more than he would. The few hours of sleep did him good. Once he woke, he and Mylitos cut more wood and began sorting through their supplies, figuring out what they could carry with them without the extra horses. With fire and food sorted, they hunkered down for a quiet afternoon and an early night. As the sun faded, the snow faded with it, revealing patches of starry sky. The snow created a gentle glow reflecting the moonlight that comforted him as they sat quietly, listening to Tigran play.

Once the moon appeared through a patch, Lucius closed his eyes and tipped his face toward Selene's moon chariot. *"My Mistress, are we safe for the evening? From the Parthians and the creatures who hunt us at night?"*

He couldn't imagine them being out in this kind of weather, but then again, a couple weeks ago, he couldn't have imagined that they even existed in the first place. The relative calm had finally returned them to his thoughts as they hid from the Parthians and the weather.

"Neither of your pursuers have any desire to be out in this weather. You are safe for the evening."

"My Mistress…" He hated to question the goddess, but the betrayal of the pater burned hot and raw still.

"What troubles you?" she asked.

"Why did the pater betray us? You…" He cut himself off before he could accuse the goddess.

"I am sorry, Lucius, but not all men's hearts are as constant as yours."

He didn't know how to respond. The mission given to pater had been too much from him, and he broke. It didn't bring much in the way of sympathy for the man, but it provided some clarity. *"Thank you."*

"You are close to your destination, my brave soldier. Follow your heart and we shall meet anon." Selene's presence lingered for a few moments, warming the depths of his soul.

When she left, he didn't feel empty without her presence. Something of her lingered and sustained him. "Mylitos, we won't set a watch tonight. We all need a full night's sleep. I have a feeling the next few days are going to be intense."

Mylitos snorted. "As if they haven't been already." He stood up. "I guess I'd better turn in and sleep while I can."

"Are we going to make it?" Tigran asked quietly.

"We will. We're almost to our destination."

"But what about after?" The boy's voice sounded small as he stared into the fire.

"We'll just have to see. I don't know what's going to happen on that mountaintop. If we make it to the after, we'll think of a plan then." Lucius smiled kindly at the boy. "You should get to bed."

Tigran nodded and joined Mylitos in the tent. Lucius wasn't quite ready to retire, needing to center himself before tomorrow's trial. If they got up the mountain, he'd worry about the temple then. As he calmed his breathing and let his eyes drift shut, he felt a soft pull toward the east, toward their destination. He was being called.

FIFTEEN

"GO!" Lucius yelled, as he held up his scutum.

The wood of the shield felt entirely too thin to stop the profusion of arrows flying toward them. He was lucky even to have it after they'd lost most of their supplies when the Parthians had caught up to them, bringing down one horse and sending the other fleeing. Focusing on getting the injured Mylitos off the ground and away, he sacrificed the horses for his comrade. They wouldn't have been able to use the horses much longer anyway as the trail narrowed and veered off into a thin, winding track up the side of the mountain.

The only thing that had saved them from further injury thus far was a hearty dose of mountain wind that sapped the arrows' power and pushed them off target. The best archers would've been able to compensate, but the wind whipped around first from one direction, then the next with a violent randomness that seemed almost intentional.

A couple of the Parthian archers, better or luckier than the rest, peppered the shield, a few arrows retaining enough power to penetrate. Lucius screamed as an arrow found flesh, plunging into the meat of his thigh. Standing there acting like a target wasn't working, so he hugged the rock face and backed along the narrow path until he rounded a sharp turn and could no longer see the Parthians.

He set the shield aside and grabbed the arrow, letting out another scream as it wiggled in his flesh. Securing its base where it met his skin, he clenched his teeth and snapped the shaft off, nearly blacking out for a second. Only the strain in his jaw and teeth pulled him back from the edge. Shouts in Parthian drifted to him on the wind.

"Lucius? Where…" Tigran stopped when he saw Lucius hunched against the rock face. "We have to go. Hurry."

Nodding, Lucius forced himself up onto his good leg and took a tentative step on the wounded leg. It screamed but would bear weight if he didn't push too hard. Though he didn't really have much of an option on a steep mountain trail with a horde of Parthians looking for his Roman blood. He cast a quick prayer to whatever gods might be watching, hoping one of them might be on their side and take pity on him. He wasn't sure, but maybe the leg hurt less. Or maybe it was just growing numb.

"Are you hurt, Tigi?" Lucius asked the boy, panting with exertion.

"These Parthian archers…" He looked disgusted and spat, but a gust of wind caught it and threw it back into his face. He didn't finish whatever judgment he'd planned to render against the Parthian archers.

Wiping his face, Tigi turned and jogged back up the path; Lucius grabbed his shield and followed. When they rounded another jagged corner, they found Mylitos hunched over, sitting against the rock face.

"Shit, Mylitos," Lucius said.

Mylitos lifted his head, his normally tanned olive Illyrian face pale from blood loss. "Leave, Centurio. I'll hold them off…"

"You're barely holding off death, Mylitos." Lucius looked back the way they'd just come. "Tigran, go see how far back they are."

The boy nodded and ran off, pulling a handful of arrows from the quiver at his hip. Lucius lowered himself as best as he could and hooked an arm and shoulder under Mylitos's arm. Together, the two injured men got to standing, forging ahead on the steep path. A moment later, Tigran reappeared, firing off an arrow occasionally.

"They're almost on us, but I sent a few tumbling." The boy let off a laugh bordering between nervous and terrified.

Lucius redoubled his efforts, trying to fight the growing pain in his thigh, blood trickling over his knee and down his calf. Mylitos's weight grew heavier as his strength flagged. The Illyrian could barely keep his head up. It lolled to the side, rolling until his chin rested on his chest.

"Lucius… Centurio, a cave…"

Lucius barely heard the whispered gasp above Tigran's shouts and the howling of the wind. "Tigran, a cave. Hurry."

He hefted Mylitos up, their armor grinding and clacking. Turning into the rock face, he found the cave. If Mylitos's head hadn't fallen to the side, they would have missed it, since the opening faced the same way they were trudging. Sidling sideways, Lucius guided Mylitos through the narrow opening. Once they made it in a few yards, the cavern opened up. Lucius found an out of the way nook and set down the last surviving man of his command, then limped back to the entrance. Gasping, he stared at a solid rock wall. The entrance to the cave was now filled with impregnable stone.

Lucius's eyes darted around as his breath shuddered in and out of his chest. They were trapped, and Tigran wasn't with him. Leaving Mylitos slumped against the stone wall, Lucius stepped closer to the where the entrance had been. The boy darted by, firing off a few more shots. From this angle, the stone plugging the entrance was partially transparent.

"Tigran!" Lucius shouted.

The boy's head turned, looking for the sound. He shouldn't have been able to hear through the stone, nor should have Lucius been able to see through rock. He reached toward the stone separating himself from Tigran. His hand trembled as he held it just above the surface before touching what should have been stone. Holding his breath, he pushed forward, feeling resistance, as if he were reaching through water instead of stone.

Tigran screamed as a hand emerged from what looked like a solid stone wall. Lucius grabbed the boy's coat before he could scramble away and pulled him back through the mystical wall. The boy struggled as Lucius pulled him through the stone. When the Lucius yanked him all the way through, Tigran's eyes looked twice as large as normal. After a few moments, he recognized Lucius and slumped to the ground, panting heavily. Stepping over the boy's legs, Lucius found solid stone to lean against to take some pressure off his wounded leg. The Parthians moved about outside, hunched over, following the messy trail of blood Lucius and Mylitos had left.

Reaching down to his left hip, he pulled his gladius from its scabbard. Soon, they'd find the rock that wasn't and push their way through, following the trail of blood.

"Tigran, draw your sword, we're going to have company soon," Lucius whispered.

The boy whimpered but scrambled up. Lucius stepped back. The entrance was narrow. He'd be able to face them one or two at a time, at least until they overwhelmed him. Trying to calm his breathing, he waited and waited... The Parthians seemed stumped as they pushed against solid rock, feeling for an entrance that wasn't there. As far as Lucius could tell, the Parthians couldn't see them, looking in every direction but where Lucius stood.

"Lucius, what's going on? Why can't they get through?" Tigran whispered.

The confusion evident in the boy's voice matched the thoughts swirling through Lucius's mind. "I don't know, Tigran."

Lucius slid down, keeping any eye on the semi-transparent stone, and rested on a boulder. Cutting the edge of his cloak, he tied it tightly around his thigh and the nub of the arrow shaft, grunting as he cinched it.

"Mylitos, how are you doing over there?" Lucius asked, letting his wounded leg stretch out to take some pressure off it.

Mylitos groaned and coughed. "Not good."

Lucius waved Tigran closer. "See if you can bandage his wounds. Cut up some of the clothes from the packs. Do what you can for him. I'm going to make sure there's not another way in. I don't fancy having company."

Tigran's eyes flashed to the injured legionnaire, the blood draining from his young face. Nodding nervously, he swallowed and knelt next to Mylitos. Lucius set his gladius down, needing both hands, and pushed himself up, steadying himself with a hand against the wall. He grabbed the sword, shook his head at the nicks on the edge. The blade had taken a lot of hard use since he'd entered the mountains of Armenia. If he couldn't get some time to care for it, he'd have to take it to a smith. With a sigh, he slid it back into its scabbard and hobbled deeper into the cavern that, for now, was their sanctuary.

After fifteen paces, the cavern took a sharp turn to the right, deeper into the mountain. Looking up, he tried to find the fissures or cracks letting the light in, but instead, the cavern walls disappeared into the darkness. The cavern glowed with enough luminescence to see, but he couldn't determine the source. His nerves, which were already on edge, ratcheted up toward the border of fear. Magical walls, unknown light sources. All the stories he'd heard throughout his life said mixing up with gods never ended well for mortals.

His commanding officer had been ordered by the imperator, who'd been told of the god's will by his pater patrum, to march into Armenia and find the temple of Mithras. Now Lucius stood in a gentle twilight, wondering where the light was coming from while he avoided thinking about what might be through the jagged opening going deeper into the cavern. Closing his eyes, he took a slow breath in through his nose and released it as he opened his eyes and stepped through the rough, narrow gap.

Keeping his head down, he pressed his hand on the rough cavern wall as the light disappeared, plunging him into a lightless terror. He stuck out his other arm and touched other cavern wall—he didn't even need to extend his arms fully to their six-foot span. As long as he had his hands on the cavern walls, and he didn't find any side paths, he would be fine. He could turn around and get back to the lighted cave. At least that's what he repeated to himself in his mind. He'd never particularly had a problem with caves, but since he'd witnessed the brutal death of his best friend Cassius in a cave in Dacia, he'd found his neutrality severely challenged. The dark tunnel felt like he might descend into the underworld. But whose underworld?

He sniffed tentatively, seeing if he could pick up any hints of sulfur that might indicate he'd taken a wrong turn. He had no desire to meet one of the gods of the underworld, not until he passed from this life, and even then, he'd prefer the otherworld of his Gallic people. When it was his time, he hoped to step onto Bag Noz and be carried to Albios to live in the light of the upperworld, in heaven. His body and mind served the Romans, but he had no desire for his eternal soul to reside in their afterlives. Nor did he want the cavern to dump him into the dark world of Dubnos.

It was said that all people, at least all Gauls, came from Dubnos, emerging from the darkness, from the earth, and that they still contained elements of the darkness within but were often blinded by the light of Albios as they walked in the middle world of Bitu. Surrounded by the total absence of light, Lucius felt Dubnos within him, the call to the earth. As a boy, he'd yearned for the sky, the clouds, and the sun, seeking the realm of Albios as he lay on his back in the forest staring upward.

Living in Bitu, the middle world, he explored the light of Albios, giving few thoughts to Dubnos. He'd ignored his threefold nature. Here, deprived entirely of the upperworld and stumbling away from the middle world his mother birthed him onto, he had no choice but to explore the third aspect of his nature, of a Gaul's nature, as he wandered through this in-between place surrounded by Bitu above and Dubnos below.

"Fuck." He'd banged his shin on a boulder. At least it wasn't his bad leg; he had no idea what added pain would do to the throbbing. His curse echoed around him, fading as it slowly bounced into the deeper recesses of the cavern.

Breathing out through his nose and trying to contain his growing panic, he sank onto the boulder, ostensibly to rest his leg but also to bring himself closer to the ground. He closed his eyes. Calming his breath, he tried to put aside the aches and pains, the nagging wounds and the exhaustion, his growing fear of the dark. He set aside the cold and the death of his friends and comrades along with those who'd perpetrated those deaths—the Parthians and whatever the brutal monsters were who looked like humans but feasted on the blood and flesh of the living.

After shoving aside the panic—he couldn't give in and crumble into himself after everything he'd gone through—he managed to reduce everything from a dull roar to whispers in the back of his mind. He let his contact with earth ground and center him. He couldn't quit. Not now. It wasn't in his nature. Selene had seen something in him that had brought her favor down upon him. He couldn't let her down. He'd started his journey in the forests of Gaul far to the west and traveled across the Danuvius River in his first years in the legions and then across the deserts and rivers of Syria and Mesopotamia and the mountains of Armenia. In his short life, he'd seen half the lands of the Roman Empire and been recognized and rewarded by its imperator. Few could say they'd done that much with their time in Bitu. Surely such deeds would allow him to ascend to Albios.

From the earth and water and darkness he was birthed, and now he would return to the embrace of the earth. The stone felt cool under his hand, firm and solid. It was just a cave—a place of the mortal realm, nothing to fear. The cool air smelled of stone and dirt and vague hints of life. It had been a while since he'd visited any of the temples of his people's gods that had cropped up as his people had been Romanized. He'd never visited one of the old groves that persisted in the deeper, darker woods where the authorities didn't go. Even if he had, it would do him no good as he sat, trying to will himself to restart his journey. This wasn't their mountain.

He'd been raised in the Romanized Gaulish religion that dominated the province. It wasn't until he joined the legions and had been inducted into the mysteries of Mithras that he'd embarked on his own religious journey. Each time he'd entered a Mithraeum, he'd descended into basements, caves, and other out of the way underground places that had been dedicated to the god who'd spread from the far reaches of Persia and beyond.

Now, as he descended deep into the cave they'd hidden in, he recalled the touch of Selene on his heart when he'd been promoted straight from the third rank to the fifth. As he thought of the goddess and the mark she'd put on him, the aches and pains fighting at the edge of his awareness receded further and brought clarity to his mind. He could do this. He could fight through the pain and terror. Inhaling deeply, he let the calm air of the cave fill his lungs and stretch his ribs. He exhaled and stood. Deeper he must go, so deeper he went.

SIXTEEN

ONE MOMENT, Lucius's hands touched the rough, uneven wall of the cavern wall, and the next, nothing but air. The ground, although it hadn't been horrible, had still been that of a cave with its irregularities. Now he stood on a smooth surface, his caligae's hobnails clicking on stone or tile.

Light exploded around him, blinding him as his eyes clamped shut. He stopped moving, listening for anything that might signal danger. After a few moments, his eyes stopped throbbing from the sudden luminous assault, so he opened them a crack, letting them get used to the silvery gold light filling the room — and it was a room.

He could see the column bases along the floor and stone benches arranged on both sides of the walls with a central aisle. Once his eyes adjusted, he opened them the rest of the way. He stood at the entrance to a magnificent Mithraeum. The columns reached up, attaching to the ceiling next to a barrel vault that looked more like a hollow column on its side with the bottom length cut away to sit on the rectangular box of the temple. With the curve coming back in at the edge, it almost looked like an Omega running from front to back in the temple.

Beautiful frescoes adorned the walls, depicting scenes of Mithras and his deeds as well as other gods. Some stories Lucius recognized, while others must have derived from tales not told in the empire. At the end opposite him, was the bull scene, though it was more elaborate and beautiful than any he'd seen before.

The stone carvings were lifelike and detailed in the larger-than-life image of Mithras subduing the bull. Lucius could see the supreme exertion of the god as he struggled to subdue the primordial world bull. Mithras wore a green tunic and blue leggings with a red cape billowing out behind him. On his head, he had the Phrygian cap rising tall, its top falling forward. His skin was tan with an olive tinge like the people of Syria, Parthia, and Persia. Black curls fell from under the cap, landing around his ears and shoulders. In one hand, Mithras gripped the bull's head, hauling back on it. With the other, he plunged a sword into the bull's neck, freeing a stream of red blood. Lucius could feel the torment of the bull being slain, its muscles practically rippling, agony filling its eyes.

Above Mithras on one side, Sol Invictus, the unconquerable sun, drove his chariot across the sky with his four white horses. On the opposite end, the place Lucius let his eyes fall last, the moon goddess drove her chariot, hauled by two great oxen, one light in color, the other dark. Selene practically glowed with silver radiance. His Mistress. The goddess who'd marked him all those weeks and miles ago in the Mithraeum in Antiochia.

Throughout the Mithraeum, gems and precious metals adorned everything. He'd never been to imperial Roma, but he imagined the opulence of this temple might even shame the temples there. Wounded, disheveled, and with torn clothes, he looked a beggar in such splendid surroundings. Despite what he looked like, this must be the Mithraeum the pater patrum had ordered Syphax to find. A pit opened in his stomach at the thought of his departed friend.

He hobbled down the central aisle, wanting to explore the Mithraeum. Before he'd managed to get a third of the way into the temple, the atmosphere shifted, becoming thicker, more viscous. Lucius shook his head. Perhaps he'd lost too much blood or it was a trick of the odd lighting, but he thought he saw the statue of Mithras move.

With growing horror, he realized the statue was moving. Mithras, the stone version, unfolded himself from the bull, leaving it in precisely the same position, and stood up. The statue grew, eclipsing the altar behind him as his head reached toward the ceiling, towering over Lucius.

"Who comes before me in my home, my sanctuary?" Mithras's voice boomed, shaking the mountain to its core, or perhaps just shaking Lucius.

He fell to his knees with a pained grunt as the arrow in his thigh shifted and dug in. Falling forward, be bowed onto the floor to pay the god striding toward him honor and respect.

"Pater Patrum, Father of Fathers!" Lucius cried out, struggling to scramble backwards in terror. He hoped the respectful address given to the most important of Mithras's adherents would work as a respectful mode of address. "Forgive me for intruding upon your sanctuary."

"Speak thy name," Mithras boomed.

"Lucius, Father of Fathers. Lucius Silvanius Ferrata, a centurio of the Roman Legions. I have been sent on behalf of Roma's Imperator and on the order of the pater patrum who servers the Imperator."

"I ordered the finest warriors of Roma to be sent to me, yet you are alone." Mithras continued his slow advance toward Lucius.

Lucius swallowed and licked his lips, trying to moisten his suddenly dry mouth. "I am not alone. A legionnaire of Roma is with me, though he is nearly unconscious and may soon succumb to his injuries, and an Armenian boy of noble blood."

Mithras looked toward the back of the temple from whence Lucius had come. **"I have no use for boys or the nearly dead."** Mithras brought the intensity of his gaze back onto Lucius. **"Rise to your knees, Centurio of Roma."**

Lucius pushed back, rising to sit on his knees, though he tried to shift his weight so it rested on his good leg.

"And what rank amongst my servants do you hold, Centurio?" Mithras inquired, reducing the power of his voice.

"I have achieved the fifth rank of Perses through the graces of holy Selene, Father of Fathers," Lucius replied, keeping his eyes on the elegantly tiled floor between himself and the god.

Stepping forward, Mithras bent over. Lucius forced himself to hold still and not pull away from the god. It took nearly all his remaining reserves to not wince away from the overwhelming presence of Mithras standing before him. While Selene was silk, Mithras was the iron fist she covered. Mithras, reaching out, placed his hands on Lucius's head, one on each side over his temples.

Lucius jolted, his eyes opening wide and his body going rigid. As his jaw dropped, a deep scream ripped from his lips, reverberating off the walls and ceiling. Mithras looked into Lucius's soul, his touch far from gentle as he sifted through Lucius's life and deeds. Lucius could feel his lungs burning for want of air, yet the scream still sounded. He could nearly feel his vocal cords tearing.

When Mithras found what he was looking for, he released Lucius. All muscles ceased functioning, and Lucius slumped to the ground, his chest heaving as he pulled air into his starved lungs. After a while, Lucius's vision cleared, and he pushed himself up onto his hands and knees. A line of spittle dribbled off his lip, falling to the stone floor below him. Raising a shaking arm, he shoved the back of his hand across his lips, wiping his mouth clean.

Lucius set his jaw and raised his head, his body unsteady. His gaze ran up the length of Mithras but stopped before meeting the god's eyes. Pushing back onto his knees, he rested his hands on his thighs, wincing when he bumped the broken arrow shaft. He wobbled in place, swaying in a sloppy circle.

Mithras straightened to his full height. **"Are you willing to serve?"**

Lucius heard the god's voice not only in his ears, but in his head as if Mithras spoke directly into his soul. "Aye, Father of Fathers." It hurt to speak through his wounded throat; his words were weak and raspy.

"Until the task I lay upon you is done?" Mithras boomed.

While those words reverberated through the room, images of the monsters that had pursued them relentlessly at night flashed through his mind, bringing with it the helpless feeling of being hunted and viewed as nothing but prey. Friends were torn from saddles and ripped to pieces. Horses shrieked until their throats disappeared at the end of the monster's claws. He'd known fear as he stood in a battle line headed into combat, but the terror the di inferi inspired dwarfed any feeling of fright he'd ever experienced. The images, at first in his mind, surrounded him as the temple faded to dark around him. When he thought he could handle no more, the images shifted until a magnificent figure stood lit in the center of chaos.

Instead of the scared Centurion fleeing before their onslaught as he tried to save as many of his men as he could, he saw a man strong and filled with wrath, standing before the blood-thirsty creatures, a black cloak billowing out behind him as he waded into the middle of monsters, laying about with his sword, slaying the creatures pitilessly. Calm confidence and strength replaced the hopeless terror he'd felt earlier. When the horde of di inferi were put down to the last one, Lucius, or the Lucius Mithras offered to make him, stood triumphant in the middle of the decaying corpses of the undead di inferi, black sludge-like blood dripping from his gladius.

Mithras's voice sounded in Lucius's mind, his tone gentler but still overwhelming. *You will become my weapon against the dark creatures who seek the blood of the living, who seek to corrupt life into the undead. You will be my avatar on this world and defend humanity from the monsters who seek to feed upon it.*

Lucius had protected the borders of the empire for almost half of his life. Now he was being called to protect humanity from a rising scourge. The high-minded ideal quickly faded and was replaced with the horror he'd barely kept contained since Gorneae. Now that he knew true monsters existed, he didn't want to spend his life soaked in the dread of running into them again. If he accepted Mithras's offer, he wouldn't be powerless before the creatures who'd dogged his trail every night and sown panic and death in their wake. They'd fear him, the bulwark that separated the monsters from humanity. He'd be able to stand against them and train others to stand with him. "Aye, Father of Fathers. I will serve until you release me."

"DONE!" Mithras reached out and shoved his hand into Lucius's chest, lifting him to his feet.

Mithras wrapped his hand around Lucius's heart, and his entire body spasmed as pain seared him body and soul. The god was the only thing that held Lucius's body upright; his arms flopped out to the sides and his knees gave way. Once again, he screamed, though no sound emerged. Every inch of his body burned as the god exerted his power on Lucius. The spot on his thigh where the arrow was lodged throbbed in agony, and a small tendril of smoke rose from the wound until the shaft and arrowhead disappeared. All throughout his body, his wounds were scoured clean with fire, and his organs felt like they were pulsing with heat as Mithras rewrote Lucius's body and his destiny through every fiber of his being. When he thought he could take no more, Mithras pulled his hand from Lucius's chest, letting him collapse into a heap for the second time.

He lay in a disheveled pile, his eyes staring blankly at the altar at the front of the Mithraeum until his body ceded back control to him. Once he could focus his eyes, he was shocked to see the altar had changed. The bull, still stone, lay dead on its side, its tongue flopped out of its mouth. A stream of blood ran from the wound at its neck.

Joining Mithras, the figure of Sol Invictus stepped down from his chariot and strode toward the center of the altar until he emerged into reality like Mithras had earlier. The two gods clasped hands, renewing their sacred covenant, then sat on the fallen bull. Mithras raised his hands to chest height, palms up. A wide, shallow bowl with two handles and a base featuring scenes of Mithras winding around the rim in red-brown clay appeared in his hands.

Mithras tipped the kylix to his lips and drank deeply before handing it to Sol Invictus to drink of the divine wine. The two gods in the foreground blurred in Lucius's vision as they drank. His focus moved to the gentle silver light emanating from the corner where Selene dismounted from her chariot and strolled down to join the two goods.

The beauty of the goddess nearly robbed him of his breath as she stood tall and elegant, the gentlest of pink coloring her pale cheeks.

"My brother." Selene bowed her head to Sol.

Even in his current state, her grace pulled at his heart.

Sol smiled at the moon goddess. "Sister."

She turned to Mithras and smiled at him. "Mihr, my friend."

For the first time since Mithras had stepped out of the stone, warmth blossomed in his eyes as he held Selene with affection in his gaze. "My dearest Selene."

Extending her arms, Selene took the offered kylix from her brother and raised it to her lips. With a satisfied sigh, she passed the kylix to Mithras and walked around the fallen bull toward Lucius.

She lowered herself in front of him and reached down, running a soft hand along Lucius's jaw until her finger stopped under his chin. "Rise, my brave soldier."

The contact of her skin against his calmed his breathing and soothed the dull ache he'd been left with after Mithras had laid his hand upon Lucius's soul. He pushed himself off the ground and onto his knees, feeling light as if the goddess were lifting him with the single finger still held under his chin.

The soft smile on her face transfixed Lucius and held him steady as she leaned to his left, placing her lips by his ear while holding her palm against his cheek. His skin tingled under her hand as warmth spread through his body. He wanted to cover her hand with his but dared not risk it.

"The night is your domain now. My gift to you is clear perception and bright vision. No more will the darkness shroud your eyes nor will the creatures who hunt the night be able to cloud your mind," Selene whispered into his ear, then kissed his forehead, clearing the last of the fogginess of pain and deprivation. Then she leaned to his other ear and whispered into it. "Now you must learn the secrets of the creatures, those shrouded deep in antiquity."

In his mind, she took him back to the depths of history, showing him the origin of the creatures who waited for him. Dark gods he'd never heard of became known to him as they plotted their vile deeds. The first creatures they created were nothing like the drinkers of blood. The lupine creatures had rebelled against their creators, seeking the protection of Selene and Artemis. Although the dark gods had failed in their first attempt to create monsters to carry out their will, their second attempt succeeded in warping humans into the soulless monsters who'd hunted him since Gorneae. For them, there was no redemption possible, not without the spark that made them human stolen from them and destroyed. The goddess's vision left him breathing heavily at the horror of the di inferi's creation, but he felt even more committed to the divine mission he'd accepted if it meant protecting humans from becoming those monsters.

When she finished her tale, she stood, offering her hand to Lucius. "Now stand, my champion of the night."

Lucius, his body trembling from the stress and the desire to hold the goddess's hand, reached up and took her hand in his and let himself be helped to his feet. Holding his hand, she led him to the two deities sitting on the carcass of the slain bull.

Sol rose and extended his right hand to Lucius who took it in his. The two shook, adding another seal to the covenant Lucius had made with Mithras earlier.

The sun god gave Lucius a neutral smile. "To you, soldier of Roma, I give you the intensity of the sun—the speed of its light, the strength of its fury, and the clarity of its purpose."

Lucius felt his body refresh as the god's hand left his, his muscles feeling light and strong after working them past exhaustion. He felt vital and powerful, more so than he'd ever felt in his life. Lucius wasn't paying attention as Sol returned to his seat, too focused on the changes in his body. However, when Mithras stood, he brought his attention fully onto the god. Lucius took the offered hand and shook it.

"My gifts to you will protect your body and extend your life. The steel that encases you shall be your sanctuary." Mithras snapped his fingers.

Lucius rocked away from the god as his armor suddenly glowed brightly, forcing him to squint as sparks flew from the steel of his segmented lorica and the manica covering his right arm. When the glow receded, he opened his eyes, grateful Selene still held his hand.

He wanted to look at what the god had done to his armor, but he'd have to save that for later when they weren't watching and waiting for him.

"Your sword, Centurio," Mithras demanded.

Lucius pulled the gladius from its scabbard on his left hip and laid it flat across Mithras's outstretched palms. As soon as Lucius removed his hand, Mithras's palms flared with light; Lucius closed his eyes. Once the light faded, Lucius opened his eyes to see what the god had done to his weapon and took back the offered sword.

The wood of the hilt guard and pommel ball remained the same dark shade while the bone handle glowed white. The blade, however, had been renewed, much like Lucius. The nicks were gone, and the metal gleamed as if it were newly polished, or more likely, newly forged. He flipped it over to look at the blank side, except it wasn't blank anymore. A beautiful sun grew from the hilt, sending its rays up the blade with one culminating at the tip. The sun continued on the wood of the hilt guard. Flipping it over, he admired the stylistic flourishes he'd added to the moon and stars Selene had placed on the blade back in Antiochia. He didn't want to take his eyes off the beautiful weapon but put it away reluctantly.

"Lucius Silvanius Ferrata, do you know the story of a rudis?" Mithras asked, turning away from Lucius and facing Sol and Selene.

"Aye, Father of Fathers. They are given to a gladiator to free them from their slavery."

When Mithras turned around, he held a wooden sword on his upturned palms. **"And so shall this one free you from servitude."**

Look took the stunning tan and dark brown striped wooden blade with its sharp, metal cutting edge and what looked like silver filigree winding down the blade to the tip. "Free me from servitude to what?"

"Death." Mithras's word echoed through Lucius's mind.

His eyes going wide, Lucius felt lightheaded at the revelation.

"Its use shall extend your life and give you the power of your enemies so you may use it against them," Mithras explained.

The sword shook in his trembling hands, his mouth suddenly dry. "How?"

Lucius had to restrain himself from flinching away from the god when he leaned into whisper into Lucius's ear.

"Place it into the heart of the monster you have defeated, then lay your head upon the pommel and whisper the incantation. It will transfer the creature's ill-gotten gains to you, giving you speed, strength, and life beyond what even Sol and Selene have granted you." Mithras stood straight.

The incantation appeared in Lucius's mind and etched itself on his heart. He felt strong and powerful, healthy, but his friend wasn't. If he now had the attention of gods, he had to use it to help Mylitos.

Steeling himself, he took a deep breath and straightened his spine and bowed his head in respect. "Father of Fathers, I thank you and Sol Invictus and Selene for these gifts, but I'd ask a boon of you."

"What else would you have of us, my brave soldier?" Selene asked, the welcoming smile she always wore spreading across her face.

Lucius made eye contact with Selene. "My friend won't live long once we leave this cavern. Can you heal his injuries?"

The moon goddess bowed her neck. "It is done."

A raven's croak drew everyone's attention toward the wall to Lucius's left. The spectral raven flew through the stone of the temple wall and landed on Selene's shoulder. Her eyes lost focus as the raven clicked its beak near her ear. When the bird had its say, the smile disappeared from the goddess's beautiful face, replaced by a look of annoyance.

She turned to address Mithras and Sol, "Our enemies await our soldier outside, a great horde."

The cavern and temple trembled, but when Lucius looked toward the braziers, they didn't so much as quiver. The tremors must have been psychically created by Mithras's anger at having his mountain sanctuary surrounded by the di inferi he'd asked Lucius to hunt down.

Sol stood up and extended his hand. "Your gladius for a moment, Centurio."

Lucius pulled the gladius from its scabbard and handed it to the sun god. Sol wrapped a hand around the hilt and covered the pommel ball with the other. He closed his eyes and concentrated. Finished, he handed the sword back to Lucius while Mithras strode toward the wall the raven had flown through. Tracing his fingers down the wall, a seam appeared, slicing a line of light down the wall until an opening appeared. A blast of cold air infiltrated the still sanctuary.

"Gather your friends and leave through this exit," Mithras instructed.

Sol held his hand up to stall Lucius for a moment. "Run, but when you have no choice but to fight, put your gladius through the heart of the first creature you can."

Lucius bowed deeply. "It shall be as you say. I'll carry out your will and fulfill my pledge."

Lucius jogged out of the rough cavern entrance he'd entered from. This time, it was only a few dozen well-lit steps until he was back in the closed-off cavern where Mylitos and Tigran were.

"Centurio, I feared you'd gotten lost," Mylitos said as soon as he saw his leader run back into the cavern.

"How are you doing, Mylitos?"

"I'm healed. I don't know what happened, but a few moments ago, my wounds stopped bleeding and sealed. I have scars everywhere, but I'm not dying. Do…do you know what… Your armor, what's going on?" The blood drained from the young man's face.

Tigran, his eyes wide and fearful, stood behind Mylitos.

"There's no time to explain. We need to go. The monsters who've been hunting us have returned; they're outside the temple. Follow me," Lucius waved them toward the opening he'd just popped out of. "There's another exit here. We're going to have to run when we get out. We only fight as a last resort. Understood?"

Mylitos saluted. "Yes, sir."

They ran back down the cave emerging into the temple. The three deities waited at the far end, but neither Mylitos or Tigran looked toward them or at any of the other splendors of the Mithraeum. Lucius nodded respectfully at them.

To the right when you exit, Selene said in his mind. *My blessing be upon you.*

Lucius stopped before plunging into the doorway and turned toward the goddess who'd marked him as hers. Holding his hand over his heart, where the moon she'd carved into his armor lay, he bowed to her, conveying his deepest respect and admiration. She smiled and nodded gracefully. There was nothing to do now but follow his friends and see what fate had in store for him outside.

SEVENTEEN

IT TOOK Lucius a moment for his eyes to adjust to the dark night sky of the Armenian mountains, though the stars blazed above and Selene graced them with plenty of her light. They'd emerged on a wide shoulder of the mountain. In summer, it might be a grassy meadow.

"To the right, north!" Lucius called to Tigran and Mylitos.

The cold winds whipped about them, picking up snow from the deep piles and flinging them about. Lucius hated that they had to descend out of the mountain at night. The conditions were made worse by their haste. The demons that had doggedly haunted their movements at night wouldn't give up simply because they fled into a cave protected by the gods, especially if the protection ended at the exit.

"Centurio!" Mylitos called, pointing to the southeast.

Lucius pulled his gladius and turned. The insidious fear he'd felt before returned, threatening to choke him. Taking a deep breath of the bracingly cold mountain, he gathered himself. It didn't matter who it was, blood drinker or Parthian or even a bear, this wasn't the time or place for company. Out of the shadows, thin figures rose over the rise, their cloaks flapping in the cold wind. Most appeared to be unarmored. Death rolled off them, nearly overwhelming Lucius's senses. Parthians they were not.

Before, when the di inferi came, he'd felt an uncomfortableness one gets when presented with something otherworldly or underworldly that quickly escalated to fear needing to be tightly contained. They'd felt like something from deep in Dubnos, something old that humans shouldn't know the truth about. Something hidden way from and older than time. Now, after his brush with gods, he felt the utter alien wrongness of the creatures.

He could feel them coming, feel them advancing in a wave, shifting over an uneven shore. At this range, he could almost feel the individuals in the surge. He longed to do battle, to remove them from this plane of existence, to send them back to the deep places where they could no longer bother humans, where they couldn't find their away to the between lands.

"Stay along the ridge, don't let them flank you. Keep moving north," Lucius shouted over the rising winds.

Lucius tried to split his attention between keeping his footing and moving away from the creatures and looking over his shoulder to ensure they didn't sweep up on them, though he could feel their proximity in his bones.

"Careful, Lucius. The path narrows here," Mylitos called.

Forcing himself to rely on his new sense, Lucius kept his attention on the path. There were no gentle tumbles on this mountain. Not from these heights. When he got to the end of the narrow pass, he turned, giving himself space, and drew his gladius. It caught the moonlight, birthing a reflection more intense than mere light on metal. Bringing his shield in front of him, he gave the gladius a little twirl. The blade sang in his hand.

It had been a fine blade from its creation, commissioned from one of the finest blacksmiths in Belgica, but now it was perfect in its balance. It felt like a piece of him, alive and filled with soul, connected up his arm, through his chest to his heart.

The demons moved fast but were forced to slow down and go over the narrow pass only a few at a time. With his wide scutum and his body vibrating with speed and strength, he could hold the pass.

The wind tugged his cloak out behind him, the cloth flapping noisily in the wind.

The first monster approached him with a raised war axe. Lucius knocked it aside with the edge of his shield and thrust his sword into the demon's guts, pulling it out with a hard twist. He stepped back, pivoted, and shoved out with the scutum, knocking the creature off the ledge. Its scream was devoured by the hungry wind. The next one was on him before the scream had even faded.

He parried a low thrust and punched out with the shield, catching the fanged monster in the face. Striking fast, he shoved the gladius into the creature's side and with scutum and gladius, pushed him after his friend. After seeing two of his cohort swiftly cast down upon the mountain, the next one came in slower and more cautiously. With a feigned charge, Lucius spooked him backward into his friends.

Now that he had a moment that wasn't kill or be eaten, he inspected his enemy for the first time. Their clothing came from various cultures and lands. Some wore armor. As the crowd shifted some, the gleam of moonlight off steel drew his eye.

"No…"

One of the creatures wore Roman armor. As his eyes flashed over the crowd, he saw more evidence. A helmet. A crest. Banded shoulder plates. He couldn't force his eyes to seek out faces in case they were men he'd known, men he'd led.

Not wanting to be cautious, the di inferi's companions hurled their comrade over the edge. Lucius took a couple steps back so he didn't get too close to the abyss. It was a double-edged weapon he'd prefer not to have turned on him. The next several tried speed of foot and hand, but Lucius's speed matched theirs and more, refocusing his mind on the fight and who might be about to attack him.

A laugh escaped his lips, his emotions leaping about like the wind, as he met and overcame his enemies, striking them down with alacrity and speed. For the first time since he'd fought against the monsters, he saw fear creeping into their eyes. Fear of the centurion besting them with ease and a laugh on his lips.

When the next one rushed him, an axe raised above his head,

Lucius darted forward and punched the edge of the shield into the chin of the demon, knocking him back and exposing his chest. He plunged the gladius into its ribs and through its heart.

Light exploded out of Lucius's hand and down through the gladius, disappearing into the body of the creature until it exploded into dust. Lucius's eyes flew open wide as the laughter died on his tongue, too shocked to do anything but stare agog. The light kept going though, finding the next di inferi and striking it in the chest as the light forked and arced through the creatures until every one of them exploded, some into dust and others into a nasty black sludge that stained the white snow with their filth. He'd smote them all, smote them as if he were a thunder god hurling forth a bolt of lightning.

He stared over the battlefield, looking at the piles of ashy dust swirling about with the snow and the dark splatters steaming in the frigid snow on the ground. Something yanked at his shoulder, and he spun about. Mylitos jumped back, barely avoiding Lucius's blade.

"Sorry, Mylitos." Lucius still felt utterly stupefied at the devastation he'd wrought.

"We need to go before more come," the soldier shouted.

"Yeah… Right…" Lucius shook his head and stumbled after Mylitos.

Tigran stood against the rock face, waiting for them. When they drew near, he turned and continued along the mountain path winding north. Shock faded, replaced by cold that shivered his body and chattered his teeth. They couldn't stay out in this kind of weather for long, but they couldn't stop, not with more of the creatures potentially chasing after them. He couldn't feel any more, but that didn't mean they weren't there lurking, waiting to strike.

He was thankful for the heavy woolens he wore, though he wished for fur. He'd have to keep moving, warming his body from within. The wind bit at his exposed face and ears.

"Halt!" Lucius called.

He untied his helmet and let it hang down on his chest as he grabbed a scarf and wound it around his head, covering his ears, nose, and mouth. It would have to do. He shoved his helmet back on, trying to get it to settle over the scarf and tied it back in place.

"Lucius," Tigran said, pointing toward the south.

Squinting, Lucius stared off in the direction of the boy's hand. "I don't see anything." He reached out with his new sense and still didn't feel anything.

"There!" Mylitos pointed off in the same direction.

"I see it."

A faint flicker of torch light escaped into the darkness. They stared into the darkness until another light flickered followed by several others.

"I don't like this," Lucius said.

"Could it be the boy's sister?" Mylitos asked.

"I don't know. Tigran? Is it Ariazate?" Lucius looked to the boy.

"I don't think so, not from that direction. She'd be coming from the north."

Mylitos turned to look at Lucius. "Is…is it more of those things?"

Lucius shook his head. "I don't think so. I don't feel their presence like before."

"'Feel their presence'? What happened in that cave, Centurio?"

"We don't have time to go into that now. Speed of foot is our best defense now." He shoved Mylitos lightly.

They broke into a slow jog, continuing their northerly path. Lucius kept an eye on the lights, now more numerous and moving toward them. He didn't know if they'd been spotted or if the lights were merely moving into the area; he wasn't inclined to stick around and find out.

"Do we keep going or look for a place to hide?" Mylitos yelled over the howling wind.

"Tigran, do you know a cave or place we can get out of sight?"

The boy shook his head vigorously. "We don't go on this mountain. I do not know its secrets."

Lucius could hear the fear in his voice. Whether it was the di inferi or the temple and its gods he didn't know, but after what he'd seen and witnessed, Tigran's caution was wise and warranted.

Lucius sighed. "So, for now, we run. Go!"

A glimpse of Selene's moon peeking through stormy clouds blanketing the sky brought a glimmer of hope and a small idea.

"My Mistress, do you see who tails us?" Lucius cast his thought to the moon.

"They mean you no good, that is all I see. They do not pay homage to me, my brave soldier."

"Do you know a place we can hide? Some cave entrance your light as fallen upon?"

"Aye, stay along the path you are on; keep the mountain on your right shoulder. You will know it when you come to it. I will ensure you are not discovered while there is still darkness. After my brother returns for the dawn, I can help you no more in the day."

Selene's voice warmed his chilled body and his fatigue ebbed. *"Thank you, my mistress."*

He felt her affection though she didn't say anything else. Plunging forward, he caught up to his compatriots, not realizing he'd fallen behind while he talked with Selene. With a plan and a destination, he stepped around them and took the lead, setting a steady pace. He knew they would find a place to rest. The thought buoyed his spirits and lightened his step. The confidence of his stride must have inspired Tigran and Mylitos who forged ahead behind their leader.

When he came upon the entrance, it was like a bell sounding in his heart, struck by Selene's benevolence. He cast her a quick prayer of thanks and found the entrance to a cave. If she'd not alerted him to it, they'd have passed it by. It stood barely four feet in height and opened such that it was nearly impossible to see from most angles.

Crouching down, he poked his head inside and breathed deeply but only got the scent of his scarf. He pulled it down and inhaled again. It smelled clean, or at least free from animals and their scents. He wished they had a torch to see what might be hidden within, but he knew that was a foolhardy wish on a dark night when enemy eyes sought him. He gave one last look over the path they'd walked down, the wind and snow quickly removing any evidence of their existence. With Selene's assurances and nature hiding their tracks, he plunged into the cave.

After a few feet, the cave opened enough that he could stand, though he walked with his hand in front of him so he didn't strike his head on a low hanging edge. The helmet would protect him, but it would still hurt. When he felt like he'd gone far enough to find air that was still and unbothered by the gusts occasionally forcing their way into the cave's mouth, he sat down and ordered Tigran and Mylitos to join him.

Pulling his helmet off he pulled his cloak up and over his head, he tugged the scarf down so he could take a drink from the skin in his satchel. The ice-cold water felt like it was going to burn the inside of his mouth. He thought he felt a few crystals of ice in it.

"Don't drink from the water. It's too cold. It'll chill you from the inside," Tigran instructed. "Put your skin under your cloak next to your body. And if you can take off the armor for now, it'll help."

"What do you think, Centurio? Is it safe enough to take off our lorica?"

Lucius nodded. "We are being watched over. They won't find our hiding spot tonight. Listen to Tigran."

They helped each other remove their armor, setting it aside in case they needed to suit up quickly. Fishing some jerky and dried fruit from his satchel, Lucius sat down to fill his belly before attempting to get some sleep. It would be a short night after spending so much of it out on the mountain side.

"Bundle up good and try to get some sleep. Tomorrow won't be any more hospitable than today." He wiggled until he found a patch of ground that would suffice and quickly fell asleep, too tired and too overwhelmed to think about all that had happened in the last twenty-four hours.

EIGHTEEN

A FAINT TRICKLE of light found its way into the cave, giving a vague outline of the entrance and the walls nearest it. Leaving his helmet off to avoid the shine of steel, Lucius peeked out of the cave once his eyes had adjusted to the light. He had to squint against the sun reflecting off the snow.

He didn't see disturbed snow indicating anyone had passed, at least not since the snow had stopped. The snow filled most of the cave's small entrance, only leaving a gap of a couple feet. They'd have to force their way out and forge their way north. If they stayed another night, they might never get out of the cave. They'd just be three corpses found in the spring thaw. The sleep had done them all a world of good, rejuvenating bodies and minds, at least enough for their needs.

"See anything, Centurio?" Mylitos asked.

"Just snow, lots of snow." Lucius returned to depths of the cave.

"We should fill our waterskins with snow so it'll melt as we go. Also, we'll want to tie some thin cloth over our eyes to prevent snow blindness." Tigran pulled out a strip from his bag and wrapped it loosely around his wrist.

Lucius nodded. "Those seem like sensible precautions."

He had seen occasional snows in Belgica as a boy, but they didn't often stay long in the lowlands forest near where he grew up. The first serious snow he'd experienced was in the mountains of Dacia. Those had been the highest mountains he'd ever seen at that point, but these Caucasii Montes soared higher. They took turns packing snow into their water skins, tucking them under the layers to melt and stay unfrozen.

Bundled up, they forged out of the cave and resumed their trek north. The going was tough as they had to force their way through the thick snow laid down over night and piled high by the wind. Still feeling the vigor of his encounter with the trio of gods, Lucius took the lead, wading through the snow to create a path for the last member of his command and their adolescent guide. As his mind drifted to the friends he'd been ordered to abandon to carry out the mission, then the friends who'd sacrificed themselves, he felt his mood dip and sour. It was only when he slipped and nearly went down the side of the mountain that he forced his mind back to the duties of surviving the present.

"At least this will slow down our pursuers," Mylitos called, breaking the silence.

"Shh." Tigran placed a finger over his lips. "You'll wake the thunder snow."

Lucius stopped and turned, waiting a moment for everyone to catch up. "Thunder snow?"

Tigran gave a curt nod. "Yes. Make too much noise and the snow can wake and come down the side of the mountain, fast as lightning and loud as thunder. You don't want to be carried down the mountain in its embrace."

Lucius nodded vigorously. "No. I don't think we do. Let's keep our voices down. Besides, we don't want them to carry to hostile ears."

"Sorry, Centurio," Mylitos whispered.

"Neither of us grew up in mountains like these." Lucius looked down at the boy and squeezed his shoulder. "Fortunately, we have a knowledgeable guide to keep us alive."

Tigran beamed at the compliment.

"Let's keep walking. We've got a lot further to go than we've come." Lucius returned to the front to plow forward and push snow out of his way.

Mylitos was right, though. If their pursuers valued their mounts and their lives, they'd be forced to dismount and lead the horses or they'd risk broken legs and dead animals, not something that would do them any good, though the fresh meat would be useful. Despite the energy from his encounters with the divine, their food supplies were growing thin, and dried meat and a bit of fruit weren't the most rounded or filling of meals. They'd have to keep going if they hoped to get a meal, assuming they didn't die from exposure or tumble down the mountain or take a Parthian arrow in the back or get eaten by one of the di inferi.

When he rattled off the short list of the current dangers, he almost wanted to laugh at the absurdity of them. The only one on the list that made sense to him was the Parthian arrow. He flexed his left hand, feeling the strain in his forearm around the scar that went through on both sides from the arrow he'd taken. The rest of the list didn't match up to the dangers he knew about as a legionnaire.

It was a dangerous business mixing up with gods. One had singled Lucius out in Antiochia, now he owed allegiance to three who'd set him on a mission. According to the oaths he'd taken upon entering the legions, he couldn't enter into any sort of contract. It was why legionnaires couldn't marry until they were discharged from the legions.

He shook his head at himself. What were human contracts to divine beings? The imperator who'd given him the mission could be dead by now. As frail as he looked, Lucius didn't see the old man recovering. He could return to a new imperator who cared nothing about the mission Trajan had sent them on.

Life was complicated enough as an officer in the legions, but now he'd made his own life immeasurably more difficult by accepting the mission of the gods. Though he probably had no choice in the matter. Mithras didn't seem a kind deity. Even if he hadn't obliterated Lucius on the spot for refusing, the god could have cast him into the snow with nothing but a mortally wounded friend, a boy, and a horde of blood drinking monsters on their scent. He'd have been overwhelmed and killed, torn to pieces, his blood turning the snow pink.

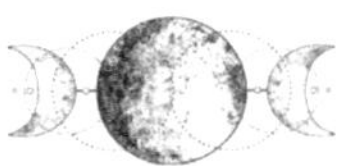

THAT EVENING, they weren't so lucky in their hiding places, but once again, Tigran, a child of the Armenian mountains, guided them. He showed them how to build a burrow in the snow that would keep the winds and encroaching drop in temperature at bay, the snow den acting as insulation, albeit a cold one.

The frigid night meant poor sleep as they huddled together, trying to combine their heat and cloaks to make more layers. When the morning sun's first light forced Lucius from his dreams of monsters and dying in the snow, he welcomed the opportunity to get out of their packed snow cave and keep moving. When he reached into the pouch where he kept his rations, he found one lonely strip of jerky and a couple of dried Armenian plums.

By the time midday rolled around, his stomach rumbled from the lack of food and the exertion of fighting through the snow. He'd put on a good layer of fat on their way from Antiochia, the legion bulking up on high energy food so they'd have reserves before going into high elevations, but his body had chewed through a lot of that already, and he had no idea when they'd make it to a place where they could get more food. If they weren't being pursued, he'd stop to do some hunting, but what was there to hunt this high up and this late in the season?

"Cent…Centurio." Mylitos caught himself and lowered his voice. "I thought I saw something behind us. A flash of light, maybe sun reflecting off armor."

"In all this snow? Are you sure your eyes aren't playing tricks on you?" Lucius joined the legionnaire and stared off in the direction he pointed.

"It's possible, sir, but once you get used to the monotony of the snow, you can start to pluck out differences."

He'd relied on the soldier's eyes before. Lucius's eyes were good, but the young legionnaire's were better, or at least they used to be before his encounter with the gods. Raising a hand to shade his eyes, he let his eyes settle so he could filter out the white glare of the snow. Even through the cloth, it was bright.

"There. I think I see it." He watched for a while longer, more slashes of light emerging.

The wind shifted and blew at them from the south. He thought he heard metal and maybe a voice or two.

"Shit. I think they've found our trail." Not that it was hard without more snow to cover it or a wind heavy enough to push about what was already on the ground.

"Do we pick up our speed?" Mylitos asked.

"No. Let's keep it steady for now. I don't want to burn our energy early and not have it when we truly need to make a break for it." He returned to the line where he'd stopped and forced his way into the untouched snow.

The path they were on descended steadily throughout the afternoon. Lucius forced a few short breaks, letting them catch their breath. Their pursuers seemed to be getting closer, possibly risking their horses to make up ground, though they couldn't go much faster than the trio. There would be no way to shake them at this point without intervention from the weather gods. Lucius hoped that when the sun went down, the Parthians would set camp, but when the torches flared to life, he gave up that hope and forged on into the darkness.

Exhausted and with growling stomachs, Lucius, Mylitos, and Tigran staggered on, their steps growing weak and unsteady. When the boy took a tumble into the snow, they fished him out, giving everyone a breather.

"If anyone has any food left, bring it out. We'll share what's there and keep going. I don't fancy our chances if they catch up to us." Lucius gestured behind them with his head.

The boy pulled out a handful of dried Armenian plums while Mylitos pulled out a few strips of jerky.

"You two share that so we can get moving again."

Mylitos shook his head. "No, you take some too. There's enough for three of us."

Tigran nodded in agreement as they split the food into three meager piles. Lucius didn't have the energy to argue, and the loud grumble of his stomach overruled him anyways. Taking the food, he shoved it in his mouth and savored the feel of it. He pulled out his waterskin and washed it down, then shoved more snow into it before returning it to his place in the front of the line.

He tried to keep his mind focused, but fatigue was fighting a winning battle, and their enemies were gaining. Soon they'd be in arrow range. But all they could do was carry on, hoping against the odds that they'd get a break. When they came around a blind corner and found a deep ravine waiting for them, Lucius thought their luck had run out.

"Lucius, look!" Tigran pointed down the edge of the ravine.

He pulled off the cloth he still had over his eyes and squinted. A shadow of a different shape appeared to cross the ravine.

"Shit! They're shooting at us," Mylitos cried pushing up next to Lucius.

"Scutum out, Mylitos." Lucius unslung his shield from the carrying case strapped to his back and pulled it out. "It looks like that's a bridge. Let's make a break for it. Tigran, you lead the way. Stay away from edge. I don't want you tripping and tumbling over." When no one moved into action, Lucius straightened up. "Go! That's an order."

They snapped to. Mylitos got his shield out while Tigran did his best to run to the bridge. Lucius pulled his helmet on and quickly tied the leather straps to snug it into place.

"Stay right behind me and keep that scutum against your body. If they get off a pot shot at this range, it'll keep you alive." Lucius didn't wait for a response before plunging forward into the path Tigran had made.

A few more arrows fell into the snow. They still didn't have the range, though it wouldn't be long before they did. It was a race — one they were ill-equipped to win.

Shouts followed them as they ran through the snow, arrows

tracking closer with each shot. A horse and rider went down in the snow, the poor beast squealing as it struggled to get up. The thunk of an arrow smacking into Mylitos's shield punctuated their need for haste.

The Parthians still weren't close enough for arrows to penetrate, but soon they would be. Ahead of them, Tigran didn't bother testing the bridge before running across the narrow span. They were almost there.

Mylitos screamed as he went down. Sliding to a stop, Lucius spun around and raised his scutum to cover his friend. An arrow landed at his feet and another stuck in the wood of his shield as Mylitos got up.

"Go! Run!" Lucius shouted, backing up to cover Mylitos's retreat.

When Lucius heard hobnails against the wood of the bridge, he turned and fled, keeping the shield between himself and his enemies. Normally, he'd take a bridge like that at a much slower pace, checking its integrity before crossing, but now was not the time for caution.

When his feet touched rock on the other side, he heaved a sigh of relief and turned around, squatting behind his shield. Mylitos stepped up, raising his to cover them like a roof. It had to be the saddest testudo Lucius had ever been a part of.

"Where's the boy?" Lucius asked, scanning the area and panting.

"I don't know."

A few more arrows thudded into their shield. The first one made it through the wood, the gleam of its arrowhead taunting Lucius and raising a phantom pain in the scars on his forearm.

"Romans!" Someone shouted in the language of the Hellenes. "Throw down your weapons and surrender."

It took Lucius a moment to realize it was a woman yelling at him.

"Centurio," Mylitos whispered. "I hear something behind us. A lot of something."

Lucius's stomach fell. They'd been outflanked and there were more Parthians behind them. Still, he held his position.

"It doesn't sound like much of an offer," Lucius yelled back.

"You can sleep by the fire, and then when we're done with you, we'll sell you into the east like we did with Crassus's men after Carrhae. Or we can kill you here and leave your bodies to feed the carrion animals. It's your choice," she called back.

It was hard to gauge her face behind the helmet she wore. She didn't wear one of the full-face masks often favored by the Parthian kataphraktoi, but a more standard helmet that drew to a point on the top with a burst of horsehair sticking out of it. The helmet had wide cheek guards similar to Lucius's, though her helmet lacked the neck guard his possessed and had a small nose guard his didn't. Like Lucius, she'd bundled up under her helmet. He could only see her eyes and thick black eyebrows. Under her heavy cloak, he caught a glimpse of scale mail.

"You'll have to cross this bridge to get to me and I can defend it for quite a while," Lucius called back.

She laughed, the surprise and mirth in it brought a smile to Lucius's lips. "You've got guts, I'll give you that, Roman."

As the thunder of hooves behind them increased, he kept his eyes firmly on the Parthians in front of them. When their horses started prancing and the riders looked about nervously, checking in with each other, the woman raised a hand and yelled an order in Parthian, drawing them back to order.

"Lucius, I think I see the boy. He's riding on the back of a horse with someone. He's waving at us," Mylitos hissed.

Lucius gave a bare nod, keeping his eyes forward. Lucius and the Parthian woman stared across the narrow chasm at each other. Occasionally the woman's eyes would flick up to the approaching horses behind Lucius.

"Back off, Parthian," another woman shouted. "I've come to collect my Romans."

A little of the tension Lucius had been holding in his body siphoned out at the sound of Ariazate's voice, though he'd never heard that note of authority in it, at least not that strongly.

"Drop your shield down next to mine, and we'll back up, shields to the fore," Lucius whispered.

"Right." Mylitos stepped to the side, dropping his shield down to help block their retreat.

"Armenia doesn't belong to the Romans anymore, little girl," the woman shouted. "It would be unwise to stand in the way of an agent of Parthia. We remember our friends and our enemies. It would be a shame for you to fall into the latter category at such a young age."

"Romans, Parthians, we of the mountains pay no heed to the comings and goings of your petty kings and puppets," Ariazate called. "Besides, you'd have to get home to report to your king. I might be a child, but I can count, and you don't have the people to keep what you want nor to take it from me." She turned her head to the side slightly. "Archers!"

At her call, people moved through the thick line of horse flesh and riders and put arrow to bowstring, but waited, bows at their sides. Likewise, those on horseback readied their bows. Lucius guessed Ariazate had the Parthians outnumbered five to one. Any attempt to make it across the narrow bridge would be met with an impenetrable wall of arrows backed up with mixed cavalry.

Lucius kept his shield up and ready, contributing his steely gaze to the mix. The wind whipped up and settled down. Lucius waited as Ariazate and the Parthian woman stared at each other.

The Parthian woman shook her head and held up her hand, issuing signals to her people. Those near the back turned and rode away, then the next row until only the woman a handful of others remained.

"You've won this round, but snows melt and spring comes, even to the mountains. We'll be back to finish this little discussion," she called before turning around and riding off.

Ariazate held her people in their line until the last of the Parthians disappeared the way they'd come. When she judged the way clear, she had a couple of horses brought forward for Lucius and Mylitos. The horses had packs behind their saddles filled with extra winter gear for them. Adding the extra cloak over his own, Lucius swapped his gloves for a thicker, nicer pair. After he removed his helmet, he wrapped his head in the thick cloth and pulled his hood over it.

Lucius joined Ariazate and Tigran in the middle of their column as they continued their northern progress. "Thank you, Zati. I's not sure I could have held them all off if they decided to cross the bridge."

Zati laughed, the sound freer than he'd heard it before. "I believe you would have, but I'm glad we showed up before you made the fool attempt."

"Where did you find all these people?" Lucius asked.

She looked about her, her back rigid and head held regally. "My brother and I still command some respect, at least in the mountain villages and communities."

"Apparently."

"There's a village a couple hours from here that'll put us up until morning. We'll continue on minus the warriors we picked up there," Zati said.

"And then?"

"That depends on you, Roman." They rode in silence for a while. "I'd suggest staying in the mountains until the spring thaw. You're alive now, but there's no guarantee two of you will make it out alive, not with Parthians crawling all over in the lowlands and your Romans pulling out."

"It's something to think about," Lucius replied.

She was probably right. The trek out would be arduous under the best of circumstance, and they couldn't just move through the mountains to avoid the Parthians, not in the winter. If they didn't want to freeze to death, they'd have to move down into the lowlands and try to navigate through the roads and towns there. Neither he nor Mylitos spoke the language well enough to pass. Someone would gladly turn them over to the Parthians to curry favor or earn some coin.

"You can stay with Tigran and me in the mountains until it's safe to travel. We still have friends in the highland villages," Zati said, breaking the silence.

"I'd be honored to accept your hospitality, Ariazate."

She nodded her head regally, though it was marred somewhat with the thick cloth wrapped around her head and body. Lucius struggled to stay in the saddle for the two-hour ride to the village. Without an enemy pursuing him and after the heart-pounding tension of the standoff, his body wanted to succumb to the exhaustion threating to topple him from his saddle. He kept himself upright and awake for long enough to get to the village.

An elderly man with a bushy beard and a merry twinkle in his eyes bowed deeply to Ariazate. "You honor our village with your presence, Princess. You and your brother may stay in our home while you remain here."

Lucius looked at Zati, an eyebrow raised. She rolled her eyes at Lucius and then nodded respectfully to the village's headman. "Thank you. You honor me with the offer of your home. My brother and I would be glad to accept it. Please show our guests to your home. I'll be along shortly."

"Of course, Princess." The man gestured for Lucius and Mylitos to follow him.

Lucius had understood the basic conversation, though he wasn't sure if he'd misheard the "princess" part or not. His Armenian was still quite rudimentary after all.

He nearly fell to his knees when he dismounted but caught himself on the saddle until he could get his feet under himself. They were escorted into a well-built home with a roaring fire. Stripping out of his armor, Lucius found a patch on the floor and fell into a deep, exhausted sleep.

NINETEEN

THE NEXT MORNING, warm porridge was brought into the house, along with steaming buckets of water so they could bathe. It wasn't the baths at Antiochia, but the hot water and soap felt divine. After he and Mylitos had cleaned themselves, Tigran and Ariazate joined them to break their fast.

"If we take off soon, we can make it to our next stop before sunset," Ariazate said, spooning some porridge into her mouth.

Lucius stood up and fetched a couple things from his bag. "I guess now is as good as any other time. Caesar's last command for you was to be free." Lucius handed the conical felt hats to Ariazate and Tigran. "The pileus represents your freedom. He also gave me money to pass on to you."

Ariazate looked at her brother, then down at the hats, then the fireplace. Tigran nodded at his sister. Standing up, she threw the hats into the fire, watching them smolder and catch. When they'd been rendered into ashes, she turned and stood in front of Lucius.

"His money, I will take."

Lucius handed her the pouch of coins. She stashed it inside her garments in some hidden pocket, then sat down and scooped more porridge into her bowl. They ate in silence until one of Ariazate's people stepped into the room announcing the horses were ready.

"I'm going to go thank our host for his hospitality. Tigran, with me." Ariazate turned and left the house.

"They didn't seem too appreciative of the imperator's gift of freedom." Mylitos spoke lowly so only Lucius could hear him.

"I don't think she thinks much of the institution of slavery. And the freedom she is granted is to be in a country that's become a proxy for Roma and Parthia to express their power. Now, because she came to our aid, the Parthians will be hunting her. Besides, these are her people. She's already free in her mountains. We are guests here, so mind your manners and guard your tongue." Lucius infused the last with the authority of his command.

"Yes, Centurio," Mylitos replied crisply.

They finished the bowls in silence and walked out to join Ariazate and Tigran so they could disappear into the mountains of Armenia to wait out the winter and the Parthians.

LUCIUS AND MYLITOS spent the winter in the highlands of Armenia with Ariazate and Tigran. Lucius used the time to improve his Armenian while helping Ariazate and Tigran get better with their sword skills.

One evening after Mylitos had disappeared to spend time with a woman he'd been chasing and Tigran had gone to bed, he sat by the fire drinking watered wine with Zati.

"Who are you, Zati? Through every village we went through, they've greeted you like a queen and Tigran like a king." Lucius had his suspicions, strongly had them, and wanted to confirm them.

"I am nobody. I am your friend, Lucius," she replied, staring into the dancing flames.

"Ariazate and Tigran are family names, aren't they?"

She didn't reply or give any acknowledgment for a while. Lucius thought she would just choose to ignore the question as he joined her in staring at the flames.

Finally, she nodded. "They are."

If they truly were the heirs of Tigran the Great, no wonder they commanded respect among the people, even if those who sought to gain power by paying homage to Roma or Parthia didn't pay them any honor. More than likely, their birth would make them a target for those seeking to curry favor with the powers who influenced Armenia. If the Parthian woman found out who'd thwarted her, Ariazate and Tigran would be hunted for the rest of their lives.

Lucius sighed. Armenia wasn't Roman anymore. The last of the legions and those local power brokers who'd bet on Roma were filtering out of the country. By now, the Parthians and their factions were in charge of the mountainous country. Lucius wouldn't be safe if he were pinned as a Roman loyal to Trajan.

Trajan—an emperor no more, dead and gone, though his works would remain. The news had even made its way deep into the mountains. It had shaken Lucius to core, another of the foundations of his life pulled out from under him. He had no idea if Hadrian would care about the mission his predecessor had sent Syphax and Lucius on, but he knew the new emperor would be dangerous to Ariazate and Tigran if he found out who they were.

He waited until he caught her gaze. "Zati, you can't stay here, not when the spring comes. The Parthians will be back, and they'll be looking for you."

"My people won't betray me."

"But are they all your people? Can you vouch for everyone? Are there some whose loyalty can be purchased with Parthian gold? I know Roman gold buys a lot of eyes and willing hands."

"What else can I do? Go begging to your imperator? I will be a slave to Roma no more. I'd rather die in my mountains than give up my freedom." She poured more wine in her cup.

"Can I present a third option that requires neither giving up your freedom or dying?" When he didn't hear an objection, he continued. "Come west with me to Belgica. My parents will adopt you and your brother. You would be my sister and Tigran my brother. Someone will need to take over the business my father has built."

"Isn't that your duty when you muster out of the legions?"

Lucius shook his head. "No. Not anymore. I have new duties now that supersede those."

He'd thought about it long and hard over the winter. If the extent of the danger was so great that gods had reached out for aid, then the task that'd been laid upon him would likely subsume the rest of his life.

"I know this is your homeland, but you will never be safe here. As long as Roma lies to the west and Parthia to the east, Armenia will be the game board for their power struggles. My mother and father are good, kind people. They'll make sure you have a safe haven. It won't be a throne in Armenia, but, and I don't mean to be cruel, you and your brother would never sit safely on one, not against the might of Roma or Parthia."

Ariazate nodded. That was the only acknowledgment of what he'd said. Together they sat in silence, drinking wine and letting the dancing flames stave off the last vestiges of the bitter mountain winter.

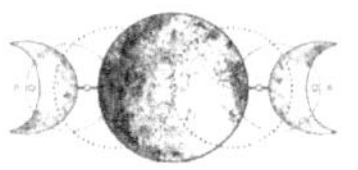

ARIAZATE HADN'T ANSWERED Lucius's invitation. He'd guessed she'd chosen to ignore it and planned to stay in the mountains and risk it, but a couple weeks later, she asked to him to take a ride with her. Riding in silence, Lucius admired the austere beauty of the mighty Caucasus Mountains.

When they found a half-frozen waterfall, Ariazate stopped and turned her horse so she faced Lucius. "Lucius Silvanius Ferrata. My brother Tigran, direct heir to Tigran the Great, and I wish to request sanctuary with your family."

Lucius nodded, a soft smile on his face. "I offer you the sanctuary of my family. You shall be as my sister and brother. All that is mine is yours."

Ariazate, who'd seemed rigid all day, relaxed. "I guess I'm going to have to learn more of your tongue."

"My father speaks Latin as well, though Gaulish will certainly serve you best. We have a long trip and plenty of time on our hands. I'm glad you and your brother chose a new path, Zati." Lucius moved his horse closer so their legs touched. Leaning over, he kissed her forehead.

"Lucius, I'm tired of being a beggar princess. I want a life where I don't have to run for my life and live on the kindness of others." She seemed too weary for one her age.

When Lucius had been her age, he'd had few real worries save for his desire to join the legions. He'd had a home and parents. He'd never been a slave to anyone or chased because of an accident of birth. With all she'd been through in her short life, she'd earned her weariness. He hoped a new home would bring her hope and happiness. Some part of her would probably always be wary of her enemies hunting her down, but this gave her and her brother the best shot of a real life.

After Lucius accepted Ariazate's request, they returned to the village. Along the way, he told her about his parents and his home. His mind drifted to the forest by their house and the bluebells he'd spent so much time lying in as a boy. By the time they made it back to his home, the season would likely be well past for the bluebells. It would be good to see his parents again before he returned to the legions to forge his future as a servant of Mithras.

After Lucius and Ariazate returned to the village, the decided that it would be best to keep the secret of their heritage hidden from his parents to protect all involved. They could disappear into the west and truly seek a new destiny.

When they judged the passes safe enough to travel, Lucius, Ariazate, and Tigran packed up and headed north, leaving Mylitos who'd decided he'd rather stay with the village woman he'd fallen in love with. Though the man was breaking his oath to Roma and the legions, Lucius didn't have the heart to make him go. Mylitos could simply be one more casualty of their expedition. There had been so many of them already. Lucius took his signaculum so that he could be recorded as dead, the last man besides Lucius from their mission.

A few of those most loyal to the heirs of Tigran the Great traveled with them to act as guides and to trade in Colchis. From there, Lucius and his new siblings would book passage on a ship heading west and make their way to Gaul and Belgica.

Still using Syphax's orders and the aegis of Trajan, Lucius was able to move swiftly, using the resources of the legions to procure horses and lodging. As they approached the village of Lucius's birth, his young friends grew increasingly nervous, as did Lucius. It had been nine years since he'd last seen his parents. That morning, the last of the journey, he'd made sure his equipment gleamed. He'd returned to wearing his Roman gear as soon as they'd reached the coast of Colchis where his rank could get them passage on a ship heading west.

Today, he wanted to show up with his centurion's crest and all the phalera. When they crested the hill that led down to his parents' property, he straightened in his saddle.

"That's it," he said.

The gardens had matured in the near decade since he'd last been there. They'd added a few more buildings during that time as well. The Roman-style manor house was far bigger than the little hut he'd grown up in with his mother, before his father returned from Britannia.

When they made it up to the house, servants took their horses without asking questions. As the preferred vendor to the local legionary forts, legionnaires seeking his father were no doubt a common site on the estate. So far, he didn't recognize the faces of any of the servants. They'd added a few more since he'd departed.

A woman, maybe in her mid-twenties, stepped out and greeted him. "Centurio, how can I help you? Are you looking for Gaius?"

"Yes, but also for Verlia, if she's home," Lucius replied.

The woman nodded. "Please, step into the house. I'll fetch Gaius for you, Centurio."

Lucius stepped into the house and took off his caligae, pulling on a pair of house slippers that were left by the door for guests. Ariazate and Tigran followed suit.

Lucius hadn't taken his helmet off yet when an older woman nearing her fifties stepped into the room.

"Welcome to our home, Centurio. Are you here for my husband?" Verlia said.

Lucius reached up, his hand trembling, and untied his helmet, pulling it off. He opened his mouth to speak but couldn't get the words to come out.

"Lucius? Is that you?" Verlia's eyes sparkled, unshed tears glistening in them.

Lucius handed his helmet behind him but wasn't sure who took it. Moving toward his mother her pulled her into a tight hug, tears of joy falling on his cheeks.

"Mother, I'm so glad to see you." Lucius kissed her forehead.

Verlia reached up and ran her hand down his cheek and jaw. "They said you'd disappeared in the mountains of Armenia. That…that…"

She stopped speaking, the tears getting the better of her.

"I did, but my friends," Lucius gestured toward the young woman and adolescent boy behind him, "saved me. We got snowed in and had to stay in the mountains until the roads were safe to pass."

Lucius helped his mother to a chair. Ariazate and Tigran stood nervously out of the way of the door. A giant of a man with wild silver hair still sprinkled with swaths of the red strode into the house. The limp he'd had the last time Lucius had been home was more pronounced, requiring a walking stick.

"Son?"

Lucius nodded and stood. His father stepped forward and pulled Lucius into a bone crushing hug, then held him back at arm's length.

"Look at you. Are those all your phalera?"

"These are most of them," Lucius replied.

"Look at your armor… It's magnificent. I've never seen the like." Ambeltrix said. "Where did you get it?"

"It's the same armor I left with. I'll explain later." Lucius gestured toward Ariazate and Tigran.

Dabbing at her tears, Verlia stood up and joined her husband and son in the middle of the floor. With a wide smile on her face, she reached out and grabbed Lucius's hand. When Tigran shuffled nervously, he drew Verlia's attention.

"Lucius, who are your friends?" Verlia smiled kindly at them.

Lucius had been too wrapped up in the joy of seeing his parents to properly introduce them. "Mother, Father, I'd like you to meet Ariazate and her brother Tigran. This is my mother Verlia and my father Ambeltrix Gaius Silvanius. Do we have guest rooms for them?"

"Of course." She walked over to Ariazate, taking her hands, and kissed her cheeks then kissed Tigran on the forehead. "Welcome to our home. I'll have rooms prepared for you."

"Thank you, ma'am," Ariazate said quietly. She was still nervous about her command of Lucius's Gaulish.

Tigran mumbled, "Thanks."

Lucius smiled reassuringly toward the young Armenians. "Zati, would you give me a little time with my parents, please? If you'd like to look around the estate, the weather is lovely."

Ariazate nodded and gave Lucius a small smile. "I could use a walk to stretch my legs after that ride. Let's go, Tigran."

"If anyone stops to ask who you are, let them know you are our guests," Verlia instructed before the two stepped outside.

Tigran walked over and handed Lucius his helmet before joining his sister outside.

"Centurio?" Ambeltrix asked, grinning broadly. "I see you have done well for yourself, son."

"Are you hungry?" Verlia asked.

"No, we stopped a while ago and ate at a tavern. I can hold out until dinner."

"Would you like a beer? Or perhaps wine?" Ambeltrix ushered him toward the dining room.

"Beer would be fine."

Ambeltrix patted him on the shoulder then disappeared into the kitchen.

Verlia found a servant to ready rooms for their guests, then sat down, taking a small cup of the beer from the jug Ambeltrix brought in.

"Tell me about your pretty friend and her brother. Is she your woman?" Verlia asked, her hand resting on her son's forearm.

"No. She's a friend." He waited until his father got situated before continuing. "I brought them out of Armenia because they ran afoul of the Parthians as they took over after Hadrianus pulled out our troops. They'd have been hunted down and killed."

"Oh, dear," Verlia said, holding her hand over her mouth in shock.

"Mother, Father. I'd like you to treat them as my sister and brother. They've become dear to me, and they need a safe place to live where they can have a chance at a life. Ariazate is very sharp, and Tigran shows promise. You could do far worse than bringing them into the business and training them to take it over."

"But, son, I'd thought you'd take over after your time in the legions," Ambeltrix said, brows furrowing.

"So had I, but I think my time in the legions might last a while longer than I thought."

"Something happened to you in Armenia, didn't it?" his father asked. "There's something different about you…"

Lucius nodded, then told them everything, save for Tigran and Ariazate's true identities. When he finished his tale, the blood had drained from their faces.

"And these…creatures are real?" Verlia asked.

Lucius nodded. "I don't know if they've made it this far west, but I fought them and barely survived."

"Are you sure they're just not wild mountain men?" Ambeltrix asked.

"No. They were once men but turned into monsters. When you kill a man, he leaves a body. When you kill one of these demons, give them a true death, they turn into dust or nasty sludge. They're stronger and faster than men and survive by drinking the blood of humans. They are very real, and I've sworn an oath to multiple gods to fight them and protect humanity. I've been marked." Lucius caressed the crescent moon over his heart. He reached down and pulled his gladius from its sheath and handed it to his father. "That's the sword you had made for me."

"It's beautiful, son."

"I still serve Roma, but I now have another purpose, one that goes beyond borders."

Ambeltrix nodded, looking stoic. His mother just looked worried. He'd never be free of danger. He'd served fifteen years in the legions and only had ten more years on his contract, but with his new mission, enlisting again would mean his mother would never know a time where her son wasn't far away, fighting the enemies of the empire, be they mortal or supernatural. He'd had a lot of time over the winter and on the long trip across the entire empire to realize what he was sacrificing for this mission—to mourn the life he thought he'd have. Someday, if he survived, his mission would end, and he could return to his life. He just hoped it would be before his parents passed into Albios.

"I'm sorry, mother. I know you never wanted this kind of life for me, and certainly not this new danger, but if I don't answer the call to protect those who need it, then many will suffer. And it's a kind of suffering you wouldn't wish on anyone." The image of his friend Cassius lying in the dirt of the cave, the creature sucking the blood from his neck, flashed through his mind.

He couldn't bring his friend back, but he could protect others from the same fate. He could train more hunters to join him. As he'd spent the winter mourning the life he'd no longer have, he planned for the mission he'd accepted. Syphax's cohort had been created for a reason, and that reason was even more important now than ever. If he could talk Hadrian into it, he'd need to raise a force capable of standing against the coming darkness, against the enemies of the gods and of humanity. Only a fool denied the gods when they made their will so plainly known. He might not have been the wisest man, but a fool he wasn't.

"No matter what you do in life, son, I'm proud of you. I knew you'd do well in life, but I had no idea you'd stand before the gods and be found worthy of their notice." Ambeltrix reached out and took his wife's hand in his.

"Gods are all well and good, but I do hope they keep you safe." She stood up and kissed his forehead and disappeared into the kitchen.

"Give her time, son. She'll come around." Ambeltrix patted Lucius's hand.

"I never wanted to cause her more worry." Lucius shook his head, then sighed.

"You have to make decisions for your own life, Lucius. Your mother knows that, even if she worries about your health and safety. But she'd worry about it no matter what."

"I know, but I still wish…"

Ambeltrix chuckled. "I know, son. I do."

"Well, I've ordered extra dinner for this evening and then a feast for tomorrow evening to welcome you home and to welcome Ariazate and Tigran to the family," Verlia said, sweeping in from the kitchen to take her place by her son, her presence pushing away the dark thoughts about his future. "Now why don't you go take your armor off and go to the baths. You smell like iron and horses."

"Yes, mother."

EPILOGUE

125 CE

PRINCEPS PRIMUS CENTURIO Lucius Silvanius Ferrata waved off the small squad of men he'd brought with him to stalk Roma's streets that night. He'd brought the I Cohort with him to Roma, leaving the other cohorts near Ravenna to await his orders while he followed a nest of the blood drinking di inferi toward Roma.

When he'd turned up in Roma eight years ago after being charged by Mithras, Sol Invictus, and Luna, though he always preferred to think of her as Selene, Hadrian and the pater patrum who served him raised Lucius up to lead his own legion of men charged with protecting the empire from the dark creatures who preyed on humans. To separate him from the power structure of the legions, they declared him the first and best of centurions — Princeps Primus Centurio. He reported only to the emperor but was allowed near complete autonomy. To maintain that autonomy so he could carry out his mission, he swore an oath by the gods to never participate in a civil war or a rebellion. And because of the oaths he'd sworn, he was the only legionary commander allowed to bring armed men into the city, though he was only allowed to bring a single cohort.

"Hold up, Centurio," Tullius whispered. "I hear troops coming."

They ducked into the shadows, pulling their black cloaks around them as the sound of hobnailed caligae and jingling gear announced the approach of soldiers. When Lucius saw the black transverse crest of one of his centurions, he exhaled in relief, his men relaxing around him.

"Report, Tasciovanus," Lucius ordered.

"Centurio." Tasciovanus gave a quick salute. "Praesutagus is giving the Praetorians a merry chase."

Lucius chuckled. "Excellent."

The Praetorians, the emperor's guards and the only legionnaires previously allowed to carry weapons in Roma, took offense to the same honor being extended to Lucius's legion. So on the few occasions Lucius brought his men near the imperial city, the Praetorians took it upon themselves to follow the Princeps Primus Centurio around as if he were going to get up to mischief.

Since Lucius didn't want to be trailed, he'd assign men to distract the Praetorians and lead them around. It had become a competition among the men to see who could lead them the farthest astray.

"Do you sense anything, Centurio?" Tasciovanus asked.

"I think so, my friend." He tried to extend out his sense of the de inferi, the drinkers of blood, as some of his men had taken to calling them. He wasn't quite used to being able to feel his enemy and hadn't encountered many since gaining the ability from Mithras. He'd spent the first few years after being promoted by Hadrian recruiting and building his legion of elite hunters. During that time, he'd seen very few of the creatures in the western reaches of the empire. It had only been the last few months that the di inferi had appeared within the empire in greater numbers.

Once he thought he had the bearing down, he picked up his black scutum with the four narrow triangular spikes pointing from each corner toward the central boss. "Form up. Let's look professional."

The sixteen men he'd brought with him for tonight's expedition stepped out of the shadows and formed ranks five deep with Lucius taking the lead and Centurio Tasciovanus bringing up the rear. A few of the men had the same spikes on their black shield like their leader, but most sported the plain black field that all new recruits to the legion received on being judged worthy of the elite unit.

As they marched through Roma's streets like soldiers on patrol, Lucius absentmindedly swished the vinerod that was the symbol of his rank as a centurion. Though he could have abandoned it upon his elevation by Hadrian to the empire's lead centurion and the commander of his own elite legion, he kept it to remember his place in the world. Often a centurion was the highest rank a common legionnaire could achieve without noble blood or high connections, and Lucius was a common barbarian from the far north.

His senses drew him deeper into the poor part of Roma, becoming stronger and more intense. Creatures dashed around the corner and burst from the apartment buildings in front of them. Lucius caught the first one in the face with the vinerod, snapping it off as it ripped away a part of the di inferi's cheek with it.

"Four wide!" he called, yanking his gladius from its scabbard.

He let the next one crash up against his men's raised shields and took the one behind it, quickly lopping off an arm while knocking a third down with his scutum. As he stepped closer to the downed creature, he brought the scutum's edge down hard on its face, crushing it.

The creatures swarmed around Lucius, trying to avoid the fury of the Princeps Primus Centurio of the Black Legion, as they were called, even though they had an official designation from Hadrian of I Aelia, named after Hadrian's family. When Lucius placed a thrust perfectly into the heart of a charging monster, it exploded into a powdery dust. The second one he permanently ended by catching in the back as it dodged past him to take a try at his men. It burst into a splat of reddish-black goo, showering the shields and the men behind them.

"Sorry about that," he called, bringing his gladius around to take a head.

When they got to the intersection, four of his men swung out wide to block off the escape path to the north. As they herded the remaining blood drinkers toward a dead end, a few tried running or breaking into one of the buildings along the ground floor, but the windows and doors had all been shut tight against the obvious sounds of violence on the streets.

After Lucius's other centurion called for a line switch to get the last group of men to the front, they hacked down the final di inferi. Lucius stood, breathing heavily and looking around to make sure they hadn't missed any and that none of the wounded were recovering fast enough to cause more mayhem.

"Well done." Lucius nodded to his men.

All sixteen stood. They'd assess injuries later, but everyone looked ambulatory and fine.

"You give the order, sir," Tasciovanus said.

"Black shields, find a body and stake it through the heart. If you can, find the one you put down. Fang shields, make sure they don't botch it." Lucius grabbed a ragged cloak from the ground, wiped his gladius on it, then sheathed it.

He knelt on the ground next to a body he'd decapitated and pulled the wooden rudis from his other scabbard. Having never had a chance to use its full abilities, now would be the time. The few di inferi they'd encountered had been dispatched quickly and efficiently in the name of training by overly enthusiastic soldiers eager to earn their spikes. But now there were plenty of bodies, and the urge to use the rudis had been steadily growing, becoming a constant nagging refrain in his mind, where before it hadn't seemed the most urgent priority.

With a two-handed reverse grip, he plunged it into the heart of the creature. Unlike a simple wooden stake, the creature didn't start its final decay into either powder or sludge. Lucius inhaled and exhaled, closing his eyes. He lowered his head, placing his forehead on the silver button at the end of the wooden ball pommel. The words Mithras imprinted on his heart in the temple in the mountains of Armenia flashed through his mind. Haltingly, he recited the incantation, not knowing what would happen when he finished.

A silvery-white light slithered down the handle and over the wood of the blade, sliding around the silver cutting edge as well as the beautiful silver filigree until it disappeared into the chest of the creature and reemerged a moment later, retracing its course.

When the light disappeared into Lucius's forehead, a surge went through his body. His heart rate picked up, and energy tore through him. Standing, he felt ready to take on an entire legion of the di inferi single handedly. Everything in the dark deadend looked brighter and crisper, as if all the details were just now made available to his eyes. Even the sounds around him seemed clearer than they had before. He repeated the process on another nearby body.

After draining the second di inferi, he vibrated.

He jolted to attention at the slightest scrape against the stone street. Hands and feet scrabbled to get its severely damaged body upright. Lucius whipped around in time to see one of the creatures use its brutal claws to swipe the leg of one of his men in its mad dash to get away. The creature moved faster than any human had a right to, far beyond anything the finest athletes could achieve. Soon, it had opened some distance between itself and the legionnaires it had caught flat-footed.

Lucius, not even thinking about what he was doing, tore after it. As quick as an antelope, he burst out of the alley and after the creature. It must have thought it had gotten away from the sluggish humans and slowed down, but when it heard the slap of leather and click of iron hobnails on stone right behind it, it gave every bit of supernatural speed it had to the chase. Lucius gained on it.

When it flashed its head around to see how close Lucius was, Lucius saw a look of pure terror, the first such glimpse of fear he'd seen from the creatures who looked with disdain at any who weren't among their number. The whimpering sounds of its fear brought a smile to Lucius's face. He remembered the bitter taste of the terror they'd inflicted on him and his men in the mountains of Armenia. Now it was time for them to be the ones afraid to go into the night.

As he brought his rudis down low to swipe at its hamstring, the di inferi went down hard, landing on its face with a groan. Skidding to a halt, Lucius plunged the rudis into its heart, repeated the incantation, and drained his third creature in as many minutes.

"Gods above and below!"

It felt like the thunderer's lightning bathed him inside and out, lifting him to the bright place, to Albios. He wasn't sure if he'd ever felt this way in his life. After a few deep breaths to calm himself before rejoining his men, he felt a slight discordant note of satisfaction that seemed to come from some place beyond, someone powerful, a hard presence he'd only felt in Mithras's temple. It was done. The covenant between Lucius and Mithras was sealed. When he'd used the full power of the rudis Mithras had given him, he'd bound his life in its entirety to the god's mission.

He couldn't say why the smug satisfaction of the god felt ominous, but it sobered the earlier jubilation. His father had said it was dangerous mixing up in the games of the powerful, and now he was bound to gods. A flash of silver settled gently on the ground in front of him, resolving into the goddess Selene.

Lucius dropped to one knee immediately and bowed his head. "My Mistress."

"Remove your helmet and rise, my brave soldier." Her words were a soft caress.

He wiped the rudis on the hem of his tunic and stowed it before rising and removing his helmet. When Selene reached out to caress his cheek, compassion and sorrow filled her eyes. Leaning forward, she kissed his forehead.

"Know that I'm proud of you, Lucius Silvanius Ferrata. You are now fully bound to Mithras's purpose and mine. I shall watch over you, my brave soldier. Keep me in your heart and I shall always hear you. In you goes my hope for humanity and those who can't fight against the dark creatures unleashed upon the world. Go with my love." She ran her fingers over his jaw and off his chin, then faded away.

The goddess's words and touch recentered him, easing the overabundance of energy that threatened to pull him apart. It also softened the edge of the vague unease Mithras's intrusion into his mind had caused. Back in control of himself, he returned to his men.

His centurion greeted him, admiration in his eyes. "I've never seen anyone move like that before, Princeps Primus Centurio." He banged his fist over his heart and dropped to his knee. The rest of Lucius's men followed suit, saluting and dropping to their knees.

"Princeps Primus Centurio!" they called, eyes trained on their leader.

The die was cast. He was a servant of Roma, but also a soldier in the gods' war against the infernal forces of the di inferi. He'd serve those gods and stand in the darkness to protect the light of humanity until he completed his mission. He was ready. Suffused with the power of the gods and the di inferi and surrounded by men he'd trained to hunt the monsters, the time to break the invasion of the blood drinkers had come.

Although time and weariness might lay him low, he'd be a centurion for all his mortal life.

LEAVE A REVIEW

Reviews are the lifeblood of every indie author. Even a simple star rating means the world to us. If you enjoyed this book, please leave an honest review at Goodreads, BookBub, or your preferred online book retailer.

Would you like to join other readers who enjoyed this book? Join my Facebook Reader Group!

facebook.com/groups/CThomasLafolletteReaderGroup

Thank you!

C. Thomas Lafollette

NEWSLETTER

The Centurion Immortal is a Luke Irontree prequel novella and is exclusive to the Dispatches from C. Thomas Lafollette newsletter. Please sign up for your free copy and you'll also receive a twice-monthly newsletter with news, book updates, recipes, drinks tips, and other fun stuff. Your email will never be given out, rented, or sold.

CThomasLafollette.com/newsletter/

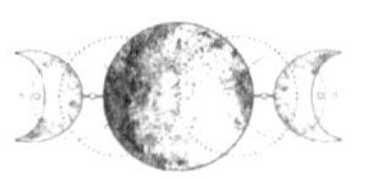

TSIRANAPOGH

The tsiranapogh (tsih-Ran-nuh-Pahgk) is a musical instrument uniquely tied to the culture of Amernia and is featured throughout **Rise of the Centurio Immortalis**. It's more commonly known by the slavic name "Duduk."

The instrument has been around for at least one-thousand-years, though it's suspected that it's far older than that, harkening back to antiquity. For the purposes of this story, it existed two-thousand-years-ago.

Made from Apricot wood, tsiranapogh translates in Armenian as "apricot horn." It's a double-reeded wood instrument that produces a hauntingly beautiful tone and has become popular in many Hollywood soundtracks such as the film Gladiator.

I have prepared a short, curated playlist of tsiranapogh pieces on Spotify that feature two players. One will play the melody while the other plays accompanying drone tones. If you enjoy the playlist, I have a much longer one available in my Spotify profile for your listening pleasure.

Rise of the Centurio Immortalis Soundtrack

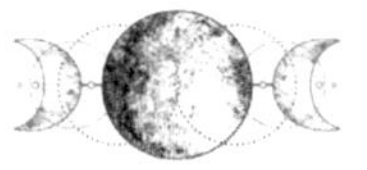

THE CULT OF MITHRAS

Mithras was a god with origins in Zoroastrianism but was known throughout Asia across many religions and traditions. Mithras had many names, depending on the culture—Mithra, Mitra, Mehr, and Mihr are some of the more common. Although the origins of how and why are obscured by time, a version of Mithraism become popular with the Roman elite, particularly throughout the legions.

There isn't a lot known about how the Roman Cult of Mithras operated, but I've tried to piece together the various known elements. Though some of the things on page are my educated creations to fill in gaps and to serve the purpose of my story.

- **The Ranks - Symbols & Imagery** (from lowest to highest)
- Corax - raven, crow, beaker, caduceus
- Nymphus - bridegroom, lamp, hand bell, veil, circlet
- Miles - soldier, helmet, lance, drum, belt breastplate
- Leo - lion, laurel wreath, thunderbolts
- Perses - Persian, hooked sword, Phrygian cap, crescent moon, stars

- Heliodromus - sun-runner, torch, Helios, whip
- Pater - father, mitre, shepherd's staff, garnet/ruby ring.
- Pater Patrum - "Father of Fathers," a title applied to particularly eminent or respected Paters.

Mithraism on Wikipedia

GLOSSARY

Auxilia - Units of cavalry, ranged, and infantry fighters who assisted legions and filled specialized roles. Roman citizenship was not required. Citizenship could be earned by completing a 25-year term of service in the auxilia.

Centuria - A unit of 80 legionnaires plus servants led by a centurio

Centurio - The basic equivalent of a modern captain. He commanded his 80 men in combat and coordinated with the other centurio and higher officers.

Cohort - A unit of six centuria, 480 men at full strength

Contubernium - A tent unit of eight men who slept in the same small tent. The basic platoon unit that fought and worked together.

Decanus - The leader of a contubernium. A corporal.

Gladius - The short sword used by the legions. It had a sharp, stabbing point that formed the main attack but was balanced and could slash just as well. Romans were trained to stab vital areas or slash at exposed flesh.

Kataphraktoi - A heavily armored cavalry unit used by the horse cultures of the Middle East and the steppes regions. Usually horse and rider both wore armor. The rider used a large two-handed lance as their primary weapon.

Legio - A legion, composed of ten cohorts. A legion usually had several auxilia units assigned to them.

Miles - The term for a Legionnaire

Optio - Chosen by the centurio to assist his leadership and to take over if the centurio wasn't available to lead the unit for whatever reason. The modern equivalent of a lieutenant.

Pilum - The specialized throwing javelin of the Roman legions. The shanks, made of softer iron than the tip, were joined to the shaft with a wooden pin. After the battle, pila (plural of pilum) would be collected, their shanks straightened and pins replaced. Each legionnaire carried two into battle—a light one that flew longer for the first throw and a heavier one for the shorter, second throw.

Scutum - The classic Roman shield. It was held by a bar in the center that ran parallel to the top and bottom. It could be used defensively and offensively.

Tesserarius - The legionnaire in charge of assigning guard duty for his centuria. The equivalent of a sergeant.

Vexillation - A vexillation was a group split off from its legion and given a special task or mission. Vexillatio in Latin.

LUCIUS SILVANIUS FERRATA RETURNS IN

FALL OF THE CENTURIO IMMORTALIS

Fall of the Centurio Immortalis

NOTE: This is an unproofed sample.

Chapter One

Lucius half dozed in his saddle as they approached the bridge over the Danuvius River, deciding to push on and hit their fort instead of camping outside the empire's borders. Although the day's march had been stiff, his men were in fine spirits as they approached the river that meant they were only a few more miles from their beds.

"Princeps Primus Centurio?" a young soldier asked.

"Boy, you don't need to use the full title," barked the grizzled officer riding next to Lucius.

"Sorry, sir. Centurio Ferrata. Legatus Pisakar is waiting for us just past the bridge."

"Hmm? What?" Lucius shook his head to clear the haze of his nap. "Pisakar? What's he doing here?"

"I don't know, Centurio. They just sent me back to inform you," the young man said.

"Just thinking out loud, Decanus…" Lucius searched for the name of the young man he'd recently approved for promotion to leader of his tent group.

"Martininius, Sir," Martininius said, aiding his Centurio.

"Decanus Martininius, thanks. Return to your station. Actually, hold. I'll join you and find out what Pisakar is up to myself." Turning to the Primus Pilus riding next to him, he said, "Tinkomaros, keep the men marching. You're in charge."

"Aye, Centurio," the gruff Gaul replied.

Between his nod of assent and the breeze, his long mustache tails fluttered in the wind. Although Lucius typically stuck to the shaved face and short hair look that was in fashion when he joined the legions under the reign of imperator Traianus, he'd let his hair and beard grow out quite a bit longer than he had in ages, bordering on unkempt. He allowed his men a certain sense of freedom when it came to their grooming—as long as they were clean, they could wear their hair and facial hair anyway they liked as befit the Empire's elite legion. His men were allowed to have their quirks and eccentricities, they'd earned them.

Lucius rubbed his hand through his shaggy, dark brown hair and pulled his horse out of line and behind the decanus, the placid gelding replying to his commands smoothly. They rode at a sedate pace along the line of Lucius's marching men, each nodding to their respected leader as he rode past.

"Remind me, son, where are you from?" Lucius asked, making small talk with his newly minted platoon leader.

"Massilia, sir," replied the handsome young soldier, his face still containing the softness of youth despite the intense training of the legions.

"What did your father do in Massilia?

"He was a clerk, sir."

"Not a legionnaire?"

"No, sir," Martininius replied.

"How'd you end up in the legions?"

"I didn't fancy quills and parchment for a lifetime."

Lucius let out a bark of laughter. "Fair enough. My father joined so he wouldn't be forced to toil in the soil outside his village in Belgica." Lucius smiled fondly, remember his father and his stories. "He said he moved more dirt in the legions than he ever would have as a farmer… Anyway, what do you think of the Lugii?"

"They seem a fine people, sir."

"Ah, politic answer. Certainly a safe option. Cautiously polite but interpretable as a small slight. Certainly a far cry from Massilia."

The city on the Gallicum Sea had been a colony of the Hellenes before linking its star to the Roman Republic five hundred years ago when they aided the republic against Hannibal Barca.

"Yes, sir. Have you been to Massilia?"

"I've passed through a few times over the years. It's a far cry from the forests of Germania."

"Yes, sir. The forests…" He seemed to be formulating a thought. "They're dark. Even in the full light of Sol. They're almost sorrowful."

The thoughtful and slightly poetic statement from the young

soldier intrigued Lucius. Most of his men were there because they were the elite legionnaires of the empire, the best fighting men in the world. Lucius could understand why the young man's centurion had singled him out for his first promotion.

"Sorry, sir, if I spoke out of turn."

Lucius waved Martininius's concern aside. "Don't worry about it. Continue. Please."

"It was just…when I could tune out the sound of the march, the wind sighed through the branches. They almost seemed weary at our passing."

"How much do you know about the history of this area?"

"Not much, sir."

"We're at a cross roads. These woods have known blood. The Getae, Dacians, Sarmatians, Macromannians, Vandals, Goths, Romans, Gauls, and probably hundreds of peoples I've never even heard of, we've all bled in these wood. All left the bones of our fallen in these woods. For centuries upon centuries. I've spilled my share of it over the years too, more than my share if truth be told.

"Those woods know me. They've long stopped fearing my arrival, instead only greeting it with weariness for what I might do. They do feel sorrow. They'd prefer to drink of the spring rains. Instead, I feed them blood."

They rode in silence for a while. The dark German woods always made Lucius feel maudlin. The tall pines were nothing like the trees of his youth in far away Belgica where the leaves rustled with laughter, forgetting the far gone wars of Caesar's conquests of Gaul.

"Sir, why didn't the Lugii accept protection in the empire like the rest of the Vandals?"

"Some men don't want to bow to the Imperator. They'd rather take their chances and be free," Lucius replied.

The hooves of their horses clattered over the stone bridge as they pulled in front of the column. At the far end of a bridge, a giant of man waited, standing and holding the reigns of his horse. He removed his helmet shaped like a roaring lion's head, revealing dark black skin, and a shaved head. He raised a hand in greeting.

"Well, Decanus Martininius, thank you for the conversation. You may return to your unit."

The decanus banged his fist into his chest plate and extended a crisp salute to Lucius. "Yes, Centurio Ferrata." He wheeled his horse around and returned to his commander to report in. Lucius nudged his gelding into a trot. The horse snorted and shook its head.

"Quit your complaining, Cicero. It's been easy duty this time around," Lucius said to his pony.

Pisakar, seeing Lucius trotting towards him, mounted up and waved his detachment to fall in behind them as they passed.

"Hamilcar, bring the rest of the men home. You're in charge," Pisakar yelled over his shoulder as he brought his stout pony up next to Lucius's mount.

"So what'd the free Vandals have to say?" Pisakar asked.

Lucius was quiet for a bit. "Ariaric and his Tervingi are moving south…in numbers."

"What does 'in numbers' mean?"

"Judging by the poorly contained panic of the Lugii? The whole damned tribe. Thousands upon thousands, Pisakar."

Pisakar whistled his dismay. "What drives them? It'll be winter in the mountains and steppes."

"Benetrax wouldn't say, specifically, but that scared him most of the all. Best I could surmise is 'demons in the night.'"

Shaking his head, Pisakar let rip a steady stream of curses.

"That's the job we accepted when we took our oath to the Black Legion."

"No, it's not that, Lucius. It's just a poor time for the Imperator to be calling you off the border."

Lucius perked up and turned his head to his friend and second in command. "What?"

"You didn't think I came all the way up here just to welcome you across the bridge? Constantius has deigned to acknowledge your existence after nearly thirty years. There's a messenger waiting for you at the castrum."

"When?"

"He and his entourage arrived four days ago."

"Well, I guess we should go see what our Imperator wants."

"You mean 'Dominus Noster'?" Pisakar said, loading the title with sarcasm.

Lucius could hear the eyeroll of his friend. Like Lucius, Pisakar didn't care for the new stylings of the new breed of imperators. They'd shed the title of "Princeps," first among Romans, and sought to elevate themselves to nearly divine status while living.

"Yes. Let's go see what the servant of 'Our Lord' wants with the Black Legion."

Lucius kicked Cicero into a canter. The horse grunted and kicked out behind him before responding to his rider's commands.

"Lucius, it's time to put that old bastard out to pasture."

"I'd watch out if I were you when we get back to the fort. He'll be aiming to bite you after that comment. He still does what's asked of him." Luke patted Cicero's neck fondly.

"Aye, he's a smart beast, no doubt, but it's getting harder for him. He's not immortal."

Lucius caught the pointed look his friend directed at him out of the corner of his eye. He sighed and patted the horse's neck. "You're probably right, Pisakar. He's probably as stubborn as I am."

"That he is, my friend, but it's time for him to rest and enjoy his days. I have a feeling we've some tough campaigning in our future, and I'm not sure the old bastard has another one in him. He'll soldier on until he drops, but why not let him enjoy some time getting fat on easy grass? He's done his duty, let him muster out."

The two men road in silence, the only sound the beating hooves of their horses and the detachment of guards riding behind them at a discreet distance. Pisakar was right. Lucius had kept Cicero around longer than was standard for the war ponies his legion and its cavalry units maintained. Cicero was one of the smartest and most cantankerous horses he'd ever ridden in the two centuries he'd commanded his legion. The old bastard had been his friend and steadfast companion since the herd master selected him to be Lucius's prime mount nearly a decade earlier.

"He should have been retired years ago," Pisakar added.

"You could say the same of me."

Pisakar laughed; the deep rumbling sound of his friend's laugh always brought a smile to Lucius's face. "You should have been dead almost two hundred years ago, my friend. But that's what happens when you put yourself in the way of the gods; they find a way to use you beyond your time."

Again, Pisakar was right. At nearly 245-years-old, Lucius had outlived everyone he knew and would probably bury all his current friends. Talk of his age did nothing to better his mood after leaving the tall, dark forests on the other side of the Danuvius.

In contrast, the village of camp followers and the families of the legionnaires he commanded bustled with activity, laughter and yells filling the air as they rode through. While the men of the Roman legions could not marry during their time under the eagle, nothing prevented them from having a companion outside the legion. Some men even started families that followed them from post to post until they mustered out and could sign the marriage contract.

The glint of sun off steel caught his eye as a young man in armor wearing the black of Lucius's legion stepped out of a small hut, a woman following him. She pulled him back into her arms, laughing when he bumped into her, nearly knocking her down before wrapping his arms around her for a passionate kiss. Lucius sighed, letting his eyes linger on the young couple.

Over the two plus centuries he'd served under the eagle, Lucius had his share of dalliances, but had never committed to anyone knowing his contract with the empire would probably never end. As his legion moved around the empire, if he met someone, he'd eventually have to move on when the call to respond to the empire's needs to fight foreign enemies, living or undead came in. His men joked he was married to his legion.

Once they crested the last hill before their fort, Pisakar raised his arm and signaled to the guards behind them. Spurring their horses forward, they closed ranks around the leader of their legion and his second in command, one of them racing forward to alert the fort to their general's return.

"Legatus Pisakar, inform our guest I'll meet with him first thing in the morning after I've broken my fast. I think I'll spend some time in the baths tonight. Have food and wine prepared for after, you can join me and update me on what's been going on while I was gone."

"Aye, Centurio Ferrata." Pisakar saluted and split off from their detachment to carry out his orders when they passed through the gates of their fortress.

Dismounting, Lucius handed Cicero's reigns to his groom. The Sarmatian was one of the few people Lucius's gelding didn't try to regularly bite or kick, probably because he was always slipping the gelding treats.

"How did the old brute do, Centurio?" Marcellus asked.

"He grumbled a lot, but he responded."

Marcellus laughed. "So the usual?"

Lucius nodded. "Give him some extra grain tonight and mix in some honey and apples."

"Yes, Centurio." Marcellus led Cicero off to be groomed and rubbed down before his evening meal.

Get Fall of the Centurio Immortalis Now!
Available May 31, 2022

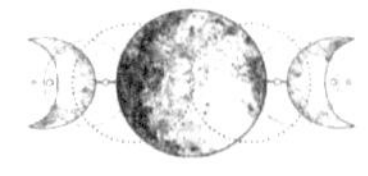

ACKNOWLEDGMENTS

I want to thank my writing group—Chris, Cina, Danni, Deborah, Marina, & Miche—for all the feedback on this book. Without you, this story wouldn't be anywhere as good as it is.

I would also like to thank my developmental editor Suzanne who is a constant cheerleader and an amazing eye, helping me fix the problems and make my stories awesome.

Raven makes the best covers and this one is no exception.

Last, I'd like to thank my partner Amy for all her support and the amazing job she does copy editing and proofing.

Without all y'all, this book wouldn't exist.

ABOUT THE AUTHOR

C. Thomas Lafollette is a writer of Urban Fantasy and Historical Fantasy and is the author of the forthcoming Luke Irontree novels. He earned a degree in Ancient History with a specialization in Classics at The College of Idaho. He's read poetry on stage with Yevgeny Yevtushenko* and dined with the Belgian Prime Minister**. C. Thomas has lived in Portland, Oregon for over Twenty years. He lives with his wife, fellow author Amy Cissell, his stepdaughter, and his three jerkface cats. He and Amy also run their own freelance editing business - Cissell Ink

*Yevtushenko was friends with a professor at C. Thomas's college. He was studying Russian at the time and Yevtushenko decided he wanted the Russian students to read with him on stage at his performance.

**This was purely coincidental. C. Thomas's host took him to dinner at a restaurant in Mons, which was Elio De Rupo's favorite spot. He'd had a pie thrown at him earlier that day and was having dinner with some friends. C. Thomas is still not sure what kind of pie it was though.

twitter.com/CTLafollette

facebook.com/CThomasLafollette

tiktok.com/@cthomaslafollette

instagram.com/CThomasLafollette

bookbub.com/authors/c-thomas-lafollette

amazon.com/C-Thomas-Lafollette/e/B09JMTR7W7

goodreads.com/cthomaslafollette

ALSO BY C. THOMAS LAFOLLETTE

Luke Irontree & The Last Vampire War

Book 0 - The Centurion Immortal

Book 1 - Dark Fangs Rising - March 22, 2022

Book 2 - Dark Fangs Raging - April 19, 2022

Book 3 - Dark Fangs Descending - May 17, 2022

Book 4 - Blood Empire Reborn* - August 23, 2022

Book 5 - Blood Empire Avenged* - September 20, 2022

Book 6 - Blood Empire Burning* - October 18, 2022

Book 7 - Blood Empire Collapsing* - November 15, 2022

Book 8 - Ancient Sword Falling* - February 7, 2023

Book 9 - Ancient Sword Unyielding* - March 7, 202

Book 10 - Ancient Sword Shattering* - May 9, 2023

The Luke Irontree Historical Adventures

Rise of the Centurio Immortalis - April 5, 2022

Fall of the Centurio Immortalis* - May 31, 2022

The Moonlight Centurion* - December 27, 2022

The Highway Centurion* - April 11, 2023

*Forthcoming

Titles and release dates may be subject to change.